D1527657

CONFESSION

ALSO BY LEE GOWAN

Going to Cuba
Make Believe Love
The Last Cowboy

LEE GOWAN
CONFESSION

[signature]

3 March '09
TORONTO

ALFRED A. KNOPF CANADA

PUBLISHED BY ALFRED A. KNOPF CANADA

Copyright © 2009 Lee Gowan

All rights reserved under International and Pan-American Copyright
Conventions. No part of this book may be reproduced in any form or by any
electronic or mechanical means, including information storage and
retrieval systems, without permission in writing from the publisher, except by
a reviewer, who may quote brief passages in a review. Published in 2009 by
Alfred A. Knopf Canada, a division of Random House of Canada Limited.
Distributed by Random House of Canada Limited, Toronto.

Knopf Canada and colophon are trademarks.

www.randomhouse.ca

Library and Archives Canada Cataloguing in Publication

Gowan, Lee, 1961–
        Confession / Lee Gowan.

ISBN 978-0-307-39683-9

I. Title.

PS8563.O882C65 2008   C813'.54   C2008-903178-4

Text design: Jennifer Lum

First Edition

Printed and bound in the United States of America

10 9 8 7 6 5 4 3 2 1

For Riley and Adam

"But that's enough, or we'll never finish—
there will always be something worse than what came before."
Fyodor Dostoevsky

ONE

Eight years since I've seen my parents' graves, and if I haven't visited it's a safe bet that neither has anyone else. Maybe a few of the curious, assuming that anyone is still curious about such things. Not a week goes by that I don't think of them there, under their shared granite slab. They died a day apart, my mother the one day and my father the next, so one stone seemed appropriate and more cost-effective. Not that I paid. I just mean that it must have seemed more appropriate and cost-effective to the man who did pay for the pretty pink rock and the engraving and had them buried side by side. They're within reach, but they never touch. How so like the world of the living.

You don't entirely appreciate how alone you are until you've lost your parents.

In the beginning, we piled stones on graves to stop wild animals from digging up the remains of our loved ones. I suppose those rough mounds served as markers as well, but the principal reason we piled them so high and wide was because we didn't want to come back to find our parents' bones strewn around like any other animal's. Nowadays, with coffins and fancy fenced-off graveyards in the middle of the city, you don't have to worry about anything eating your dead parents. We've almost completely run out of things to worry about.

I'm kidding. I wouldn't even mention it, but down east here, people tend not to know when you're kidding.

My mother's father was a baker, and he was not a kind man. That was about all she ever said about him. There was an empty place in my mother that couldn't be filled up with any amount of love or nastiness, and I was always pretty sure it had something to do with her father, but there was no way of getting at what he might have done to her. It was like she spent her whole life hiding from him, always glancing over her shoulder. One time, when I tried to get more out of her (I was probably seven or eight years old), she told me he was like the giant that Jack meets at the top of the beanstalk. I guess my father was Jack. He met her at a meeting in a Denver basement in 1964. She was seventeen years old and he was over forty. It was the monthly gathering of the Secret Society, an anti-communist cell operating in Denver. She had been hired to dance and take off her clothes for them. (She told me this when I was sixteen, after she'd pulled out my bottom drawer and found a magazine full of young women who had taken off their clothes. She said I could keep the magazine, but I couldn't stand the thought of her knowing it was there, so I burned it.) The Secret Society didn't pay her much to take off her clothes. The man who hired her, a friend of her father, said it was for the cause of freedom.

The morning after the last performance of her dancing career, she was heading north in my father's pickup truck. He was the most exciting man she'd ever met, a war hero from an exotic northern king-dom. Queendom. He'd lost his arm fighting the Nazis, and she was escaping with him from the giant and from Denver and from the United States of America, and she would never be unhappy again.

Nine months later I was born.

I'm only twenty-nine years old. People generally think I'm older. I'm not sure why. Maybe because I've suffered more than most in twenty-nine years, and that's made me act or appear older than I am. Don't get me wrong: there's no pride in my claim of suffering. Mostly I suffer from shame, and there's not much percentage in being proud of your shame. I'm a janitor here at an elementary school in Toronto, Canada, and I'm also a bit of a philosopher. The thing that marks me most is my unusual relationship with God. I've killed for Him, and He, in turn, has killed for me. That, I believe, is an unusual relationship.

I like being a janitor because it's plain and simple, one of those jobs that's never noticed unless it's left undone or not done well enough. When somebody compliments me on my work, it's most often because she wants to feel good about herself for noticing. I'd just as soon not be noticed. The highest compliment is when they forget you exist. If they can't see right through you, you're not using the right window cleaner. This afternoon, for instance, I happened to be emptying the trash barrel in the corner of the schoolyard when I heard the voice of this lawyer's son, a boy I have not gained a good opinion of. I turned to see that he had another kid cornered.

"Give me the ball, you little faggot."

These kids were both in grade four, the same grade as Caroline. There's no way he'd have let a teacher hear him say that, but he didn't take any notice of the janitor. I was of no more consequence than a rat rooting around the garbage. Less, in fact. A rat is far more deserving of attention than a janitor. And if the cornered kid hadn't been a friend of Caroline's, I'd never have got myself involved. I watch out for Caroline and her friends. Caroline is my daughter.

"I said, give it here, you faggot. Why don't you go play with your girlfriends? Maybe they've got a Barbie doll for you."

Caroline's friend has more backbone in him than little Mussolini expected, and he shook his head and wouldn't give up the ball. Didn't say a word, though, and you could see he was pretty scared.

"Give it here, faggot!"

"Watch your mouth," I said.

The lawyer's kid spun around to look at me. Caroline's friend was gaping at me too, but he looked just as scared as before I stuck my nose in, like he thought I was on *his* case for not watching what he wasn't saying. For a second there, they were equal: two scared little boys.

"I don't like to hear that kind of talk," I said.

By this time the lawyer's kid had realized I was only the janitor. "Mind your own fucking business, freakoid." He turned back to Caroline's friend. "If you don't give me the fucking ball—"

I picked him up by his shirt collar at the scruff of his neck, as if he were a kitten, and turned him around to face me. "I told you, I don't like to hear people talking that way."

He started wriggling, and for a second I thought he was going to take a swing at me, even though I had him by the back of the neck. The laying on of the hands wasn't what made him drop his fists. It was my eyes. He could see something in my eyes that made him hang still and pee his pants. He could see me wondering whether God wanted him dead. Caroline's friend saw too, and he ran.

I set the boy down and walked away.

Caroline's friend went right to the teacher in the playground and told her. I'm not sure which teacher, because I'd gone down to hide under the stairs in my room with the red door. Had a coffee. What could be safer than drinking coffee in a room under the stairs behind a red door? A knock came, and I opened up to see that the principal herself had come for a visit. She looked me over for signs of chaos and depravity.

"How are you, Jonathan?"

"Fine. Just having a coffee. Would you like a coffee?"

"One of the students said you were involved in an altercation in the playground."

I knew I should not have lifted him off the ground. Less than three months on the job. They could get rid of me for less.

"Just now? Oh. Yeah. A couple of boys arguing and I told them to stop. Hope I didn't scare them."

She studied me and I looked at the floor.

"Did you touch him, Jonathan?"

"Touch? No. I don't think so. No."

"What happened?"

"The one called the other a name."

"What name?"

"I don't remember."

"It's better if I know what name."

I looked around to make sure no one else was listening. "Faggot."

"You see, Jonathan, that's important. There's a strict policy against that kind of thing. But you have to come to me immediately. And you'd better not have touched him. We've had to deal with his father before. You'd better tell me the complete truth about what happened so that I know what I'm dealing with here."

I shrugged and then, because it was obvious she wasn't buying, I added, "Just dealing with garbage."

I smiled and she shook her head, not appreciating the humour of a janitor dealing with garbage.

"I need to know, Jonathan," she said. "I need to know exactly what happened."

"Never touched him," I said. "I told him to watch his mouth, and the kid he was tormenting ran away, so I left."

She looked me in the eye and I forced myself not to look away.

"That's strange," she said. "The boy you helped was under the impression there was some kind of physical intervention involved."

"That is strange," I said. "Maybe he wished it were so."

"Maybe," she said.

"It certainly makes for a better story."

She studied me some more and waited. She has eyes so blue that even in the basement they make you remember the sky.

"I like this job," I said. "I wouldn't do anything that would mean I could lose it."

Caroline looks like her mother. Like her mother and like my mother. It's hard to put a finger on the particular resemblances. My mother's eyes and mouth, for sure. Her mother's nose and chin and cheekbones. The resemblance goes beyond the face, though, right into her tiny skeleton: the way she stands on her left leg and curls her right foot behind her left ankle. Her mother used to do that too.

Caroline's mother, Gloria Irvine, was only seven when I first met her in Mrs. Field's grade two classroom. That was far from Toronto, in Broken Head, Saskatchewan, a place Caroline has no conception of, I'm sure, though that's where she was conceived. Not so strange really: out of squeamishness, we all tend to avoid a conception of our conception. But my mother wouldn't allow me the luxury.

"It was Calgary, Eisenhower." My name was Dwight then, but my mother usually called me Eisenhower or some other silly made-up name. It was a game she liked: she'd call me Eisenhower and she'd ask me how I got a name like Eisenhower and I'd tell her it wasn't my name. "That dingy little bachelor apartment your father had there. A furnished room, and we slept on the pullout couch. Galley kitchen, with the table tucked into the L of the main room. Bathroom and showers down the hall. There was that couch you were made on and a desk in the corner."

I was nine, Caroline's exact age, when my mother told me this story. We were on the farm near Broken Head where I grew up, sitting in the dark kitchen (the west windows had been smashed in a hailstorm and Dad had boarded them over and left them that way) with the bright red walls. Vermilion, she called them. Her favourite colour. She kept pointing to the couch in the living room as if it were the very one she was talking about. I remember her bright red lipstick. Her lips were the same shape as Caroline's.

"You happened in that apartment on that couch, and I remember the exact moment. I'll never forget that orgasm. I was seventeen and it was my first and I've never had one like that since. He must've drunk just the right amount that day: not enough to make him useless; just enough to slow him down. It was like he flicked a switch I never knew was in me. It was like the top of my head come

6

off. It blew me apart, and the sperm that was *you* had nothing between it and the egg."

She ran her fingers through my hair. You mustn't underestimate my mother, even though she dropped out of school to run away with my father. She was smart, and she wanted to make sure I knew things. She'd already long ago explained to me what an orgasm was. I'd asked her where babies came from, and she'd outlined the mechanics and started piling on vocabulary. Penis. Vagina. Copulation. Ejaculation. Reproduction. That was years before, and she was gradually layering on the details.

"That's what an orgasm's for in a woman. They've got an obvious purpose in a man. In a woman it's not so obvious, but that doesn't mean there's no reason for them. Contrary to popular belief, they're not purely for pleasure. Scientists have done studies, and they've found that a woman is much more likely to have a baby if she has an orgasm. It opens her up so wide. Not surprising. Unfortunately, Eisenhower, nothing's ever purely for pleasure."

I've spent most of my life imagining the scientists doing those studies. But I never became a scientist.

The principal did stay for coffee, even though she always tells me I make terrible coffee. She sat on an orange plastic chair, legs crossed at the knees, holding her chin in a professional way. Choppy came in smelling of the smoke he'd had in the alley and found her sitting on his chair, and even though he said he was just as happy turning over a pail and sitting on that, all of a sudden she had to go. When she was gone, Choppy sat where she'd been sitting, cleaning his fingernails with a jackknife and flashing me dark smiles.

"She wants you, boy. Why don't you give it to her right down here in our cozy little room? Just hang a 'Gone Fishing' sign on the door and I'll leave you be."

"She's a married woman, Choppy."

"What difference does that make? She's bored with the husband.

7

You saw him at Breakfast with Santa: any woman'd be bored. He's gone a little thick around the middle and a little thin around the top. Gives her a bit of a thrill fantasizing about doing it with the caretaker, I'll bet."

"You're the one fantasizing, Choppy."

"I'm only thinking of *you,* boy. Going around day after day with that hangdog expression on your face. You make *me* want to cry. Anyone can see that all you need's a little loving. The principal can sure see it, and she's more than ready to give it to you."

"Thou shalt not covet thy neighbour's wife, Choppy. Thou shalt not commit adultery."

He picked his nose and eyed what he'd discovered. "The Bible's got its place, maybe, but it's not much good for getting your dick wet, is it? We'd better be getting back to work." He stood up on his tiptoes and stretched his arms up to the ceiling.

"You remind me a bit of my father, Choppy."

"Is that so? Well, Johnny my boy, you are more like a son to me than my own son, that bastard. You are indeed. And I'm sure your old man's a fine, upstanding specimen of humanity."

"Was," I said. "He passed away."

"Oh," he said. "Sorry to hear that."

I shrugged. "We were never that close."

Caroline and I are closer in age than my father was to my mother. Mom was only eighteen and Jacob Froese was forty-two when I was born. It's pronounced *Froze,* which is why I chose that name for myself. I call myself Jonathan Froze: I have all the official identification so that nobody will ever know Dwight Froese and Jonathan Froze ever occupied the same body.

Jacob Froese lost his left arm somewhere in Belgium. My mother told me that, and at first I wondered if we might ever go over there to look for it. I don't know if it was a grenade or a shell or a very large bullet. He never talked about it. I watched him shred targets to test a new weapon he'd made, and I saw him kill a gopher a hundred yards away with a .22, but he never said much about the war. This once, I must have been eight, in the middle of supper he stopped chewing his steak and looked me in the eye and said, "At boot camp, there was this sign above the barracks door: Kill the Enemy." Then he looked towards the window as if he'd been interrupted by a magpie shrieking out there and started chewing again.

Another time, they were screaming at each other and Mom's nose was bleeding, and he grabbed me by the arm as he was marching out the door and shook me hard and said, "She was mine until *you* come along!"

He should have had a new prosthesis by the time I was a kid, but somebody or something warned him that the government would use monitoring equipment in the newfangled prosthetic to keep track of his movements, so he made do with the old one, making repairs of his own when anything went wrong. He was handy. He made guns in our basement on a metal lathe. I liked to watch him work, liked the smell of hot oil and smoking steel as I peered through the spaces between the basement stairs, the single light bulb dangling down on a wire above him glinting off the narrow ribbon of metal that lifted off as the cutter licked slowly down the length of the shaft. Periodically, to cool the cutter, he would squeeze a drop of oil from the can he held in his good hand. There was a big red button on the lathe that he pushed when he was finished, and when he pushed it, the lathe always stopped. I'd sneak down when his back was to me, but as the shaft slowed he'd turn and take off his safety glasses and stare through the darkness under the stairs straight into my eyes, and he'd say, "Red means stop."

Unlike my mother, he wasn't much of a talker, but this one time when he was drunk—more often than not, he was drunk—he told a very strange story.

"We were living in this fleabag apartment in Calgary, and I got this letter from a lawyer," he said. My ears perked up because I knew he was talking about the apartment with the pullout couch my mother had told me about. He was telling the story to a friend of his named

Chandler who was a gun dealer and bought the guns he made. I was hiding in the pots cupboard beside the fridge. Listening. There wasn't any good reason to hide. I hadn't done anything to piss him off that day, but if he'd found me he would've been mad enough to take his belt to me. I was only hiding because I knew he'd make me go out to the shop and sort bolts if he saw me. I guess I was also keen on hearing what he and Chandler talked about when they talked.

"Letter from this lawyer said my dad dropped dead of a heart attack and left me half a section of land. Didn't know what to think: leaving me land when I had every reason to believe I'd been decently disowned. I was a bit suspicious. Greeks bearing gifts and all that."

Chandler laughed. "Your dad weren't no Greek: he was a damn Mennonite."

"Mennonite *preacher*. So I couldn't figure why he'd leave land to the boy he'd shunned. Hadn't said more than two sentences to anyone in the family since the day I stole the horse and rode to Broken Head to join the army."

"Oh, right. You Mennonites didn't believe in going over there to kill other Krauts, did you?"

"Nothing to do with Krauts. Didn't believe in killing the man who was holding the gun to their heads. Pacifists. Turn the other cheek and let him blow your brains to the far side of never mind."

"But you were cut from a different cloth. Right, Jake? So you joined up. You want another splash?"

Chandler'd brought the whiskey they were sharing, and Dad must have nodded, because I heard him push back his chair and go to the fridge for more ice.

"So they shunned me. Not that I gave a damn. But I was sure thrown for a loop when I got that letter from the lawyer. Jumped in the truck and drove the six hours here to have a look at the place before I sold. Had no intention of keeping it. No desire to live here."

"What changed your mind?"

Dad's chair scraped back into place at the table, and I heard him strike a match to light a smoke. "Well, I came and took a look around. Walked through the pasture. Went for a swim in the creek. Skinny-dipping, like I remembered doing when I was a kid. Left my arm lying there on the bank. When I got out, I lay down on the ground stark naked and closed my eyes, and when I opened them again, my dad was standing over me, looking down into my eyes. He asked if I liked it."

"What? Liked it? What are you saying? Who asked?"

"My dad."

"I thought you said he was dead."

"Yeah. But there he was, looking down at me, and he asked me if I liked the place, and I said I thought he was dead. 'I'm not your father,' he said to me. 'I come to you in his form because my real form would strike you stone blind.'"

"Uh-huh?" Chandler said.

"'Is that so?' I said to him. 'Who are you, then? Elvis Presley?'"

Chandler thought that was funny.

"He spat on the ground right beside my head where I'm lying there, just the way my dad would have done. Then you know what he said?"

"What did he say, Jake?"

"He said, 'I am Yahweh.'"

"He's who?"

"Yahweh. God. That's God's original name. He's had a few, you know?"

"Really?" Chandler said. "Why does He keep changing it?"

"Dunno. Too many bad cheques. So I'm looking at his spit dripping down from a blade of the prairie wool, and I'm thinking, *Is that really God's spit?* And so you know what I said to him?"

"What did you say to him?"

"Prove it."

"Prove what?"

"I told him to prove he was God."

Chandler coughed before he spoke. "You did? And what'd he do?"

"Well, he stepped on his own spit, right beside my head, so the toe of his boot was practically in my eye, and I'm staring at this scuff on the toe of his boot that's shaped like a butterfly and I'm wondering if it's going to turn into a real butterfly and flutter away, and then he said, 'I'm not here to make miracles for you, Jacob Froese. I'm here to warn you that the son who'll be born to you in three months will one day kill you.'"

I sat up straight and bumped my head against the top of the cupboard. Neither Dad nor Chandler spoke for a long time. I held my breath.

"Did you hear that?" Dad finally asked.

"Yeah, I heard. Eva was pregnant," Chandler said. "That was Dwight he meant would kill ya?"

My name back then was Dwight. Not Jonathan. Not Eisenhower.

"That must have been who he meant," Dad said. "That's who was born three months later. 'Your son who's growing in that young prostitute,' is what he said."

"Dwight? He told you Dwight was going to kill you?"

"Yeah. And I stood up and asked him if that was his proof he was God. 'That's your proof you're Yahweh?' I said. But as I was standing, he was growing, so he was still looking down at me from way up above. He was smiling. I don't remember my father ever smiling. His yellow teeth were showing. 'If you want to take my warning as a miracle you can, but that's the only miracle I'm giving you,' he said."

"Dwight?" Chandler said again.

"And I said to him, 'You were always clucking on about God, but you were never before honest enough to admit you thought you were him.'"

"He said that Dwight was going to kill you?"

"And he said, 'I've given you my warning, but you're such a faithless fool, you won't know it's true until you're dead.' And he turned and walked away. I watched him for five whole minutes until he'd climbed out of the valley and disappeared over the horizon."

Inside the dark of that cupboard, I saw God disappearing.

"Jesus, that's one hell of a bad dream," Chandler said. "But how did that dream make you decide to stay here?"

"Who says it was a dream? I was awake. It wasn't a dream."

Chandler started coughing again, and then he started to laugh. "Come on, Jake. You think it was real? You don't *really* think it was real."

"I don't *think*. I know it was real. I was awake."

Chandler's laugh got a little more nervous. "So you moved here with Eva and had the kid and raised him? I don't get it, Jake. Why would you do that if you thought it was real? If God told you the kid was going to kill you, why didn't you flush him down the toilet the first chance you got? And why would knowing that make you move here? You said you didn't even want to live here in the first place."

I could hear Dad drumming the fingers of his good hand on the table.

"I'm not scared of God. I don't even believe in God. That's why I moved us here. How else was I gonna prove to him that I don't believe in him?"

There was this long moment of silence where you could hear the birds singing outside, and then Chandler laughed so hard that after a while he started coughing again and it took him a long time to stop.

"Whatever you say, Jake. Whatever you say."

I talked to Caroline's nanny with the pierced nose out by the garbage bin after school today. Pretty young to be looking after her, but she seems nice enough. Not sure what Caroline's mother's thinking, putting her life in the hands of someone so young. Black hair, dark complexion. I thought she was Mexican, but apparently not. She told me Caroline had lost her red toque and wondered if she'd left it in the playground and if Choppy or I or one of the teachers might have picked it up and put it somewhere. I went into the school and looked through all the lost and found boxes, sifting mounds of smelly boots and shoes and coats and hats and dirty lunch kits. Couldn't find it. What I did find was a sunhat I remembered her wearing the day I first saw her in September and a few days after that. I thought about taking that out to the nanny, but realized it wouldn't be wise. I went and hung the sunhat on her hook in her empty classroom and went out and told her nanny I couldn't find a red toque.

"Oh, fuck," she said. She saw me flinch. "Excuse my French. Her mother always gets on my case when she loses something. She's constantly losing her hats, and I'm constantly getting blamed. As if there was anything I could do about it. She doesn't like wearing them, but her mother insists on jamming them on her head every morning as she's going out the door. And then she tosses them off *any*where and I'm supposed to keep track of them and I'm the one who gets blamed when she loses them."

"Maybe it'll turn up. Her mother must be . . ." I didn't know where to go with that, and she was standing there looking at me. "I guess I'll have to make allowances for your French, considering you're not even French," I said.

"I am," she said, without so much as a blink. "Nez Perce." She gave a little tug to the ring in her nose.

I shrugged and scratched at a sudden itch on my own nose before I got embarrassed and dropped my hand.

"I have no idea what I am, really," she said. "I was raised by foster parents. My mother was some variety of Indian, but she gave me up. After I read *Bury My Heart at Wounded Knee,* I always wanted to be Nez Perce. You heard of them?"

"Don't believe I have," I lied.

"They were this tribe from the west coast of the U.S. who had their land taken away and fought the cavalry halfway across the continent trying to join up with Sitting Bull in Canada to help overthrow the white invaders. But eventually the cavalry slaughtered most of them and they had to surrender. So I always wanted to be Nez Perce, even though my white foster parents were very good to me. Actually, Caroline's parents are good to me too. I get paid better than any of these other nannies. But I still complain. I'm such an ungrateful little dirtbag."

I shrugged and scratched my nose again. "I thought you were Mexican," I said.

She looked at me like I was a bit of an idiot. "Shows what you know."

She smiled a smile that showed me her crooked white teeth and walked away.

I took the Queen streetcar home after work, as usual. Home is a room above a barbershop on Queen East that I imagine isn't much different from the apartment where I was conceived. I sleep on a pull-out couch. The bathroom's not in the hallway, though. There's this desk I'm writing at in the corner by the kitchen. I have a computer they were throwing out at the school.

Caroline's my daughter, and I wish I could be a real father to her. But I can't even tell her who I am or how I feel about her because if I did they'd fire me and I couldn't be close to her anymore. I've already missed too many years to allow that to happen again. I want to leave this account of myself so that she can read it someday when she's old enough. I want her to know the truth about where and whom she comes from. There's too much that her mother and her family wouldn't want her to know. I'm afraid that otherwise she'll never even know I existed.

I guess I'll begin by telling about the day I killed her grandfather.

After I'd done it, I drove straight to Broken Head to tell the police. Past stubble fields bleached white by herbicide. No tillage. Poison and fertilizer instead of leaving the land fallow, the higher purpose supposedly to avoid disturbing the earth so it wouldn't blow away, the real goal to squeeze a crop out of the soil every single year.

At the rural detachment of the RCMP, I pulled into the parking lot, walked inside and told the man behind the window that I had another death to report. Two officers came to question me, but all I'd tell them was that my father was dead. After taking me to the hospital, where a doctor looked at my ear and a nurse bandaged it, the police asked me to direct them back to where they'd find his body, and I did that well enough, though I had a feeling he'd be gone when we got there. He wasn't. The flies were already at the blood and mess. I was glad that the day before I'd taken my mother straight to the hospital.

Even though I believed he'd killed her, I no longer felt the least bit of pleasure in his look of surprise.

Instead of arresting me, they asked me if I'd be willing to see a psychiatrist, and I said that I would. The psychiatrist asked me many questions about my mother and father and how they'd both died, and I told him everything I knew. He had me admitted to the psychiatric wing of the Broken Head Union Hospital. The police did not charge me immediately, as they said they needed to complete their investigation. These men were friendlier than they'd ever been before. It was because I'd killed my father. They didn't like my father. I didn't tell them anything about the duel because, when one of them asked me about the duelling pistols, another told me it might be better for me to talk to my lawyer before I answered, as if they didn't want to hear what I might have to say. It was as though in the killing I had become my father, telling the story he'd told me just before I killed him, the story about how he'd been trained to kill over there in Europe— trained to seek out the movement of a man from a great distance and draw his crosshairs on that stranger's chest or head and pull the trigger. And the policemen looked at my father's body, with the bullet hole through the forehead and out the back of the head, and they nodded and said they understood. They showed more mercy to me than I had shown to him, my own father.

In the hospital, I had my own soap-green-walled room with a barred window. There were fluorescent lights and a single metal chair for visitors and a washroom by the door and my own personal officer outside to make sure I did not try to escape. It was very hot, and a pretty nurse put a fan in the room that blew a breeze at me. There was a woman next door who talked constantly, and so loudly, even when she was alone, that sometimes I wondered if she was speaking to me.

"Time to be a-goin' home now. Frank's waiting for me. Get his supper ready. Better be goin'. You've ben so nice. I like the soup. Good soup. Very good soup. Wonderful soup. I like the carrots too. Frank doesn't like carrots, but I've always liked 'em, ever since I was little. Used to steal the carrots from Mom's garden. And the peas. Nothing better than fresh peas right out of the pod. Oh, Mom was mad when she caught me. She paddled my bottom, she did. I really should get home. She'll be very mad. Or, I mean, Frank will. Mom's dead now. I know she's dead now. I know that. I know my mother's dead. I know that for sure."

My ears rang. My father's bullet had taken a large piece of the left one. The remains were bandaged so that when I looked at myself in the bathroom mirror I saw a veteran of some simple, perfect war. I believed Dad had killed my mother, and I had avenged her death and discovered that vengeance would not return her. She was gone and everything about her was gone, and no matter how much I expected her to walk through the door and take me in her arms, she would not be coming back. Sometimes the nurses came and gave me pills, which I took, and asked me questions nurses ask, like "Have you had a bowel movement today?"

The pills didn't help the ringing in my ears, which was beginning to drive me insane. It wasn't a long drive. I wished that, instead of going to the police, I'd got another of my father's guns and put it in my mouth and pulled the trigger. How stupid to have given up that chance. Sometimes I imagined getting up and getting dressed and walking out of the room and past the guard and all the way to the farm and finding a suitable tool and finishing the job properly. I didn't want to be locked up and forced to live out the rest of my miserable life.

Other times I wondered if it might not be so bad in jail. This hospital room with the barred window was not so good, but maybe

I could learn to be happy in a cage, like those animals you see in the zoo that are watered and fed and care for nothing. I'd have plenty of time for reading Dostoevsky. The thought of the other prisoners worried me, but could it be any worse than high school?

Please try to understand. I believed my father was evil. I believed he'd killed my mother. I wouldn't have killed him otherwise. I wouldn't have left him lying there for the flies. Though flies are beautiful in their way: the iridescence of their wings. Like feathers and silk. And oil and gasoline. As a janitor, I'm not supposed to have any place in my heart for flies, but I can't deny their beauty.

A man not all that much older than me who called himself my lawyer came to my room, shook my hand and sat down in the metal chair, with his briefcase resting on his knees. He said it was good to see me again. I didn't admit that I had no recollection of ever having seen him before. He started asking me strange questions: "Are you sure that five minutes passed between when he shot you and when you shot him? Couldn't you have been mistaken? Maybe it just seemed that long. Time seems to slow down at times like that."

I gave him a long, steady look that made him squirm. "How would you have any idea what time does at times like that? It was five minutes. But how did you know it was five minutes?" I asked, and he looked at me through his Coke-bottle lenses.

"You told me," he said. "You told me the whole story. I hope you didn't say that to the police. Are you sure you didn't tell the police?"

He had painfully combed hair and a smattering of acne on his forehead. When I didn't answer, he looked even more worried. He wasn't quite able to look me in the eye.

"The thing is, I have unfortunate news," he continued. "Your mother's death has been ruled an accident." He looked out the window at the elm tree growing across the street before switching his gaze to the floor. There were bars on the window to make sure I didn't jump out. Not just me: every person who'd ever been in that room had wanted to jump out that window. Even my lawyer wanted to jump out that window. "According to the autopsy report, she must have been standing on the bank of the river and fallen backwards and hit her head on a rock and drowned."

"Creek," I corrected him.

My lawyer cranked his eyebrows a notch higher.

"Fell into the creek," I said.

He nodded. "Fell into the creek and hit her head and drowned."

"What report?"

My lawyer opened his briefcase, as if to check his notes for the answer. "The autopsy report."

"And how would they know what happened? Were they there?"

He handed me a few sheets of paper clipped together. "Here's the report. You can read it over yourself, and you'll see how they reached their conclusions. It'll complicate things. But in the end, it doesn't change the fact that you had good reason to believe your father had murdered your mother. That's very important. And your injury is also very important. He tried to kill you." My lawyer pointed to the bandage on my ear to show me what he meant.

I looked at the cover of the report. It was written by Dr. Andrew Irvine. I knew who he was. Everyone in Broken Head knew who he was. The father of a girl I had been in love with for many years and who mostly did not know I existed. The father of Caroline's mother, Gloria Irvine.

"I want to talk to him," I said. "I want to talk to Dr. Andrew Irvine."

My lawyer looked puzzled. He smiled and nodded and stammered that he didn't think that was possible.

"Of course it's possible. Why wouldn't it be possible?"

He shrugged his shoulders in a way that made me want to crush him into the floor and sweep him away. My lawyer had an unfortunate talent for making people want to crush him.

"Go and tell him I want to talk to him," I said.

"He's likely to be a witness for the prosecution. Professionally, he can't . . ."

"Go and tell him. He must work here somewhere. Wherever they keep the bodies. In the basement?"

My lawyer said he'd speak to him. He closed his briefcase and shook my hand again, all the time looking at the food tray beside my table in a way that made me wonder if he was hungry. To be hungry for that congealed mess, he'd have to be a very hungry man. I suspect he was only trying to avoid my eyes. He said he'd see me again soon and hurried away.

That evening the door opened and Dr. Andrew Irvine walked in and sat down in the chair where my lawyer had sat. He didn't speak. I was lying on my side, facing the door, but the light was out, so he might have thought I was sleeping. He wore a sleek black suit and a very sad expression. I even wondered if he might begin to cry. He sat looking at the fan in the corner panning slowly back and forth. From the next room, we could hear the woman talking, and Irvine tilted his head to listen.

"Emily, you're a fool. Don't know what to say to ya. I'd just as soon you was dead. We go on and on like this and nothing changes. Remember that dog? Daddy gave him to me for Christmas and he disappeared. Never knew what happened. Fell through the ice, maybe. That's what Daddy thought, 'cause the last time he saw him he was chopping a hole in the ice for the cows to drink from. But it could have been coyotes too. They like eating dogs. They'll eat anything. They're hungry beasts."

While we were listening, I raised myself on my elbow and looked Irvine in the eye.

"Hello, Dwight," he said. "Andrew Irvine."

He stood and offered his hand, and I pulled myself to a sitting position. It was a hand made for holding scalpels, with long fingers and soft skin. Nothing like Dad's hand.

"My father killed her," I said.

"Pardon?"

"You've made a mistake," I said. "My father killed my mother."

Irvine sighed and nodded as though considering what I'd said. "You don't need to worry about the arrangements. I've handled things for both your mother and father. There's a plot for them in Memorial Park, and they'll share the same headstone. It's not a large stone, but it's very tasteful. I hope it's okay I did that?"

Dr. Andrew Irvine was well known in Broken Head for his causes and general philanthropy. His donations and acts of grace and brotherhood. What I mean is, he was a churchgoing man and famous for his Christian charity. I was flooded with a terrible shame that I had not even considered my parents' final arrangements.

"My father wanted to be burned," I said. "He told me that. He didn't tell me much, but he once asked to be burned. They shouldn't be buried together. He killed her."

The woman next door interrupted. "A pretty little dog. Black and white."

Irvine looked away from me, listening to her voice.

"She's talking to herself," I told him. "She's all alone."

"Yes," Irvine nodded. He lowered himself once more into the metal chair. "I understand how you feel right now, but I think that in time you'll be glad they're together. Your father didn't kill your mother. It was an accident. I hope you'll forgive me for making the arrangements without consulting you first. Of course, if your father expressed other wishes—if you want it done differently, there's still time. The funeral, as they've told you, will be tomorrow. You'll want to be there."

No one had told me, or if they had I didn't remember.

"No," I said. "I don't want to be there. My mother's gone. It doesn't matter where she's buried. Even with him. But you're wrong. He killed her. That's the important thing. I want that straightened out."

"That's not what you told the police when you brought her body here. That's not how it appears."

"I didn't want the police to arrest him. I wanted him for myself. I'm telling *you*, my father killed her."

He put his hand over his mouth before he let it drop to his lap. "I understand your insistence, but I also think you need to know it isn't true."

"What makes you so sure it was an accident?"

He studied me through the gloom of the room, the fan ruffling his hair as it pivoted in his direction.

"I shouldn't tell you this. I'm not supposed to be talking to you at all. Do you understand that?" I nodded, though I didn't understand. He looked towards the door and leaned forward and whispered, "The contusion was caused by a stationary blow: her head hit the object and not the other way around. She wasn't struck. There's no sign of a struggle. There was only one other sign of trauma, which was to her right leg. It indicates that she stepped into a hole, fell backwards into the creek and struck her head on a stone. A badger hole. I went out with the police, and we searched upstream from where you found her, and we found the hole and the stone with traces of her blood on it. The stone was below a steep embankment, and it was just big enough that the tip was above the surface of the water, and there were traces of her blood. I took samples. And her lungs indicate that she was unconscious when she drowned." He looked away. "She fell and hit her head and drowned. Your father had nothing to do with it. I'm sorry."

I stared at him until he crossed his legs.

"Did you see something?" he asked.

"How do you know my father didn't push her?"

He gave me a long look and cleared his throat before speaking. "You saw your father do this?"

"I heard him threaten her many times. I know he did it."

"Did your father tell you he killed her?"

"No. He didn't tell me anything. He *never* told me anything."

He sighed and nodded. "Your mother fell. Her death was an accident. You should be at their funerals tomorrow."

22

He closed his mouth and stared at the floor, and I became all too aware of the ringing in my ear.

"An accident," I said. "Could have happened to anyone."

He held his silence for another moment, looking at me strangely—looking as if he were a little afraid of me. "Yes. It was an act of God." He reached up and rubbed one of his temples with his fingertips.

"God? God? And where does that leave me?"

"I'm sorry?"

"I had to kill my father to avenge my mother's death. If she died by an act of God, where does that leave me?"

"Avenge? I see. I'm sorry. I'm not sure. I can't answer that. I accept that you did what you did because you believed your father was guilty. But it was not for you to judge or seek vengeance. And I can't tell a judge or jury that your father was guilty. Maybe he was guilty of other things, but not of your mother's death. I suppose you mean legally? Where does that leave you legally? I really don't . . . I can't say your father was guilty. I know that he wasn't."

Abruptly, I swung my legs over the side of the bed. He flinched, and the police officer was immediately on his feet and standing in the doorway.

"You say it was an act of God. So where does that leave me?"

Irvine turned to the police officer and nodded, and the police officer looked me sternly in the eye and disappeared from sight. Irvine stood and closed the door. "As I said, I'm not a lawyer. But I do think perhaps we should find you a better lawyer. I'm already looking into that."

"What does a lawyer have to do with it? Where does it leave me with God?"

Again his nod, as if he were expecting all along for me to say just this. "You could pray."

"Pray? You tell me God killed my mother. Why would I want to pray to Him?"

23

He stopped nodding. "You're on the wrong path," he said. "God doesn't murder. It isn't for us to understand the acts of God. And certainly it's not for us to judge them. That's pride. Not that I don't understand what you're feeling. I'm a proud man too, and sometimes it feels to me that God isn't just. I have the same kind of thoughts myself every single day. Believe me. But you have to accept that there are reasons beyond our understanding for God's actions. You should be there with your parents tomorrow. If you can't pray, would you allow me to pray for you?"

"No. He killed my mother. God killed my mother."

He looked away, and I wanted him to meet my eyes, but he wouldn't.

"My father's death was an act of God too. Did you know that? Before I was even born, God came to my father and told him I'd kill him. I had no choice. God set me up to kill my father."

Irvine coughed and looked up at the ceiling. "You should be at the funeral," he said.

"No," I said. "How can I?"

"Just ask the Lord's forgiveness and go."

"Not until He asks for my forgiveness."

"He already has. He died for you and was born again."

I pulled myself up straight again to look him in the eye. "Good. Then tell God I don't forgive Him. How could I possibly pray to such a disgusting . . . ?"

His eyes shamed me enough that I did not finish the sentence. He shook his head. "I'll have that lawyer come to see you as soon as possible."

He pulled himself to his feet, nodded once and walked out the door without looking back. The fan swivelled to watch him go.

On that day, I was forced to consider the possibility that my father had not killed my mother. I didn't want to believe it, but Dr. Andrew Irvine poured some small drop of faith into my ear. God pointed His finger at me and stuck it through my heart. I thought of my father once telling me I was special in some way, and I saw that this was what he had foreseen. He knew I had been chosen. He'd done his best to refuse to believe in God, but what good had it done him?

I slept all the next day. They didn't wake me for the funeral. Nobody but Irvine really wanted me there anyway. How could I go and let everyone watch me make a spectacle of myself saying goodbye to the father I'd killed? I told myself that they were parting together and heading in opposite directions: my mother to heaven and my father to hell.

Very likely there wouldn't have been many to watch me if I had gone. My parents were likely almost alone as they were lowered into the ground. Who would have gone to be there with them? Those whose duty it was to be there: a minister, one or two representatives from the funeral home. And maybe Irvine.

TWO

The new lawyer came two days later, much older and more confident than the first. He came all the way from Regina, sweet capital of fair Saskatchewan. After pumping my hand and repeating his name three times, he excused himself, stepped outside and insisted that the policeman move down to the nurses' station and watch my door from there. To my amazement, the cop obeyed. Once he'd got his way, he closed the door, sat down in the chair, pulled out his tape recorder and asked me to tell him the whole story. As I talked, he didn't always seem to be paying attention. He jotted down notes, flipped through files from his briefcase, checked his watch and stopped me three times because he needed to go somewhere to make a phone call. This was not long before cellphones started taking over the world. After he returned from the calls, he'd apologize and make vaguely insulting comments about the people he'd talked to. The only thing that made it clear he was actually listening was that every so often he'd ask me a question relating to what I'd just said.

He asked if there was anyone besides my father who I could imagine might have killed my mother, and I said there wasn't. "Except maybe her father."

"Her father? How well do you know her father?"

"I don't. Never met him. Don't even know if he's alive."

When I'd finished telling him the story, he put his notepad and files back into his briefcase and told me there was nothing to worry about: I would not see the inside of the courthouse, at least not for a murder charge. The missing piece of my ear would guarantee my freedom. "Your father seems to have made a very bad impression on the local constabulary." From what he'd gathered, the police didn't want to press charges, but the crown prosecutor was still sniffing around. "But don't you worry about him. We had a drink last night. He's an old buddy of mine. Old enough that I know more about him than he'd like anyone to know. He's just a little worried about possible political ramifications with your case."

I couldn't see why any politician would give a damn about me, but I didn't ask what he meant; instead, I told him that it was my idea that my father shoot first and that I wished he hadn't missed, and I reminded him of my father's perfect aim: if he'd wanted to kill me, I'd be dead. My lawyer tossed his hundred-dollar haircut with a solemn sort of shake and asked if I'd mentioned any of this to the police.

"No," I said. "I didn't tell them much of anything, except where to find his body. I never liked talking to police."

"Good. Don't you talk to anyone but me."

"Not even God?"

It was the only time I ever saw him look even slightly uncomfortable, and it was only for an instant.

"There's a saying that a man who represents himself has a fool for a client, and I don't see why it would be any different with God on the bench." He smiled, revealing a mouthful of teeth so white they could not possibly be real. "But you talk to God if you like. Just let me do the rest of your talking."

I told him that Dr. Andrew Irvine had already volunteered to talk to God for me.

"Irvine?" he said. "You know that if they do charge you he'll be speaking for the prosecution? But on the other hand, he arranged for me to represent you, didn't he? He said you didn't deserve to suffer any more after what you'd been through. He's a good man, Irvine. Yes, you let Irvine deal with God, and I'll do the rest of your talking."

Within a few weeks the Crown announced that I wouldn't face charges. My new lawyer accomplished this by turning me into a hero. I had no television, and they didn't bring me newspapers, so I didn't get the chance to watch myself while it was going on. The first thing I noticed was that the nurses got friendlier. When I didn't eat my Neptune Surprise, one of them snuck me in a hamburger. The best kind of hero kills scary monsters. The nurse described how the television told the story with a voice talking over pictures of Dad's mug shot and a picture of Mom—I don't know where they got it—and my high school yearbook photo, along with shots of our house. It was obvious to everyone but Irvine that Dad had something to do with my mom's death. We were both his victims, and it was only after Dad shot off a piece of my ear that I put a hole between his eyes. All of Canada was on my side. Broken Head fell in love with the new idea of me, and the prosecution had no difficulty dropping all charges.

It wasn't until later that I realized I'd done something that made me real to people. For the first and last time, I was something more than me. I was pitied and loved and admired.

Once it was over, the lawyer shook my hand and went away, and gradually I disappeared from televisions and newspapers everywhere.

My ten months in the psychiatric unit were mostly spent sleeping, and I'm left with a strange, ethereal sense of that time. On the one hand, it seemed like ten years; on the other hand, I don't have enough memory of it to fill more than a few days. The nurses' particular rituals dragged on and on, and the psychiatrist visited me or I visited his office almost every day. Despite that, he has no face. I mean, I've completely forgotten his face. I think he was about forty. Or maybe sixty. He insisted that I talk about my feelings, so I told him about wanting to kill God. This always pleased him. He'd ask me to talk about my mother and my father, and I'd do my best to satisfy him, even though I didn't know what to say. I wasn't sure what it was he wanted to hear.

One of his favourite stories was about the time I heard my father telling how God had prophesied I'd kill him. He asked me to tell him that story so many times that I got tired of it. After about the tenth telling, he asked if I thought maybe Chandler was right and my father had dreamt the whole thing. I laughed. It seemed funny to me, wondering if Dad had dreamt it after it had come true. But he kept prodding and wondered whether I thought my father might have set things up so that it would eventually come true.

"Oh, I see. You don't really believe in God. You think Dad dreamt the whole thing and then spent eighteen years trying to make it happen until I finally obliged him."

"It doesn't matter what I think. I just wonder what you think. You don't believe it's possible that your dad was dreaming?"

"Oh, sure. Anything's possible. But have you considered that maybe Dad didn't dream it at all? Maybe I made the whole story up so I could kill Dad and blame it on God."

He sat there, waiting for more. I remember that he had a brown leather chair he always sat in, but I can't remember his face, so I substitute Sigmund Freud's.

"Is that what you think?" I asked him.

"What do you think?" he said.

"Might be what happened. That's not how I recall it. I remember being crammed into that cupboard so that my neck had a kink in it for two days afterwards. I remember him telling that story. I remember it all like it was us talking here. But who knows whether this is happening? Maybe I'm just making you up."

"Maybe you are," he said.

To change the subject, I'd tell him about the crop that I knew was growing in the field and about the cattle eating grass and drinking water in the pastures, and he'd assure me that they were being looked after, and I'd explain to him that they didn't need much looking after at the moment (it was still summer) but that they would soon enough and that I didn't believe I could face it. I couldn't go back there and see what had become of me, the killer of my own father. How could I inherit his land by killing him? It was still my father's land, and I didn't want to become my father, who I still didn't want to believe was innocent of my mother's death. The doctor said it was completely understandable that I should feel what I was feeling.

But at the same time, I knew that I was only saying what I thought he wanted me to say, and that I was not even getting close to rooting out the numbness. I wished I *could* feel. I was ashamed and afraid to talk about what I didn't feel. I knew that in my position any decent person must feel some kind of guilt and grief for his murdered father. He was a man, after all, with years ahead of him, and I had taken those years away. But every time I told myself so, another part of me insisted that he deserved to die and pointed out that I hadn't even been born when God had chosen me to kill him. Who was I to question God?

The only real feelings I remember were a bottomless loneliness and an all-too-ordinary sadness that clung to every waking moment. The green walls and the bars on the window. The memories of blood and brain matter. I had lost my mother. She was the only one who'd ever loved me, and already I had difficulty picturing her. Her red lips. The way she held herself upright, with her shoulders thrown back, her breasts jutting forward and a hand on one hip. I started remembering her face again only when I saw Caroline.

Yahweh did not visit me there, though I expected Him at every moment. Sometimes, in the early morning when the sun was slanting through the blinds, I would squint my eyes and pretend I could see Him sitting in the metal chair where Dr. Irvine had sat, His face shining back at me. But He never came.

It was Dad who named me Dwight, after the WWII general who became president. Mom wanted to call me Jonathan, after her older brother, who didn't come back from Vietnam. When she ran away with my father, she felt like he was her brother come back from the dead for her. But he wasn't. Dad said *Jonathan* was a boring name.

They didn't agree on much. Their arguments were so noisy that I often worried he might kill her. I saw him twist off a pigeon's head. I saw him shoot a sick calf without even flinching. It wouldn't have been any more difficult for him to kill her. My earliest memory is of waking to hear him screaming in the night and walking down the hallway to their room, clutching my bear, Murgatroid. I touched the doorknob, remembering that I had been ordered never to open that door without knocking, but deciding that Mom didn't mean this particular moment when she told me *never*. He shouted again, just a single word—"No!"—and I opened the door.

The bedside lamp was on. Mom was lying on the bed and he was kneeling over her, his right hand on her throat.

"Dad?" I asked.

Somehow the question got through to him, and he unlaced the fingers of his hand from her neck. His left hand was still poised in the air above her, like an eagle's or a lizard's claw. It was fashioned of cables and levers and metal shafts.

Mom shook her head at me, terrified that I'd seen her terror. "Daddy was having a bad dream," she said.

I shrugged to tell her that this was evident and inevitable and not relevant to the nature of my visit. Dad stared blankly at me, apparently still in the dream.

"I can't sleep," I said.

Mom sat up straight and nodded, rubbing her neck with her left hand. "Well, it's late. You go back to bed now before you upset Daddy."

And I nodded and turned and pulled the door closed behind me and ran as fast as I could back to bed. I lay there awake for a long time, listening to the coyotes howling.

We were alone on that farm. My father never made amends with his family, and he had a way of making people nervous, so we didn't have neighbours dropping over for coffee. His only friends were gun dealers like Chandler who sometimes visited. Even when he should have been farming, he spent most of his time drinking and working on guns, or building shops to store machines and other treasures he bought when he went away on business, and then making passage-ways out of Cindercrete blocks to connect the shops with each other or with the house so he didn't have to go outside to get around. He even built a passageway that covered over the window in my bed-room, so that I could no longer see the stars when I looked out through the glass.

Mom arrived knowing no one in Saskatchewan and, being newborn, neither did I, so we were best friends in a way that mothers and their sons are usually not. She was really just a kid, only turned eighteen when I was born. She started teaching me to read when I was three. We played games where we draped the blankets over the furni-ture to pretend we were pioneers riding wagon trains west or astro-nauts travelling through outer space to other planets. And we played a lot of hide-and-go-seek. I thought I was the greatest hide-and-go-seek player in the history of the world, though I was not really a good seeker. Once Mom hid under a blanket six feet from my counting post and I walked right past her—practically stepped on her. She was home free in three seconds. It might have been a record. But they don't keep records for hide-and-go-seek.

My mother was proud and beautiful and she was clever, but she was not a great hider like me. She took too many chances. After Irvine told me Dad was innocent, I began to wonder if her father might really have found her and killed her. Sooner or later she was bound to get caught. I tried to teach her, but she was a poor student, and there's just so much to learn about hiding. For instance, a good hiding place isn't everything. Once found, no matter how well camouflaged, it's ruined. Never share a hiding place with anyone, unless you plan on killing him. Or her. You have to remember that eventually the other hiders are bound to be seeking you. Be especially careful not to be seen leaving your hiding place at the end of the game, even if it means you have to wait until everyone gets bored and goes away. Or dies. Eventually, everyone dies.

A talent for hiding is no small thing. The importance of hiding goes all the way back to the Bible. As God walked through the Garden of Eden, Adam and Eve tried to hide from Him because they had eaten the apple from the tree of knowledge and learned that they were naked. They were ashamed and so they covered their skins, but their hiding gave them away and He banished them from His Garden. With their shunning, we lost the Garden, but we gained knowledge. We became like the gods in every way, except that we were not immortal.

I quote from Genesis: "Then Yahweh God said, 'See, the man has become like one of us,'" (have you ever wondered who God was talking to when he said this?) "'with his knowledge of good and evil. He must not be allowed to stretch his hand out next and pick from the tree of life also, and eat some and live for ever.'" And so he kicked us out of His Garden and hid Himself away behind his cherub guards and the flame of a flashing sword.

And now He hides from us. But never forget that if we stop looking for Him, He hunts us down. He's getting warmer. I hear Him outside the window, over the rumble and the screeching of the Queen streetcars, humming a tune I can almost recognize. What'll happen when He finds me? He wanders the streets, mumbling to His reflection in my window. He's been very lonely since the other gods died: lonely, and irritable when crossed. No one but me could have avoided the wrath of His eyes for so long.

But I'm talking nonsense, of course. You can't hide from God. He's the limitation of our freedom. But He should be the only limitation. We should be able to shed our clothes and walk out into the street and shout, "Here I am, God. I'm beautiful. Come and find me!"

But if we did, they would come and arrest us. That is the world of our making. We hide for a living and we live by what we hide. Some hide wealth, some hide power, some hide love. I hide dirt and other refuse from school hallways. I make garbage disappear. Did you know that in old England a "hide" was defined as the minimum amount of land required to support one family unit? And consider that when Adam and Eve were booted out of the Garden, they began killing their old friends the animals not only to eat them, but so that they could use their *hides* to cover their own; not only out of embarrassment, but because outside the Garden it got very chilly at night.

Sorry about that. Sometimes I can't stop babbling. I can't get over Him telling Abraham to kill Isaac or gambling with the devil over Job's soul. How could he possibly have made a bet with the devil and then allowed the devil to do that to Job, just so He could win his bet? I want so much to believe in Him, and at the same time I wish I could do away with Him for good. He's the devil I know and the Saviour I don't. I'm even more confused about God than I am about women. Ignore it if you can. Treat it like pencil marks and sketches in the margins, where you try to work out the answers. I'll erase everything I don't need once I'm sure there's no point in its existence.

The principal called me up to her office today.

She was out when I got there, but Mavis, the secretary, motioned me in and I sat down and waited. She has these pictures of flowers hanging on the walls to make things appear soft and comfortable. When she came in, she wouldn't look at me as she settled herself behind her desk.

"Mr. Gayton has lodged an official complaint," she said.

"Pardon?"

"He says that you assaulted his son."

"Oh?" I said.

She still didn't look at me. She picked up a pen as though there was something she needed to remember to write down.

"I told him that my investigation had led me to believe that his son was bullying another boy. I suspended his son for three days. When he started shouting, I told Mr. Gayton that perhaps he should be more concerned about why his son thought that bullying was acceptable

35

behaviour. I told him you'd assured me that you hadn't touched his son. It's his son's word against yours, and I told him that, considering his son's record of lying and bullying, I preferred to believe you."

"Thanks," I said.

She dotted an "i." Or maybe an exclamation mark.

"So we'll have to hope he doesn't hear the other boy's story. Won't we?"

After thirty seconds of silence, it was clear she wanted me to leave. I thought it was clear. Maybe she wanted me to take her in my arms and let her cry on my shoulder. I left.

I walk by the brick house at the edge of the ravine only once each week. Always on Friday, always at the same time in the afternoon, when school is out, so that if people notice me going by, they'll notice that I go by on Fridays at exactly the same time every week. I wear my sunglasses and a hat so Gloria and Nick won't recognize me if they happen to see me wandering by. Caroline's bike sprawls in the driveway. A cat in the front window looks out at me. Once I saw Gloria, because she gets home early on Fridays. She parked in the driveway and got out of the car and walked into the house.

Her house is in the opposite direction to the school from where I live, but I always go shopping at a grocery store on the Danforth and take the subway and bus home with a few bags of groceries. Her nanny shops there on Friday afternoons too. She was perusing the bananas yesterday when I approached, pretending I hadn't seen her.

"Hello," she called to me.

I nodded and scanned her overflowing cart. Frozen waffles on the top.

"Hi. Shopping?" I asked.

"Good guess," she said.

I lifted my basket. "You eat a lot more than I do."

She rolled her eyes. "Shopping's part of the job description," she said.

"Oh. I figured you were shopping for yourself for the weekend."

"I have no weekend. I envy you your weekend."

"You can have it. It's all yours."

"Not mine. I live in. Buy the food, do the cooking, laundry, everything. Actually, they do let me have some time off on the weekend, just so long as they don't need me to babysit, which is rare on Friday and Saturday nights. But at least I'm not expected to cook for them on Saturday and Sunday. Not usually, anyway." I just stood there nodding at her, not sure what to say, so she went on. "I shouldn't complain. They're really pretty good to me. I want to go to university, so they set up an education fund for me, like I'm their own kid. What nanny has that?"

"You're part of the family."

"I have a suite in the basement."

I nodded. "Really? The basement?"

She nodded. "See ya later," she said. And she pushed off on her way.

I saw her again in the cereal aisle, but she just smiled and rolled by.

They would let me out of the hospital for walks so I'd get my exercise, and I'd wander through the streets of Broken Head, watching the world change to fall and then winter and looking at houses and avoiding the eyes of people. I was famous, so people were excited to see me, but I didn't understand what I meant to them, and nobody spoke to me. They were afraid or too polite to tell me. Most days I'd visit my parents' graves and sit there on the yellow grass and try to think of what I'd say to them if they were still alive. I also liked to walk over the overpass and stop to watch the trains shunting below, a habit that caught the attention of my doctor and brought about much consternation until I convinced him that it was only the beauty of the straight lines of the rails running off the horizon that attracted me.

Emily, next door, was moved to another part of the hospital, and some time later I heard she'd passed away. I made the mistake of telling the doctor I missed her voice talking in the night, and the next thing

I knew the nurses were encouraging me to visit with an old man down the hall named Emmet. His wife had just died, and he'd tried to hang himself, but his belt snapped and when he hit the floor he broke his right hip. He had one daughter still living in Broken Head, but when she came to visit he wouldn't speak except to tell her to go away and leave him alone. I went and sat beside his bed, expecting and hoping he'd tell me the same thing. Instead, he asked me, "Are you the boy who shot his father?"

I said that I was.

"What was that like, then?"

I didn't answer.

"Must have been something. I was in the war. Never got to fight, though. Sent me down to Ontario for training and then sent me over to England, but by the time I got there it was all pretty much over. Hitler blew his own brains out in his bunker. He shot you too, I heard."

I knew he did not mean Hitler.

"Yeah," I said. "My ear." And I pointed out the missing section of my ear. He sat up straighter to take a closer look.

"What was that like, then?"

I shrugged. "Loud."

He smiled at that. "Guess it would be."

I nodded. He waited for more. It was such a responsibility: shooting and being shot and talking to an old man who wished he was dead and felt he'd missed out on something in a war he never got to. Not knowing what to say to him. I thought of my father and of something of Dostoevsky's I'd been reading over and over again.

"I bled a lot," I told him.

He nodded encouragingly. "What was that like, then?"

"I don't know. It was like bleeding. These big drops of blood were falling onto the ground, and I was watching them falling and spattering the grass, and I kept thinking that my blood would seep right into the soil and that flowers would grow there. From my blood. And my father's."

His mouth was open by the time I stopped talking. "Flowers?" he said. "You think? Well, I guess." He turned and looked out his window. "We could sure use some rain, couldn't we?"

After that day, the nurses would sometimes wheel him down to my room and he would tell me how much he had loved his wife and how much he hated his daughter for not visiting when her mother was dying, even though she lived only fifteen miles away, and why some tractors were better than others and how many rocks he'd picked out of his fields in his life and why he'd given up washing his hair even before his wife died and how many friends he'd lost over the years through no fault of his own. It was all right because I didn't have to do much talking; he didn't seem to care whether I said anything or not. He didn't ask me about shooting my father again, but sometimes he'd roll himself over to my bed for a closer look at my ear.

"Loud," he would say, chuckling to himself.

One day I opened my eyes and Chandler was sitting in the metal chair.

"And how would you be?" he asked.

Why did it have to be Chandler? I wished it were Yahweh. It wasn't quite a fair trade.

"Fine," I said.

He nodded and those bulbous eyes of his threatened to pop out and bounce around the room. "Heard ya shot yer dad. With the pistols I sold him."

He was smiling a smile so wide the lines on his cheeks almost hurt me.

"One of them," I said. "He shot me with the other."

"Fair fight, then. Hospital's not much fun, is it? Havin' my own problems. One of my testicles swelled up bigger than a potato. Hurts like hell."

Neither of us spoke for a long time, until I'd begun to hope that he was only curious and might leave without saying another word.

"Jesus. I could use a smoke, but they don't let ya smoke in here. Don't you smoke?"

"No."

"Your daddy never taught you to smoke? Didn't he teach you anything useful?"

"Did he kill people? For a living?"

He looked me over. "Your dad? Nahhh. He wouldn't've had so many cash flow problems if he were in that line, would he? He made guns and he sold them. And he liked to collect junk, which was the real monkey on his back. His junk was always gonna make him millions when the next Great Depression came, but it never did arrive."

Chandler grinned fondly as he told me this. I imagined my father sitting at our kitchen table, sipping whiskey and smoking his roll-your-owns and confiding to Chandler about the money he'd make from the junk when that next depression came, and I thought about the possible reasons he'd been so careful not to reveal his dreams and desires when I could hear them. God had told him I would kill him, and he didn't want to make himself vulnerable to me.

"He never killed anyone since the war," Chandler went on. "Until your mom. That was a bad piece of business."

"Apparently it was an accident," I said.

Chandler nodded slowly. "The thing is," he said, still smiling that ridiculous smile, "your daddy owed me some money when he died."

I made the mistake of meeting his eyes. "I don't know nothing about that," I said.

"There must be insurance or something, I'd think, so I figured I'd better discuss it with ya. Twenty thousand dollars. Thereabouts. I've got it all down on paper, of course. It's something over twenty, but I'm willing to settle for twenty. Your father was a friend of mine."

"When would you want it?" I asked.

We agreed that any time in the next week would be acceptable, and he shook my hand and went on his way.

The year before I was supposed to start school, when I wasn't yet five, Mom's belly began to grow and eventually swelled up even fatter than Mr. Schmidt's, the Pool elevator man (I sometimes went with my father when he hauled wheat to the elevator, and I was always impressed by the way Mr. Schmidt's belly hung over his belt). She told me that soon there'd be a baby coming and warned that the baby would take lots of her time—there wouldn't be nearly so many opportunities for hide-and-go-seek as there used to be. Or for playing Jane and Anne: I'd dress up in one of her slips and we'd pretend we were a team of girl detectives, like Nancy Drew. Or the Hardy Girls. She was Jane and I was Anne. That game always made Mom nervous, because once Dad caught us and told her if he saw me wearing a dress again he'd burn it. The slip, I guess.

I wondered how she could have allowed the baby to happen. How had it managed to get inside her? When I asked, she explained that she had built a nest inside herself and laid an egg and that my father had put his penis into the place between her legs to fertilize the egg with his seed and this had made the fetus who would become my brother or sister.

How could anyone possibly believe such a ridiculous story?

Still, Mom insisted that this was how it had happened, and someday soon the baby would come out through that place between her legs and be born just as I had once passed through that narrow tunnel. I still didn't believe her. So she pulled up her top and lay down on the bed next to me and let me touch her belly.

"Feel it kicking, Eisenhower? There. I think it's wearing cowboy boots."

At first I was more interested in looking at the tattoo on Mom's pelvis: it was something she called a gryphon, which looked like a cross between a dragon and an eagle, and it seemed to be coming out of the place she said I'd come from. She'd had the tattoo done in Denver, and so I'd named the gryphon Denver. I'd seen it

41

before, but I didn't usually get to look at it up close. It had green eyes and a pointy red tongue, and the swelling of her belly was making Denver grow.

"Put your hand here," she said, placing my hand where she meant. There was a line there, running from her belly button right down through Denver to the place she said I'd stepped out of.

I felt something. And then I actually saw something: a ripple moved across my mother's belly like a shark's fin breaking the surface. My mother laughed and said the baby must like me, because she was waving.

"It's a *she*?" I asked.

"It," my mother said. "We don't know *what* it is yet, so we have to call it an *it*."

She took my hand and put it on her breast to let me feel how she was filling with milk and told me that the baby would suck her breasts and eat the milk from her just as I once did. I asked her if I could have some of the milk and she let me try, but I couldn't get anything and she ran her fingers through my hair and explained that the milk wouldn't come until the baby was closer to being born.

Against my better judgment, I was beginning to believe her.

"I'm going to have a baby inside me someday," I told her. Mom laughed and told me I was a boy, and that boys couldn't have babies. I started to cry and told her that I could too if I wanted to, but she said that I couldn't, pointing out that I didn't have the place between my legs where the seed gets in and babies get out. She was right. All I had was my penis, which looked like a little white worm. Mom told me that she liked my worm. She called him Mr. Worm.

"I still wish I was a girl."

It wasn't the first time I'd told her this, but when I said it that day she gave me a long sad look and started to cry.

"What's wrong, Mommy?"

"Nothing's wrong, Eisenhower. You're just so sweet. It makes me so sad that you're not happy with who you are. I'm afraid that's going to make your life very sad. I don't want you to be unhappy. I want you to be happy more than I want anything else in the world."

She tried, but she couldn't stop crying.

That night I didn't sleep well, and the next morning at breakfast I promised her that I wasn't unhappy. I'd decided that I didn't want to be a girl after all. She gave me a big hug and told me that was the best gift I could ever have given her.

We never played Jane and Anne again.

When it was time for the baby to come out, Mom went to the hospital. I was none too pleased, as I'd wanted to watch it arrive, but Mom said she had to go because the baby liked it inside her so much it didn't want to come out and only the doctors and the nurses knew how to lure it into the world.

She went away for a very long time. Now that she's gone forever, it sometimes seems like she never came back from that time in the hospital and I'm still waiting for her, and for all that time it's been only me and my father. In the morning he makes me get up and eat my cereal before eight, and at eight he tells me it's time to go out to the shop and sort bolts from nuts and place them according to size in metal trays. There are many different sizes of nuts and bolts, but there's nothing very interesting about sorting them so they're all alike in their special trays. I don't even know why I'm doing it. He works on something else while I sort—at one of his lathes or building another passage out of Cindercrete blocks—but when I stop sorting to draw pictures in the dust, using iron filings for curly hair or to show there's magic in the person I'm drawing, he appears and yells at me to get back to my sorting. When I try to ignore him or tell him that I'm not going to sort any more bolts, he slaps my face and kicks the pictures to pieces with his boot and tells me that I'd better. Then he goes back to whatever he's doing.

I want to tell him that I want Mom to come home. I wonder why the baby won't come out, and I imagine the doctors and nurses placing toys and sweets just outside the opening between her legs to attract it from its lair. But for some reason it will not come. What's it doing in there? Floating, Mom told me before she went away.

I imagine the baby is a dragon that looks something like Denver. After all, dragons live in caves. When it comes out, it'll breathe a shaft of fire and eat all the doctors and nurses. Or maybe another dragon inside my mother is keeping the baby a prisoner. Maybe the baby is in there sorting bolts from nuts and according to size.

Sometimes when I'm sorting bolts, Dad's friend Chandler comes to buy guns. Chandler's eyes are a little spooky: they look as though they might pop out of his face if you pushed a button in his stomach. One day Chandler comes to buy a small machine gun Dad made that Chandler calls a Tommy gun. I follow them out behind the barn, where Chandler tests the gun by lacing a woodpile with bullets, the logs dancing as the lead draws a dotted line.

"Beautiful!" Chandler says. "Beautiful!" He has a look of perfect happiness, but all at once his face becomes very serious. "But, Jake, I'd be taking quite a risk tryin' to move somethin' like this."

Dad smokes a cigarette and looks up into the sky, watching a hawk ride the air currents above the field across the grid road.

"Collectors would kill for it," he says.

"Sure they would, Jake, but the problem is finding the buyer and gettin' it into his hands and out of mine. It's got to be a buyer I can trust, cause if he brings it out at Christmas and accidentally plugs his mother-in-law—well, I could have a problem on my hands."

Dad spits at his feet the way Yahweh once spat. "How much you give me?"

Chandler laughs and shakes his head. "Make me a bologna sandwich and we'll talk about it."

But instead we have Campbell's tomato soup. I tell Chandler that Mom says not to slurp your soup, and he laughs at me and slurps even louder. He likes his tea cold, and he slurps that too. The two of them sit smoking cigarettes while I eat my dessert and then Dad gets down the whiskey bottle from the cupboard over the fridge and tells me to go back out and sort bolts while they talk.

Sometimes Dad takes me to the field and I ride round and round on the tractor until I get so bored I start to fidget and Dad stops the tractor and puts me in the truck. The truck's hot and dusty, and there's the smell of gasoline; it's as boring as the tractor, but quieter. I draw pictures in the dust on the dashboard and on the seats and on the floor. These are the longest days of my life. There's nothing but my pictures to break the monotony, and pictures aren't enough. I walk in circles around the truck. I lie in the box, watching the clouds drift and jet streams trace parallel lines across the sky, wondering about the people Mom told me are inside the tiny metal projectiles. Briefcases and sparkly jewellery decorate these people. I catch grasshoppers and make them fight to the death, the right-hand one against the left-hand one.

When the sun begins to go down, Dad finally stops the tractor and gets in the truck and drives home and makes a supper of split sausages and fried eggs and toast. I wolf it down, working on a picture of a dragon on my brown pad of paper beside my plate. Sometimes I ask Dad to draw me a horse and sometimes he does. He draws horses far better than I can. After supper I go straight to bed without a bath, even though I have never been so dirty.

When she finally comes home from the hospital, there's no baby and my mother's eyes are as empty as Dad's and she has to stay in bed for weeks and the sorting bolts and the trips to the field go on as though she hasn't returned. The only difference is that I'm sometimes allowed to go in and visit her after I eat my Campbell's soup and before I go to bed. But when I visit her, it's as if she's not all there. Some part of her has escaped with the baby. I tell her I've missed her and try to give her kisses, and she nods and looks away and says that she's tired and could I go and let her sleep? I ask her if I can have some of the baby's milk, and she starts to cry. Dad comes in and tells me to get out of her room. When I ask what happened to the baby, Dad tells me not to ask questions I don't want to know the answer to, and when I ask again he picks me up by the collar and carries me to my room and drops me on my bed and tells me to stay there until I get enough sense in my head not to ask stupid questions.

The baby must have got away and nobody knows where it went. Mom's belly isn't swelled up anymore, so I know it isn't inside her. Maybe it's inside somebody else now and we'll have to fetch it back when it comes out.

What if it's inside me? I feel my tummy, but all I can tell for sure is there's *something* in there.

I wonder what it must be like to live under the skin: dark and warm and never, but always, alone.

Besides Chandler and Emmet, my only visitor at the hospital was Dr. Irvine, who sat by my bed every now and then and talked to me if I felt like talking. He brought me books by Russians, for which I was grateful. I asked him to bring me Russian books because for years I'd wanted to be Russian. I'd already read some Dostoevsky and Tolstoy and Solzhenitsyn's *One Day in the Life of Ivan Denisovich* and Lermontov's *A Hero of Our Time,* the last of which I found mentioned in Dostoevsky and tracked down in our school library. I read it three times. I doubt it's only Canadians who spend their lives wishing they were from somewhere more interesting, but it's certainly a Canadian way of thinking. Most of the kids at school wanted to be American. My mom was American, so I could have gone that route, but I didn't like most of the kids at school (and they didn't like me), and when I found out that my father's ancestors were from a village that had become part of the Soviet Union, I decided that meant I was Russian. I know that sounds pretty stupid. It made my dad shake his head and spit. He'd always worried that the Russians were taking over, and there I was telling him *he* was a Russian.

Dr. Irvine also brought me the Bible, King James Version, and explained to me that we were living in a world occupied by Satan's forces, but that God would one day come to liberate us. I told him that I hated God and He should not look for me to soldier in His army, and he told me that the doctor had told him I had given Emmet the will to live. I told him it wasn't true, or that if I had, it was only by accident.

"Accident?" he said. "I would have thought that if anyone would recognize the power of *accident,* it would be you."

I had to turn away from him. He'd so easily exposed my ignorance.

"The flowers will grow," he said, and he smiled. "I confess that I envy what you did for Emmet. I can see a gift in you that I wish I had. It really is envy on my part, and I ask the Lord's forgiveness for not being satisfied with my lot. But I envy your life's potential. You acted rashly, but you have been forgiven. The people of Broken Head have forgiven you. God is watching you and smiling."

I still didn't respond, wondering where all this was coming from, and afraid to admit to him that flowers growing from blood or tears was something I'd stolen from Dostoevsky. Because I wouldn't speak or look in his eyes, he said goodbye and went away.

The next day I told the doctor I no longer wanted to kill God. I told him I'd forgiven my father and I wanted to be able to forgive myself. I didn't want to die. I wanted to be saved. I was searching for some sign of Christ within me. Though he congratulated me, the doctor seemed a bit disappointed. I was disappointed too. I didn't really feel anything. I didn't feel what I knew I *should* feel when I closed my eyes and saw my father's eyes looking up into nothing.

Chandler came back a week later and asked me for the money. I told him I'd forgotten the whole thing the second he'd walked out the door. He sat there in the shadows, those eyes of his all over me.

"I guess I'd better talk to somebody about it," I said. "I'm not sure who."

Chandler licked his lips with his yellow tongue. "We've got ourselves a serious situation here," he said. "I don't think you understand exactly how serious. That's something your father and I always had an understanding about. He owed me money a lot of the time, and he always understood the seriousness of the situation when he did. That's one of the things I appreciated most about your father. I respected him, even when he owed me money, because I knew he understood the seriousness of the situation. But I don't think you understand, Dwight. I'm getting the definite feeling that you do not understand the seriousness of the situation we find ourselves in. And that's disappointing!"

He barked the last three words so loud that I flinched, and that made him smile.

"I think you're the one who doesn't understand," I said. "You're nothing. You're less than nothing. I'm not even the tiniest bit afraid of you."

He sat up straight. "Is that so?" His grin only got bigger, his remaining yellow teeth jutting out of his mouth in their various directions. "Well, well. Isn't that interesting? What did you think you saw when your dad shot off your ear? Or I s'pose you talk that way because of where you are. But you won't always be here. Sometimes we're not afraid enough of what we should be afraid of because we don't have the proper imagination to appreciate the seriousness of our situation."

It was cloudy outside, and I was hoping we might even get some rain, which we hadn't had in weeks. The curtain was open to let in some light, and a fly bounced against the window. I watched until it finally settled.

"There's nothing serious about you, Chandler. There never has been. You're a joke. Didn't Mom tell you? She must have." He didn't respond. "Could you go away now? I'm tired."

The fly rose and began bouncing against the window again.

"I fucked your mother," Chandler said. "You know that? I fucked her good." He smiled his smile and stood up and started for the door.

"I could crush you like a fly," I said. "Did you know that?"

He turned to me with a look of surprise that slowly faded to a look it took me a few seconds to recognize as fear—a look that, on his face, was so surprising it made me feel better than I had in months.

I thought he was going to say something, but all he did was shake his head vigorously, as if trying to detach a biting insect without using his hands, before he walked out the door.

I was fifteen the last time Mom and I visited Chandler's cottage in the Cypress Hills. It was in bad shape. Some beast had dug through the shakes on the northwest corner of the roof, looking for shelter in the attic, and a water stain shaped like the chalked marking of a body appeared on the north wall and the plywood floor in the northwest corner. I climbed up and saw that Chandler had tacked a piece of tin over the hole. Despite his effort, the room smelled fustier than ever— smelled like something had died. Some animal must have got trapped inside the attic when Chandler had done the repair.

Chandler inherited the lot from his father and tore down the building that was already there, which I imagined as a pretty little log cabin with a cheery fire burning in a stone hearth. He planned to build something grand. He'd gotten this far, but could never find the time, money or inclination to finish his summer temple of love. The kitchen was a hotplate on top of a tiny propane fridge in one corner. There was no running water, so it had to be lugged from the public tap on the street. The two beds had rusty springs that squeaked every time you breathed, and the mattresses had absorbed the damp and smell of the rest of the room. The outhouse smelled even worse than the cabin.

Still, Mom was determined to pretend we were in paradise. She bought a pile of magazines we usually never read (I mean, we didn't usually read magazines period), for some reason thinking I'd be inter- ested in reading the specs of various models of automobiles. Even the blondes draped over the machines looked metal. But maybe the car mags weren't really for me: Mom still had fantasies about sports cars and speed, and before long the women's and the news magazines bored her. The only one we fought over was the copy of *Esquire* with the label "Hot." She started pestering me about what I saw in the young lady with so much skin and such silly hair, and I gave it up for the Bible. She liked to tease me about reading the Bible, but she let me do it, just so long as Dad wasn't around. We both knew he wouldn't be happy with me reading the Bible.

Four hours after we arrived, we were on the veranda, Mom stretched out on a chaise longue and me slouching with one leg over the arm of a lawn chair—she'd brought along some plastic lawn furniture my father had collected on one of his business trips—when Chandler pulled into the driveway in his El Camino.

"How's everybody doing?" Chandler called as he stepped out of the car, shading his eyes against the noon sunshine. I dropped the Bible under my chair and shuffled a copy of *Time* over it before Chandler had climbed the five steps. Mom's eyes fluttered open as Chandler's shadow fell across her face.

"Well, aren't you a sight to heal a sick man's wandering?" Chandler said.

"Can't heal a wandering," I said.

Chandler swivelled his head and aimed his eyes at me, as though he'd only just noticed my existence.

"Well," I shrugged. "Is a wandering a wound? Did you mean it's a wound?"

"It's a sickness," Chandler said. "With a woman as beautiful as your mother waiting at home, a wandering is a terrible and unexplained disease. It's a shame, and a shame is worse than an illness."

"This isn't home," I said, shrugging a second shrug to show Chandler I was barely interested enough in what he was saying to bother pointing out the holes in his logic. I almost picked up the *Time* magazine before I remembered what it was hiding.

"Chandler," Mom finally interrupted. "You said you were going to the States. What are you doing here? Oh, don't even tell me. The thing is, we need coffee. How could I forget coffee? Could you go up to the store and get us some?"

"I just got here." Chandler crossed his arms on his chest.

"I decided to check in on you before I go south. I think I'll leave tomorrow morning."

"Tomorrow morning? I can't give you coffee unless you get us some."

"That's all right. I don't need coffee."

"But, Chandler, I do. I need coffee. And you do too. You're just not owning up to it."

Chandler thought about this, lifting himself up on his tiptoes and staring out towards the lake through the veil of lodgepole pines, trying to get a clearer view of a bikinied woman paddling by in a canoe.

"Is that so?" he finally said. "Not owning up to my needs. Well, I s'pose you must be right. Women are always right about these things," he told me. He turned and descended the five steps. "I'll be back before you can say titteroonee."

He got into the car and slammed the door.

"Titteroonee," I said.

Mom was on her feet by the time Chandler's El Camino had reached the street. She leaned down over me and kissed the top of my head. "I'll see you later."

"Where you goin'?"

"I'll leave you to deal with Chandler when he gets back. It'll probably be easier to get rid of him if I'm not around."

"What?"

"You said you'd get rid of Chandler if he showed up. Right?"

I had said that, but only to show her I was on her side and not my father's. He'd refused to come with us to the cottage. I'd only said it to stop her from crying. She said we couldn't go without my father, because Chandler would show up and bother us, and I said I'd get rid of him if he did show up. It was a stupid thing to say. It was Chandler's cottage. We were the guests. I'd hoped she was wrong and Chandler wouldn't appear, and I thought if he did Mom would humour him for a few hours and send him on his way. She was good at that kind

of thing. Hadn't she managed to send him off to the store two minutes after he'd arrived? So why would she leave it up to me to deal with
a problem she was so much better equipped to tackle?

Of course, I couldn't very well point any of this out to her. She
was already retreating along the path towards the lake, waggling her
fingers over her shoulder.

"Make him a cup of coffee."

"I don't know how to make coffee. Except instant."

"Well, let him make some, then. Otherwise, he might be upset
at having to go buy it for nothing."

"Where should I say you went?"

"Wherever you think." She shrugged and blew me another kiss
before disappearing into the tall pines.

There was nothing to do but wait. I picked up *Time* and began
to flip through. The Americans were campaigning for some election
or other. Somewhere people were rioting and killing and being killed.
An abortion doctor in Florida had been wounded by a sniper with a
high-powered rifle. I wondered if Dad ever went to Florida. There was
an article about it getting close to 1984 and talking about what Orwell
had got right and what he'd got wrong. I'd only read *Animal Farm*,
but Dad liked to talk about Big Brother watching you. He wouldn't
even let me get a social insurance number because he didn't want
the government to be able to keep track of me. Mom didn't have one
either. The only reason Dad had one was because you couldn't avoid
it if you joined the army. And Big Brother wouldn't send him what he
called his "honourably maimed money" if he didn't have one.

Chandler was clutching the can of coffee in his hand when he
climbed the steps again.

"Do you want to make yourself a cup?" I asked him, doing my
best to sound hospitable.

Chandler stared.

"I don't know how," I explained. "I only know instant."

"She inside?" Chandler started for the door.

"No. An old friend just dropped by and she had to take off."

"Old friend?"

"Yeah. That woman from Maple Creek? Melva?"

Chandler shook his head. "Where did they go?"

"Fort Walsh, I think. That's where they usually go every summer." Fort Walsh is a tourist attraction in the Cypress Hills. It's the birthplace of the RCMP. They've rebuilt the fort, and they have people dressed up like they were living a hundred years ago to make you feel like you're walking into the past. "She and Melva went. They might have gone to Melva's. She's from Maple Creek. Her husband's a cop?"

"Is that so? A cop? What's old Jake think of that?"

I shrugged. "Make some coffee, if you want. I won't have any. I like the smell, but it doesn't agree with me."

"You're too young for coffee," Chandler said.

I nodded. "That must be the problem."

Chandler disappeared inside for a while but came back without a cup of coffee and reclined in the chaise longue. Lying back that way only made him look uncomfortable, like a turtle on its back. He scratched his forehead and looked around, searching for what it was people came there to find.

"Something got in your roof," I offered.

"Yeah. Squirrel. When you think she'll be back?"

"The squirrel?"

"You said she might be at Fort Walsh?"

"Oh, Mom? I don't know. Sometimes she stays the night at Melva's. Sometimes Melva and her husband bring her back the next day."

"What? She leaves you all alone overnight?"

"Oh, I'm fine. I've got magazines."

Chandler studied me, realizing at last that he was in danger of getting stuck babysitting the kid who Jake had been warned would kill him. "So where's your dad?" he finally asked.

"Florida."

"Florida? What's he doing in Florida?"

"I don't know. What's anyone do in Florida? Business."

"Business," Chandler said, settling back into the chair, lounging on the longue. "You know what your dad's business is?"

"Garbage. He buys other people's garbage."

Chandler laughed. "Yeah, I guess that's right. I guess that's what he does. You're not so dumb, are ya, kid?"

"No."

"Nope. Not so dumb," Chandler repeated.

A cloud floated between us and the small blue window of sunshine framed by the green pines. We both looked up.

"And he burns it," I said.

"What?" Chandler turned from the sun to look at me.

"He burns garbage," I said. "Down in the pasture. That's his business. He gets a good hot fire going, and that's the end of the garbage. I watch him."

Chandler opened his mouth and closed it. "Do you like your dad?" he finally asked.

I was rather taken aback by the question. It wasn't a question anyone was supposed to ask. "How do you mean?"

"I don't know. I'm just wondering . . . if you're close."

I picked up a magazine. "He's my dad," I said, and for good measure, turning the page of my magazine, I said it again. "He's my dad."

Not much later, Chandler rose and said he had to be getting along to a gun show down in Montana and to say hi to Mom when she got back.

"Enjoy the cabin," he said, stretching a hand skyward before he stepped into his El Camino.

She was back ten minutes later, by which time I was flipping through *Esquire* again, ogling the breasts of the women in the pictures. All the girls in *Esquire* were beautiful.

"Are you still reading that stuff?" She sprawled back into position on the chaise longue.

"Got something better to do?"

"Yeah." She grabbed the magazine from my hand and threw it off the veranda. It landed on the roots of a tree that was almost a hundred years old and almost a hundred feet high: a great fire had destroyed this forest a hundred years before and reseeded the whole thing in the destroying. I tried to punch her shoulder but she grabbed me by the wrist, and I tried to grab her arm with my left hand and she grabbed my left wrist, and we were wrestling. She outweighed me, though, and always won. She kept telling me that any day now I'd reach puberty and shoot up to six feet, but at fifteen I was still only five feet tall. She was sitting on top of me, her hands pinning my wrists, leaning over me so that I was staring straight up into her cleavage.

"What are you looking at?"

"Nothing," I said, craning my neck so that I was looking away. She smiled. "I want to do an experiment."

"What kind of experiment?"

"You'll see."

She got off me and went into the cabin. I went back to the Bible. When she came out again, she'd changed into a halter top and a pair of denim cut-offs that were both a couple sizes too small for her. Using a tiny mirror she got out of her purse, she painted her eyelashes with mascara.

"What kind of experiment is this?"

She tilted the mirror to look at me. I got up for a closer look at the brush she used to apply the mascara.

"Just want to see if I can make my eyelashes as pretty as yours."

"Shut up."

Her reflection winked at me. "How do I look?"

"Good," I said. "You're a very handsome woman." I had read someone saying this somewhere. I felt a little shy, like I was talking to a stranger. She looked like one of the high school girls on my bus. "What are you gonna do?"

"Go for a walk."

A steady hum of cars cruised around the lake, radios blaring, the air a half part essence of lodgepole pine and a half part exhaust. I'd walked around the lake after we arrived and been passed by the same car—an orange Nova carrying two teenage boys and a dangling pair of plush dice—seventeen times in the one circuit, Alice Cooper confessing his love for the dead out the window. I know that, for Caroline, going up to that cottage on an island in Georgian Bay must be a sort of retreat to the wilderness, but to a farm kid like me, cottaging felt like a weekend in Toronto.

Mom gave her instructions before we left the veranda: "All I want you to do is walk a ways behind me, so that you can see what happens but nobody knows you're with me."

"Why? Why can't I walk with you?"

"Because it'll wreck the experiment."

I walked behind her, watching her bum move. An experimental wiggle. That wiggle had never been there before, but it looked as though she'd been walking that way her entire life—it looked far more natural than my own walk felt.

She hadn't wiggled half a block before the Bunsen burner of her bum set off an explosion in some young men's Erlenmeyer flasks. Five teenagers, lounging on their patio, drinking a few beers, spotted her going by. They hooted and whistled at her, and she turned and blew a kiss at them. One went over the railing of the patio and raced down the path towards her, and the rest of them followed. She ran. They jumped into an old red convertible and started after her. She was wise enough to cut through some yards and head for the lake, but they spotted her, and by the time I caught up, one of them had her trapped at the end of somebody's dock, and the others were sitting in their car at the top of the path. Every so often the driver yelled, "I want you to have my baby," and the car rocked as all four of them bounced around and howled like werewolves.

They noticed me standing there watching them, and one

pimply-faced boy got out of the car and approached me. "Is she your sister?" he asked.

"No," I said. "She's my mother."

He laughed. "You got a beautiful sister," he said.

"Beautiful," I said.

"Does she have a boyfriend?"

"No," I said. "A husband. You'd like him. He's a hired killer. He just shot an abortion doctor down in Florida."

The guy laughed and opened his mouth, but he began to look nervous. "He's a killer, is he?"

I didn't answer. Down at the end of the dock, it looked like my mother was crying. She hid her face in her hands and kept shaking her head at whatever the guy said to her. He tried to put his hand on her bare back, but she batted the hand away. Finally he gave up and left her alone, and the pimply-faced guy who had spoken to me said, "See ya 'round." They both got into the convertible and drove away, the horn bleating as though they were leaving a wedding.

I walked down the dock to my mother. She still hid her face in her hands. "Are they gone?" she asked me.

"Yeah."

When she dropped her hands and turned to me, she was grinning a wide grin.

At the cabin, she washed off the makeup in the enamel hand basin.

"What was that supposed to prove?"

"Nothing. It proved what it proved."

"What if I tell Dad?"

She turned to me, her makeup running, and for a moment she looked very sad. Then she smiled again, an angry smile that went straight to my stomach, and she said, "Oh, please don't tell Daddy on me, Dwight. Please don't. He'd kill me if you did. I'll do anything if you promise not to tell. Anything. I'll let you feel my titties . . ."
And she yanked the halter top down so that her breasts pointed at

me. I looked up into her eyes, more than embarrassed, but still wanting to look again.

"Go ahead," she said. "Feel them. You used to suck them. They've never really been anyone's but yours."

I turned away until she covered them again, and when I turned back, she said she was sorry.

"Why do you do stuff like that?" I said.

"I said I was sorry. It was stupid. I don't know why. Bored, I guess. Boredom is my mate, and you're my baby."

We went back out to our plastic furniture on the veranda, but after a minute she started to cry. "I'm really sorry, Dwight. I shouldn't have done that." When I ignored her, she grabbed my head between her hands and made me look at her. "I'm sorry I did that to you."

When I didn't respond, she released her grip and I turned the page of the Bible.

"Relax, Mother," I said.

The rest of our vacation went pretty well. Those boys figured out where we lived and drove by a lot, but they didn't bother us. Mom thought it was pretty funny.

The week after Chandler threatened me, I spent a lot of sleepless nights trying to figure out what I'd do about him and imagining what he was planning to do about me. The nurses tried to make me take pills, but I wouldn't. I knew I'd scared him, and his strategy could be to get me first. I thought he'd come while I was sleeping.

He wasn't a man to be messed with. I remembered him once telling Dad how he'd castrated a man who refused to pay back a debt. I didn't believe it, but I spent a lot of time thinking about that story.

I used to hold the calves down while Dad castrated them.

I didn't believe Dad actually owed him any money. If anything, it was more likely he owed us money for some of Dad's guns.

I imagined shooting him through the forehead. I imagined his brains on the wall behind him before he fell.

———

Emmet crutched himself into my room one day to tell me he was leaving. His cattle needed him, as their calves would be coming soon, and it was time he got home to watch the expectant mothers. He couldn't trust his cousin who'd been looking after them all winter, and he thought he could face the house all right without her there.

"She's there," I said, wanting to play the part that Irvine said God had set out for me.

Emmet peered down at me and said, "In the flowers?" He shook his head. "No flowers in March."

I wished him well and he wished me the same.

"Emmet," I said. "A friend of my father's wants to kill me."

He nodded and smiled. "You'd know more about that than me. Maybe the flowers'll save you."

He nodded once more and was gone.

"I think I have a problem," I said, after I'd told Irvine about Chandler.

He frowned. "Donald Chandler?" he asked.

I didn't know his first name.

"The man who sold guns? He was a friend of your father's?"

I nodded.

"He lived at the Elite Hotel on Main Street? Did you not hear about that? Did you not hear the sirens? It burned down the night before last. They believe it started in his room. They think he fell asleep while he was smoking in bed. He must have woken up, because he managed to crawl out his door and down the hallway a few yards, and in the end he wasn't even burned. A fireman carried him out, but it was too late. He died from smoke inhalation. I have him downstairs right now."

"He's dead?" I asked.

Irvine nodded, and when I didn't say anything else, he got uncomfortable and started talking to fill up the silence. "Smoke inhalation victims are particularly interesting. They don't need much makeup for the funeral. Smoke inhalation makes the skin look pink.

Gives a nice healthy glow." He sniffed his fingertips. "I wouldn't worry about the money," he said. "Your father's estate will have to look after it. If there's anything on paper. Was the man a friend of yours?"

I didn't know what to say, and after a few moments Irvine came over to my bed and placed a hand on my shoulder. "I'm sorry," he said. "God's will."

I shook my head but still couldn't think what to say.

Instead of relief, I had this strange, empty feeling I can't entirely explain. I was afraid God had tricked me into another contract. I'd plotted a thousand ways I might escape Chandler and another thousand of how he might kill me. I'd thought my way through it and decided it was better to tell Irvine and let him help me out of it than it would be to try to find my way through it on my own. It was the right thing to do. I wanted to do the right thing.

But God had dealt with him. Crushed him like a fly. God had either repaid his debt to me or chalked up one more debt against me that he'd expect me to repay in kind. I wasn't sure which.

THREE

Aside from the Chandler thing, when my time in that hospital room was finally past, the whole of it left about as much impression as the smoke drifting up from a candle. One day I woke up from a heavy sleep and Dr. Irvine was sitting in the chair, the same place he always sat. When he saw I was awake, he said, "We've got a suite in our basement. Kitchen. Private entrance. I had it put in for my mother when she lived with us, but she passed away a couple of years ago."

"I'm sorry," I said.

"You're welcome to stay with us for as long as need be. I can arrange a job for you."

He waited for an answer, but I didn't give him any. I wasn't entirely sure he was actually there.

"I just want to help," he finally said.

"I can't remember my mother or even my father's face. Whenever I try to think of my father, I see Chandler."

"I'm sorry about that," he said. "That must be very difficult."

I couldn't think of what else to say, and after a while he stood.

"We'll talk about the suite again soon."

He walked out the door.

Maybe we did talk about it again. If we did, I don't recall. I only remember my doctor asking me how I felt about Irvine's arrangement and telling him I didn't understand why he'd do that for me and all of a sudden feeling tears in my eyes. I had to get up and leave the doctor's office. It could not have been many days later that a nurse shook me awake and told me I should get dressed because it was time to go. I asked her where I was going, and she smiled and said I was being discharged and told me again to get dressed before she closed the door between us. I didn't remember Irvine's offer at all, and as I pulled on my pants and buttoned my shirt, I kept imagining getting into my father's truck and driving back to the farm and finding my mother and father there waiting for me. But when I stepped out of my room, the first thing I saw was Irvine and my doctor and the nurse standing near the nurses' station, talking in serious tones. They saw me coming, and all three smiled at once. I approached them warily and the nurse said I was looking well and Irvine shook my hand and my doctor asked me how I felt.

"Tired," I said.

The doctor said I needed exercise and it would pass.

"Shall we go?" Irvine asked.

I put my bag in the back of my Fargo pickup, which had a special spot in the hospital parking lot, but Irvine motioned me up the street, so I picked up the bag again and followed him. The Irvines lived close by: only a block away. Once I had known this, and as I walked behind Irvine it came back to me. I sometimes used to drive by, hoping I might see Gloria, imagining her life in that big house. It was one of the oldest houses in Broken Head, built right back near the turn of the century by some doctor or lawyer. It was brick, and there weren't many brick houses in Broken Head. I think the man who built it was dreaming of some London district where women carried parasols and went about on men's arms, but when Irvine led me around back, there was a very modern kidney-shaped swimming pool surrounded by a perfect little garden. Gloria Irvine and her boyfriend, Nick Campion, were sunning on metal lounge chairs beside the pool while a woman I recognized from choir recitals as Mrs. Irvine misted the flowers with a hose. She stopped to look at us, raising her nose a little higher as we approached, but continued what she was doing.

Gloria saw me. She pushed her sunglasses up to the top of her head and smiled. I was in her backyard. Gloria Irvine's backyard. The most beautiful woman in the world, and I was standing there in her backyard, holding a battered suitcase, and she was smiling at me. I hid behind the suitcase, and then I wanted to hide the suitcase.

"Oh, good, you're both out here," Irvine said. By "both," you could somehow tell he meant only Gloria and Mrs. Irvine. Nick sat up. Mrs. Irvine released the cock on the hose so the water stopped flowing. She waited, her eyebrows arched. Gloria swung her feet to the ground and draped her towel over her shoulders. "I wanted to introduce you to Dwight Froese. He's going to be staying in the basement suite for a while."

There was an awkward silence before Gloria sprang to her feet. "Dwight! Dwight was in choir with me. Weren't you?"

"Yes," I said.

"I miss choir," she said. "Do you miss choir?"

"Yes," I said.

I'd joined the choir to be near Gloria Irvine.

"I was two years ahead of you. I don't really remember meeting you," Nick Campion said as he stepped forward and offered his hand.

"No," I said, though I did remember him, of course. That chin of his that goes on forever. The tiny mole on his cheek that looks like he might have painted it on. His yellow sports car in the school parking lot. I took his hand and he tried to squeeze the life out of mine. When he let me go, I stepped backwards and looked at Gloria. She was the most beautiful woman on earth, and I had invaded her backyard, the centre of her world. I knew it was not right and felt I should apologize.

"I do miss choir," I said.

And she said, "Me too."

Even with the towel draped over her shoulders, I could see these lovely hollows at the base of her neck that I had never seen before. And then she shifted the towel, wrapping it more tightly around her shoulders, and I looked away.

"Gloria's just finished her first year at McGill," Irvine said.

Gloria opened her mouth, but before she could speak, her mother interrupted. "I thought we'd agreed we weren't going to rent out your mother's suite." She was talking to Irvine, but she was staring straight at me.

"Hello?" I said.

She didn't respond.

"We're not renting it," Irvine said. "Dwight needs a place to stay."

I was relieved when Mrs. Irvine turned her gaze on her husband and away from me. He met it with a similarly unrelenting expression, and at last she turned back to the garden and recommenced her misting.

"It's this way," Irvine said, motioning for me to follow. I nodded to Gloria and Nick as I walked away. Gloria gave a nervous little wave.

The private entrance was shielded by an arbour at the side of the house. We walked down through the laundry room and across a cement floor to another door. Irvine pushed in a key, opened the door and reached in to flick on the light. He handed me the key.

"There you go. The key works on the outside too. But we never lock the door. You can if you like. It's your space."

It was a six-inch step up onto a floor covered with beige carpet. The apartment was one room: the sink, refrigerator, stove, a chrome kitchen table and three matching chairs were at one end and the continental-sized bed was at the other. There was also a dresser, a bedside table and a pressboard bookshelf. The ceiling was intersected by a large beam, painted black, between the kitchen and the bed. Two small windows at ceiling level let in a little light. A lush potted fern in a metal plant stand stood below one window.

"Watch your head," Irvine said, motioning to the beam as he walked across the room. "You're much taller than Mother."

"Thanks," I said. "For everything."

Irvine shrugged. "It's no palace. You can start the job next week. It's only janitorial work, but it'll mean you've got a little money until you decide what to do with the farm. I'll give you a ride if you want. Or you can drive yourself, I guess. Or you can even walk. It's not far."

"Thanks," I said again.

"It's nothing. Place to stay until you get your bearings."

I tried hard to think of something else to say. "Thanks," I said once more.

Irvine patted me on the shoulder and left, pulling the door closed behind him. I set down my bag, looked around at my new home, took a step forward and slammed my head on the beam. I sat down on the bed, rubbing hard to force the pain away. My ears rang, my father's bullet still whistling by.

A while later I went for a walk. As I was leaving, I passed under a window and heard the Irvines arguing. Before I could make out more than Mrs. Irvine saying the word "murderer," I hunched my shoulders and walked away. I heard her say it twice: *Murderer, murderer.* I didn't want to listen, because I didn't want to hear that it was me they were arguing about. It made me think of my own parents, though it didn't really sound anything like them. But I kept imagining my mother arguing with my father about the fact that I'd killed him and how it served him right for treating her the way he did.

Sprinklers twirled on lawns. It was another dry spring. I remember thinking that if they didn't get some rain soon, there'd be nothing to harvest. I circled the block and headed back to where I'd started.

A couple of hours later I was in my room when Irvine knocked on the door to bring me a frozen dinner and offered to drive me over to the grocery store. I thanked him, but said I'd manage well enough myself. He offered money and I accepted.

I'd never bought my own groceries before, but had sometimes trailed around the store with my mother. It was a strange feeling, deciding what to buy, piling things into the cart, the Muzak ebbing and swelling. A couple of women kept glancing at me, whispering to one another, and when I walked by them, I nodded and they smiled.

I forgot the obvious things like butter and salt and pepper. As I decided which cupboards to put things away in, I discovered sugar, flour, rice and macaroni in the canisters lining the back of the kitchen counter. There was salt and pepper in a pair of shakers shaped like toadstools.

I slept for much of the next week, but I had bad dreams. Dreams of drowning. I'd wake to find myself sitting bolt upright, straining for the surface, gasping for air. Another dream that wouldn't leave me alone was a visit from my mother. Once she woke me by walking into my room without knocking, delivering fresh peas and beans from the garden and pickles and canned spaghetti sauce. I said she should tell Dad to confess that he'd killed her. She picked at the bandage on my ear and asked me how the job was going. I told her it was great. She told me she was going to change the dressing and started to do just that. It felt like she was really there, really alive, and I only had a vague sense that there was something mysterious and precious about her presence. She kissed me on the top of the head and I woke up. I lay there staring up at the black beam crossing my room.

A few months after Mom lost the baby, she smiled her old smile at me one morning and I thought the world would go back to the way it was meant to be. I started helping her instead of Dad, cleaning house and folding laundry and making meals, and we picked up where we'd left off with our games of hide-and-go-seek and our home-schooling. She drilled me on multiplication tables while I helped her make pie. She made me read out loud when I went to bed at night. A picture book that told the story of Homer's *Odyssey* was one of my favourites. She read me stories about Peter Rabbit and the Knights of the Round Table and the Wizard of Oz. I started writing my own simple story books that year, when I was still five. They were heavily influenced by Thornton W. Burgess, King Arthur, the Hardy Boys, Homer and

L. Frank Baum. Sometimes she'd point out the school bus driving by and tell me that next year I'd be on it, but when it was time for me to start grade one, my father wouldn't let me go.

"What could they teach him that we can't?"

"It'll be good for him to be with other kids," Mom insisted.

We were eating our supper, the radio playing the news, the late August sun cutting a swath in the kitchen's gloom.

"Why? All the crap they'll put in his head. He's already reading every book you can find him. What's he need school for?"

She'd bought me a Robert Louis Stevenson book when we were in town to buy groceries, and he'd wondered how much it had cost but let it go when she told him. Now it was open beside my plate, and even though I'd found the vocabulary was really a little beyond me, I kept staring at the words while they talked, pretending I wasn't listening.

"Maybe I need a break," she said. "Are you gonna teach him?"

"I already do teach him. I teach him to fend for himself."

"You don't even talk to him. You never give him a word of encouragement."

I could hear him chewing on that, and I wanted to look up because I could feel his eyes on me, but I didn't dare. He lit a cigarette. Then all at once he reached over with his good hand and closed my book, and I couldn't help looking up into his face.

"This world's full of idiots," he said. "The town of Broken Head, where your mother wants to send you off to school, ain't nothing but a crowd of morons chasing their own tails. You're different from them, Dwight. You have something inside you that makes you different from anyone else in this world. You can be something better. Something special."

He stopped talking and I nodded and waited for more, but he looked at Mom and so I looked at her too. She was staring at her plate.

It was peculiar, that speech, coming from him. As much as I may have hated myself at times in my life, once he'd told me of my specialness I never really stopped believing what he said. Even when other kids at school were humiliating me, in some way I always felt above them. I believed that somewhere inside me was the glint of greatness.

And so because my father did not want me corrupted by the world, I stayed home and Mom taught me for almost two full years, until one spring morning Dad wanted us out to help with the rock-picking. Mom and I both hated picking rocks more than anything, and I hid when it was time to go. When he couldn't find me, she said that I had school work to do anyway, and he could bloody well pick rocks by himself.

"Isn't it about time he graduated?" my father said.

I was hiding under the couch and no one had ever found me there.

"He'll graduate, all right. You know it's against the law to keep a child home from school? If they find out, they'll come and take him away from us. Maybe the police'll come and have a look around too. Is that what you want?"

They'd had this fight before, but on this day Mom had a certain edge to her voice and Dad was fed up with both her and my lack of willingness to help around the place, so he slapped her face hard and said, "Send him off to school then, and maybe they can teach him to kill his father. That's what God wants. So you better do it." And then he headed for the door.

"You don't believe in God," my mother called after him, not giving him so much as a tear or a drop of blood in reward for his slap.

"No," my father called back. "But the teachers at the school likely do."

Mom must have already figured out the number she'd need to phone to make the arrangements, because the next day when she drove me to the school on the south edge of Broken Head, the principal and the teacher were expecting us. They didn't believe what Mom told them about my prior learning, but they gave me a book and I showed them I knew all those words, and they asked me my multiplication tables and I told them the right numbers. Mom and the teacher, Mrs. Field, walked me to the grade two room. Mrs. Field introduced me to the class and everyone stared at me. She pointed to an empty desk and I shuffled to it, sat down and looked back at Mom still standing in the doorway. She blew me a kiss and disappeared.

I remember Gloria Irvine sitting near the front of the row next to mine, her blond hair shining like a halo in the sunlight falling through the window. It was that day I started desiring. I wanted her to glance back for a look at me, like some of the other kids were doing, but she stared straight ahead at the blackboard, twirling a lock of her hair around her finger.

Sometimes I wonder if Choppy might be right that the principal desires me, but even though she's friendlier than a principal maybe ought to be to a caretaker, I don't think it's true. Men like Choppy understand desire only through their own eyes, and from what I've seen, women tend to desire in different ways than men. Still, they do desire, and I don't pretend to understand a woman's desires. I used to want to understand, but I have given that up, just as I have given up on desire. My father used to say that religion caused all the world's problems, but it's really desire that destroys us. If it weren't for desire, we'd have no need for God.

The lawyer's son is back at school. He sneered at me this morning when I made the mistake of looking in his direction, then looked scared when I kept my eyes on him. That's a mess, I know. A good janitor's like a ghost. The kids should be able to walk right through you while you're mopping the floor. On the other hand, he's behaving himself with the other kids better than I've seen in the past. Maybe I've put a little religion in him.

I pray for him. I worry that he won't show up one morning and the principal will call me in and tell me that he's been hit by a bus.

The church Gloria takes Caroline to on Queen Street is a nice enough place. There's a lovely stained glass Mary they'd never have allowed in the church they went to back in Broken Head. Nick still doesn't go to church. The nanny goes to the same church Caroline does, but not on Sunday mornings. She goes on Tuesday evenings, wearing loose clothing and carrying a canvas bag. In the service she takes part in, they play strange Asian music or recordings of the ocean tide, and sometimes they chant. Kripalu yoga. It's a religion about becoming aware of your own body. I went to my first session last Tuesday, and took a place in the back row, where I could watch what the others were doing. The nanny waved when she spotted me. She was in the front row, right below the cross.

It's all about stretching and relaxing your muscles and bones and concentrating on feeling how the stretches burn in your body and into your mind. At the end of the service everyone chanted, their hands clasped before them, and the instructor tilted her head to us and said, "I bow to the light within you."

Afterwards the nanny asked me how I liked it and invited me to go for a coffee, but I told her I had to be getting somewhere.

The job Irvine found me was cleaning toilets in office buildings. I was the low man on the totem pole, so I got that job, and the young woman who'd had it before me would sit and smile at me while we ate our lunches. I thought at first it was simply gratitude for coming along and by my very existence raising her a little higher in the world, but actually she was impressed that I had been on the news and had killed the monster that had made my mother's life a living hell and murdered her in the end. That's what Patty told me when she tried to talk to me. The other women paused in their conversations to listen, and I shook my head and said I didn't really want to talk about it, and the other women looked away. Patty smiled sweetly and nodded that she understood.

It was there that I started learning my trade and began to love what I do. What could be more elemental than mopping and wiping and rinsing other people's shit and piss and vomit from porcelain and linoleum and tile? When I was through with a bathroom that first week, Mrs. Spalding, the middle-aged woman who was my boss, would check out my work to see if it passed muster. Mostly I did just fine, though sometimes she made me redo the chrome on the fixtures.

"Sparkle," she'd say. "I need to see sparkle. They pay us for sparkle."

In that job I found my calling; I was accomplishing some small necessity in other people's lives that they took completely for granted but that was nevertheless very important to them. I wiped away germs and filth and centuries of plague and pestilence. I gave them sparkle, whether they noticed or not. It was a feeling I'd had before, as I swathed a field of wheat, but there was something in the humble nature of my offering that made this work feel even more sanctified. I had moved to the opposite end of the food chain, and there was a power down there.

I was a janitor. I am a janitor.

Our shift was from nine in the evening to five in the morning. After work, I'd have breakfast and go to bed and sleep until four or five in the afternoon. Then it was time for supper and soon time for work again.

I'd lie in bed in the mornings, trying to untangle the creak of Gloria's footsteps from the other noises overhead. Sometimes I'd hear the mumble of what had to be her mother's voice quarrelling with Irvine, and sometimes I'd hear Gloria mixed up in those fights too, and though I couldn't make out what they were saying, I couldn't help but imagine Mrs. Irvine saying *murderer,* and I'd think of my father pushing the red button on his lathe and turning to say, "Red means stop." I knew I couldn't keep living there, in the Irvine house, with Mrs. Irvine wishing me away. Sooner or later I'd have to go back to the farm.

One Saturday afternoon I got into the Fargo and drove that gravel road I'd driven so many times before, watching the landmarks pass: climbing the hill to the flat above Broken Head, back down into the valley, the Grentner place, back out of the valley, the old railway tracks, Mitchell's Corner, and down the last stretch back into the valley and home. The neighbour who'd rented the land had already finished the seeding, but without rain the shoots had only poked through the soil into the pale herbicide-bleached stubble and begun to die. His nitrogen fertilizer was burning his crop before it could even get started, as though he'd dumped a great river of piss on it and expected it to drink. He was a no tillage guy, so at least there was no dust.

The cattle had all been sold to pay off Dad's outstanding debts. All that was left to me was the house and the land and the rusted machinery. I walked through my mother's garden, kicking over a row of peas that had withered on the vine last summer. I got some pickles and tomato sauce from the shelves in the basement next to my father's lathe.

I sat in a corner of my old bedroom and cried that day. I cried until there were no tears left in me. There's no emptiness like an empty home. Little by little, nature grows up to claim it, making you regret every memory that would deny nature its rightful place. Once you've seen that nature has no need for you, it's easy to see why you need God and He needs you. The weeds have no gods. I couldn't stand it there. Even the Irvines' basement room was less lonely, with the creak of footsteps above me. I decided that I should sell it all and use the money to get away from Broken Head and get on with life.

But instead of heading straight back to my basement, I drove farther west to the Hutterite colony. I've already mentioned how I wanted to be Russian: because of that particular desire, I had an interest in the Hutterites, them being our local communists. I don't know that I'd have admitted, even to myself, why I was going there that day, but for years I'd had a kind of fantasy about joining the colony and making myself over that way. A group of men all dressed alike, in black jackets, black pants and black caps, were unloading a large, shiny four-wheel-drive tractor from a flatbed when I pulled into their yard. I wondered why they'd be buying a new tractor in the middle of a drought. A young man with a beard walked over and greeted me with a handshake. I asked if I might have a tour. He motioned over another young man without a beard, who agreed to show me around.

The reason my guide had no beard was that he was unmarried,

and in all probability he'd been selected as my guide because I looked to be in the same state. I knew this, but I asked him about it anyway, and in his Low German accent he explained to me that Hutterite men grow their beard when they marry, which happens only after they are baptized. Their baptism is the most important decision in their lives, and usually happens in their early twenties, after a decade of study. He would soon be baptized, he told me, and would marry a girl from a colony in Manitoba.

He showed me the church and the school and the dining room where everyone ate together, the men first and, once they were finished, the women and children. I was given a slice of fresh bread by a woman with a polka-dotted black and white scarf.

"Very good," I said when I'd finished chewing a mouthful. The woman smiled, showing her white teeth, and she was beautiful.

My guide showed me the pig barn and the chicken barn and the dairy barn and a huge Quonset full of machinery, including a row of tractors like the one they'd been unloading out in the yard. He told me that they had 250 sows, 12,000 chickens, 60 dairy cows, 350 beef cows, and 9,000 acres of cultivated land.

"A lot," I said, feeling a bit uncomfortable for him because he was obviously so proud of this rather capitalistic accumulation of wealth, even if it was collective wealth.

"Ve're doing bery good," he said. "But vee need sum rain."

I wanted to tell him about my life, about my basement room and my job as a janitor, about my rituals and beliefs. I wanted to say that my background was Mennonite, and so we were related in that way, as my roots were Anabaptist too. I wanted him to see that I had not let the world get the better of me.

He asked me if I'd like to try a little dandelion wine. "No, thank you. I don't drink," I told him, and he shrugged and kicked the dirt.

"You nevers go to bars?" he said. "Pretty girls."

Before I knew it I was back at my truck and he was sending me on my way with a jar of honey and a dozen eggs I'd bought for five dollars. I drove back to town, to my room in the Irvine basement, cooked myself three fresh Hutterite eggs, and went to bed to read. I wasn't really tired, of course. Though it was evening, I still had half my day ahead of me.

I've still never been baptized.

Being sent off to school meant that at seven and a half years old I was finally pushed into the world and found that it had been going on my whole life without any need of me and it wasn't willing to slow down and let me catch up. The school work didn't leave me behind: Mom had made sure I was considerably ahead of the game on that score. It was the general rush I couldn't adjust to. Breakfast, for instance. My nutritional intake wasn't nearly as interesting to me as it was to Mom. No matter how she urged and whined and scolded and nagged, I always dawdled over breakfast, not the least interested in cereal and milk and fruit, drawing pictures of horses and dragons with crayons and the pad of brown paper she allowed on the table beside my bowl. I negotiated mouthfuls of cereal in return for being allowed to keep the pad and crayons when she threatened to take them away. Then, always before either of us expected it, but always at the same time, at 7:20 in the morning, we would see the headlights of the school bus swinging into the yard, and she'd scream at me to get my shoes and my coat on and grab my lunch. She'd ask if I had remembered my homework, and if I hadn't, which was to be expected, I'd run back to my bedroom, the horn honking out in the yard, Mom scream- ing about how much I'd upset Mr. Hahn, the driver, and finally I'd burst out of the house, my jacket dragging behind because I'd only managed to get it on one arm, my papers spilling out of my back- pack. I might even trip on the bottom step as I climbed onto the bus and bang my knees on the next step and drag myself to my feet to meet Mr. Hahn's frustrated eyes and then the blank, sleepy stares and giggles and occasional scowls of my busmates as I walked down the aisle to my place in the fourth row.

"Dwight the Mennonite," the year-older-than-me boys would say. They didn't know or care that I wasn't a real Mennonite—that I'd never so much as walked through the door of a church. My last name was enough to label me. God has His ways of claiming his chosen.

My seat on the bus wasn't officially mine, but was official enough in its own right. When I got on the bus, the seat was empty, but not for long: I shared the swatch of green Naugahyde (bordered by white piping) with Johnny and Ruth Geisbrecht, who really were Mennonites. Johnny was well over two hundred pounds and much older than Ruth, and when they got on the bus Ruth would slide in beside me and Johnny would swing his hips to crush Ruth and me into a smaller space so that there would be enough room for him on the seat. My left side pressed against the metal side of the bus, the window at my cheek. My right side could not help touching Ruth.

Even though she really was a Mennonite, I liked Ruth. She smelled of some kind of flowery soap that her brother never used. I imagined she kept it hidden in a box in her bedroom. I tried to imagine her bedroom. She must have shared it with two or three of her older sisters. The Geisbrecht house was the only house on the bus route that looked almost as sad and unloved as ours, grey and lonely on the bald prairie, without even a tree in the yard to shelter it from the wind. Rusted farm machinery parked along a battered hedge of caragana behind the house. There were five kids who filed out and got on the bus some mornings, but Mom told me that Dad had told her there were really nine kids in the family. Apparently there were two older boys who'd already quit school to work on the farm and a younger girl who wouldn't start until next year and a new baby. Every morning I'd stare at the house and the one lighted window, and I'd try to imagine what it was like in that little house with nine kids and their mother and father. I imagined a bench at their table instead of chairs and I imagined Johnny swinging his hips to make a space for himself and knocking Ruth right off the other end.

When I got to school, I forgot all about Ruth.

Gloria Irvine was responsible for kindling my interest in God and the Holy Bible. There was a competition in grade four, reading poems aloud. I picked something about a snail by A.A. Milne and made it past the classroom recital to a higher level of public ridicule: morning assembly, in front of the entire school. I lost. I deserved to lose. Gloria read the twenty-third Psalm, and everyone believed that she actually was walking through the valley of death with the Lord by her side. They gave her the prize, which I think was a gift certificate to a restaurant in the mall. The next day, on the playground, I shuffled up to tell her how much I liked her reading and her poem and asked what book it came from. She looked at me like I was green and didn't say anything before I skulked away. A day later she set a black book on my desk and said that I could have it. She gave me this look like she felt really sorry for me—like I was one of those starving kids in Africa and she was giving me some bread—before she hurried away. There was a ribbon for a bookmark, and when I opened the book, it was at Psalm 23.

When Mom saw the book, she told me I could keep it, but that I'd better not let Dad see it, and so I hid it under my underwear in a corner of my sock drawer.

After school, I didn't have even Mom to organize me, and there wasn't much time to get my books together and my outdoor runners and my coat on and stumble out the door, shoelaces flying, and onto the bus.

You'd think a kid would speed up as he got older, but things didn't really improve much as time went by. A few years later it was late fall and still dark outside, the sun a hint of red on the horizon, and Mom was still pestering me to eat my breakfast. My stomach didn't work in the dark. Maybe my stomach hadn't woken up yet. When the bus came, I remembered that I'd left my reader in my room and ran up to get it, Mom screaming at me to just leave it, and as I was running back down the stairs and through the kitchen, the bus drove off without me.

"You see!" Mom shouted. "I told you he wouldn't wait forever.

Now look what you've done! You've missed the bus. Now what are you going to do? What is your father going to say?"

The basement door opened and Dad took a step into the room. Mom finally shut up. Though he'd been in the basement, Dad wore a lime green cap smeared with black grease that made the green all the brighter. Maybe he'd already been to the shop. He'd built a passage to connect the back stairway directly from the basement up into the shop, and he might have gone there without stepping outside, but it was unlikely, as he wasn't wearing his jacket and it was a cold morning. There was a stove in the shop where he burned old tires that he ground into fuel, but even when it was heated the shop wasn't particularly warm. It was built of Cindercrete blocks, and there was no insulation.

"I thought I heard the bus," he said.

"You did, Jake. Hahn just left on him. I'm gonna phone and complain. He only gave him a second."

"Sounded to me like he waited longer than that."

"No longer than usual. There was no need for him to drive off like that. He's just—you know what his problem is? He hates kids. There's no way he should be driving a school bus."

Dad reached up with his prosthesis and scratched the inside of his ear. "Never put anything smaller than your elbow in your ear, Eisenhower," Mom once told me. That always made me imagine someone trying to put his elbow in his ear.

"Hahn's a good man. Maybe he got tired of all the waiting." The bus driver, Mr. Hahn, was a gun collector and an acquaintance of Dad's. Sometimes he'd come with Chandler to check over the merchandise. Dad withdrew the prosthesis from his ear and examined it for any evidence it might provide. "It would be understandable, don't you think? Don't you ever get tired of all the waiting?" I didn't answer at first, but he stared such a long, unblinking stare that I figured I'd better nod. The whites of his eyes were yellow and spider-webbed by blood vessels. "Me too," he said. "God tells me I'm gonna die some day. Sometimes I get tired of all the waiting."

He turned and descended back into the basement, slamming the door behind him, his footsteps heavy on the stairs.

"Now see what you've done?" Mom asked me and answered herself because I never knew what I'd done. "You've gone and made your father mad. You've gone and pissed him off, and I've got to live with him. What am I going to do with you? Get your boots on. I'll have to get changed and take you myself."

A few minutes later we were out in the old Fargo, Mom grinding the starter until it caught. Just as she'd shoved it into gear, Dad appeared in the black rectangle of the shop door and waved at us to stop. She put her foot on the clutch and rolled down the window. "What?" she called.

He walked to her window, but instead of looking in at us, he was peering straight up into the sky. "Where you going?" he asked the clouds, which were billowing and white and the shape of a small difference set against blue.

"I'm taking Dwight to school."

His eyes were aimed so high that all I could see were the yellowed whites at the bottom of his eyeballs. "I might need the truck," he said.

"Need it when? I'll be back before noon. Maybe before eleven. I just figured I'd pick up a few things while I'm in."

Finally he looked straight into my eyes, and I had to look away, down towards the pond, where the diamond willows had lost all their leaves.

"What's he need to go to school for, anyway? He could learn a lot more around here."

"You want to teach him? I don't need him hanging around my neck all day, but if you want to teach him something, then you can go right ahead."

"I gotta go somewhere."

"Are you going this morning? How long will you be gone for?"

"I don't know. Maybe a week or two."

"A week or two! Where the hell are you going?" He didn't answer.

"Jake, if you're going for that long, you'll have to fix the car so that I've got some way of getting into town while you're gone."

"What's wrong with the car?"

"I don't know what's wrong with it. It doesn't work. It doesn't start."

"Starts fine for me."

"Well, that's great, Jake, but you're not going to be here, so could you fix it so I can start it or show me how you start it or something?"

"All you gotta do is look at it right so that it knows you have its best intentions in mind."

"Is that right? Okay, well, you show me how to look at it right and I'll take it to town right now and you can get on to wherever the hell it is you're going." She opened the door and got out of the truck and slammed the door and leaned on her one leg the way she leaned on her one leg. I wondered whether I should get out too. "Where are you going, Jake?"

"What are you wearing under there?" He pointed to her jacket.

"What do you mean?"

"I see you put your lipstick on to take him to school. What have you got on under there?" With his real hand he unzipped her jacket, revealing her red sleeveless blouse.

"When I go to town I get dressed up a bit. You don't want me to go around looking like a hag, do you?"

A skull grinned from the top of her right breast. Her only other tattoo was Denver. Her red blouse was my favourite. Vermilion. She zipped up her jacket.

"Where'd you say you were going once you dropped him off?" my father asked.

"I've got groceries I need to buy. We need groceries. The boy needs to eat. I need to eat, even if you've decided to go off somewhere."

"Why do you need to dress like that to buy groceries?"

"Like what? It's a nice blouse. It's my favourite colour. The same colour I painted the house." She waved her hand at the house, as though to prove her point, but the house had long since begun a serious peeling. She'd used some paint he'd brought back from one of his expeditions, and it was the wrong kind for the outside of a house: interior latex. There were only patches of red clinging here and there to the grey siding, and even those patches had been almost erased by the Cindercrete passages Dad had built to connect the house with the shop. He reached out with his real hand and unzipped the jacket again and touched a strap of Mom's blouse, testing the material between two fingers. Mom swatted his hand away and zipped up the jacket again.

He looked at his hand with much the same expression as he'd had earlier when he checked out his prosthesis after scratching his ear. This time, though, I imagine he was thinking about the feeling; about the one hand that touched things without feeling them and the other that could sting from the swat of my mother's hand.

The prosthesis began to rise. The thumb levered open and closed on the clasp of her zipper and very slowly pulled her jacket open to her belly. Mom let this happen. She stood very still, her face expressionless; she allowed it to happen, almost as though she enjoyed the way he slowly pulled open her zipper and let in the late October air.

Dad glanced at me as I stood there shuffling from one foot to the other. Without even being aware of it, I had got out of the truck. I couldn't lean on one leg the way Mom could. The one leg got numb when I tried. So I shifted back and forth from one leg to the other to keep the blood flowing. I wanted to tell them I'd try to do better. I realized that all this was happening because I didn't like school and so I'd dragged my feet and missed the bus. It was all my fault.

My father turned back to my mother, the prosthesis still gripping the clasp of her zipper at her waist. "If you cheat on me, you know what'll happen," he said. "You know that, don't you?"

Slowly, almost as slowly as he'd lowered her zipper, Mom shook her head. "I don't cheat on you, Jake. I've never cheated on you."

"I know nothing. I know about what you did with your father, and we both know how lucky you are to be here. But if I ever do know you've cheated on me, you know what'll happen, don't you?"

"I'll never cheat on you, Jake. You know I'll never cheat on you. I just wish you'd show me how to look at the car so that it'll start so that you can go away on your little vacation and Dwight and I can still get into Broken Head when we need to for groceries."

"I'm not going on vacation!" He shouted straight into her face from six inches away, and I thought he would hit her. "I'm working. I'm working so that you'll have some money to buy groceries for the boy and for you."

Mom kept her eyes low. "You're working. I'm sorry. But I'll still need the car while you're gone."

Dad spat at her feet. "You take him to school in the truck and get your groceries. I'll have the car fixed by the time you're home."

"That'd be great. That's all I'm asking. Thanks, Jake." She stood up on her tiptoes and kissed him on the mouth. He shrugged and glanced at me as she kissed him, his shoulders moving up and down as if he were telling me some terrible secret about her lips.

When I got home on the bus that night, my father was gone. He often disappeared that way. Working. An empty chair at the table, the shadow of his eyes still moving across the walls.

Chandler came to visit that night. Chandler generally showed up as soon as Dad left on one of his trips, which I thought was strange since Chandler was supposed to be Dad's friend, so why did he always visit as soon as Dad left? Mom put up with him, but she didn't like Chandler much. Chandler liked Mom, though. He said Mom was an angel fallen to earth. This time, Chandler brought a paper sack full of Halloween candies for me and a leather tooled box. He placed the box on the kitchen table and opened it to show us two pistols with ivory handles nestled on red velvet.

"Oooooh, they are pretty, Chandler," my mother said. "Aren't they, Dwight?"

Chewing on a toffee, I reached out and brushed my finger on the velvet. It changed colour, revealing the trace of my touch.

"Never seen anything so beautiful," Chandler said. "Besides you."

My mother turned her back on us. She was washing some dishes at the sink. I didn't like the way Chandler stared at her bum.

"They must be worth a fortune," Mom said. "We can't afford them."

"You already bought 'em. I guess Jake wants 'em to copy. I'm just makin' the delivery."

"What?" She turned around to face him. "What did Jake pay you for those?"

Staring at her breasts, Chandler chewed his bottom lip for a moment before he spoke. "I thought he'd be here. Where's he off to?"

"No idea."

"Old Jake likes to roam, don't he? But who can blame him when he brings home prizes like you."

"What did he pay you for those things?" she demanded. Chandler shrugged. Mom turned back to the sink and dunked her hands in the water.

"I hope they're not late," Chandler said. "I hope he hasn't gone off somewhere and challenged somebody to a duel without his pistols."

"Is that what they are? Duelling pistols?"

"That's what they are. French. A couple of hundred years old. The Frogs used to settle all their arguments that way. Slap the other fella across the face with your white gloves and tell'm to meet you in the woods at sunrise and *bang*, problem solved, one way or t'other." He picked up one of the guns and aimed it at my mother's bum and mimed the recoil.

"You're not supposed to point guns," I told him.

Chandler eyed me in his spooky way, his eyes bulging out of his skull. He slowly panned the gun from my mother to me. Then he laughed hard and put the pistol back in its red velvet case and lit his fourth cigarette. The other three butts were resting there in the saucer my mother had given him for an ashtray.

"You're absolutely right. Should never point a gun. Your daddy teach you that?"

I nodded.

Chandler took out a handkerchief and polished the smudge of his fingerprints off the handle of the gun. "Well, he oughta know." The laugh came croaking out of him again until it turned into a painful-sounding sour cough. When Chandler finally got control of the cough, he raised his eyes slyly and said, "Your daddy oughta know."

It was strange that Dad bought those pistols. He didn't really love anything, not even guns, and he never collected them himself. When I got to be a teenager and decided I wanted to be a Russian, I came across those pistols in practically every Russian novel I read, and so I developed a whole new appreciation for them. When I touched those pistols, I felt a connection to Dostoevsky.

Dr. Irvine invited me to his church, and I decided to accept. I thought maybe I'd ask about being baptized. I also thought it might be a way to watch Gloria sing. It was the first time I'd ever been in a church on Sunday: our school choir had sung in churches, but never on a Sunday. When I arrived my first Sunday, the sermon had already started, so I snuck in and sat in the back row of pews. A few people noticed me there and smiled and nodded. I was starting to get used to this reaction. Patty at work had told me I was a hero. I spotted Dr. Irvine, but Gloria wasn't with him. Neither was her mother. Pastor Tuttle, the minister, talked about Christ in the desert for forty days, and how the devil came and offered Him the earth and Jesus turned him down. When it was over, I almost managed to sneak away, but Irvine called me to meet the pastor and a few of the faithful.

Pastor Tuttle had ghostly white hair and a complexion to match. "Oh, yes," he murmured. "We've read about your trials, Dwight, and

Andrew has told me about your struggles to overcome. Praise the Lord you've emerged with Christ in your heart."

A small crowd of faces watched me, waiting for some appropriate response. I blushed and looked at the floor.

"Froese," he said. "It's a Mennonite name, isn't it?"

I confessed that my family had never gone to church.

"Well! Welcome to ours," Pastor Tuttle said, clapping me on the shoulder.

I thanked him. When he walked away, the crowd began to disperse. Irvine said there was someone else who wanted to meet me.

"Dwight, this is Mrs. Greene." She was a pretty young woman with delicate features and long yellow hair combed behind her ears and straight down her back, but her eyes were so blank that even when she smiled at me there didn't seem to be anyone living inside her skull.

"Oh, I'm so pleased to meet you," she said. "I feel like I know you already. I watched you on television. It was terrible what you and your mother went through. And Dr. Irvine told me what you did for the man in the hospital." Her blank eyes met mine, and neither of us spoke. I felt God watching me. "You've got Jesus in you," she said. "I want you to come and meet my Jimmy."

"Mrs. Greene has a son who is very ill," Irvine said. "How is Jimmy doing, Mrs. Greene?"

She coughed into her hand and looked at her palm, studying the germs she'd captured there. "He wasn't at all well last night, but he was sleeping when I came away this morning."

By the time I left the church, we had agreed I'd visit on Thursday.

The Greenes lived in a wooden bungalow on the south side of Broken Head. I liked the walk across the overpass to get there: something about the way all the rows of rails gleamed off into the horizon in either direction. I planned to be there at sunset on the equinox, so I could watch the sun set into those rails.

When she answered the door, Mrs. Greene's eyes were glazed in that same way as the first time I'd met her. She didn't seem to recognize me.

"Hi. I'm Dwight Froese?"

"Froze?" she said, looking around for snow or evidence of winter. Her brown eyes steadied on the sight of the sprinkler going next door. She stared at the water arcing back and forth for so long that I thought she'd forgotten I was there.

"Yes. Dwight Froese. Mr. Irvine introduced us?"

She turned back to me but stared at my chest when she spoke. "Of course. I know who you are. From the television. You've come to see Jimmy." She motioned me inside. "He's in the living room. We moved him downstairs. Gerald wasn't sure, but they thought it was a good idea and I convinced him. It's one of the things they recommend. He's not so far away then, upstairs in his bedroom, and there's no danger of him falling down the stairs. He's part of our daily lives. I think Gerald was more comfortable with him up there, out of sight. But Jimmy likes it down here."

I followed her into the living room, which smelled slightly of urine and strongly of disinfectant. In a hospital bed facing the window, a pale boy lay sleeping. He was bald and thin, his skin the yellow of newsprint that has been exposed to the sun.

"Oh, he's resting. We should leave him be. You can sit and wait, if you like." She still would not look me in the eye. "Don't feel you have to. He's expecting you, though. I told him you were coming."

"No . . . that's . . . I'll wait."

"All right. You can wait here, or if you'd prefer we can have tea . . ."

The kitchen was a cheery yellow room with a breakfast nook in the corner by the window that revealed the backyard. I squeezed into the nook and she floated around preparing the tea and setting out china on the table. Tiny flowers were printed on the blue dress she wore, and when she leaned over the table, I saw the line of pale skin on her breasts where the sun hadn't reached. I looked away.

She said nothing and I did the same, thinking our silence was in consideration of the boy sleeping down the hall. But when the kettle started to whistle, she stood there watching it for thirty seconds before she lifted it from the burner and poured the water into the teapot.

"There we go," she said, plopping the pot on a knitted trivet and manoeuvring in beside me until her leg was touching my leg. When she turned to me, her nose was only inches from mine. "It's nice to have you here," she said.

"It's nice to be here."

"I watched you on the news every night."

"I didn't see any of it," I said. "I didn't have a television in the hospital."

"I think of you and your mother all alone out there on that farm. Jimmy and I are alone here most of the time. Waiting. There's nothing to do but wait."

I nodded and started to talk about the weather. She listened for a while before she interrupted me. "They told me I needed to make the most of the time Jimmy and I have, but it's only time, and I didn't know how to make more of it than what it is. Until I saw you in the church. You were sitting there, staring up at the cross with your hands in your lap, and all of a sudden I knew. You're so beautiful, and you have no idea, do you? I realized that fact all of a sudden. When we're young, we never really see the beauty in ourselves. It's so pure. I remember when I was a teenager I'd search my face for pimples and think I was ugly, but when I look at my pictures now, I can see how beautiful I was. I was so very beautiful. Naked, I was even more beautiful. I don't have any pictures of me naked, but I really was so beautiful. And I didn't even know it. I wasted my beauty because I didn't know what I had. No one saw it except Gerald, and he doesn't even remember. He looks at me and all he sees is the way I am now. All softening and wrinkling and dying. Don't waste your beauty, Dwight. You are so beautiful. Everyone is so beautiful when they're young. Except Jimmy.

He looks so old." She took a breath, drawing a fingertip down from the centre of her forehead to the tip of her nose. "You have such beautiful eyes," she said.

I nodded and swallowed, thinking of Red Riding Hood and the Big Bad Wolf. "Thank you," I said. "You have nice eyes too."

They were pale brown eyes, and once I'd said this I immediately noticed that, despite the tranquilizers, they really were very lovely eyes.

"But your hands . . ." she said. "It's your hands I can't get over. They're such beautiful, beautiful hands." She touched my left hand where I'd rested it on my folded arms, leaning on the table. "Long fingers. And so strong." With the tip of her index finger, she began tracing the skin between my middle and index finger. "They're the most beautiful hands I've ever seen in my life."

I could not speak as she brushed the length of my middle finger.

"The thing you have to understand is that I don't want to be your mother. Do you understand that?"

I nodded.

"I have my own child. I don't want to be your mother. I don't need another son."

I nodded again and she slowly leaned forward and kissed me and began rubbing her palms over my back. It hurt a little, and I wondered if she could feel the acne there, even through my shirt. Kissing wasn't something I had any experience with, but I did my best. A moment later she was pushing her tongue into my mouth.

We kissed that way, there in the kitchen nook, for a while, the tea cooling, undrunk, and I began to rub my hands over her back the way she was doing with mine. I could feel her bra strap through her blouse. What was most in my mind was her tongue pushing into my mouth and how I imagined her breasts might look and whether I might have the chance to see them. Would that mean I would have to remove my shirt and show her the acne on my chest and back? And if I did, once she'd seen me that way, would she be so revolted that she'd put her clothes back on?

She stopped and sat back and looked at me sadly, and I thought it was all over. "We'd better go upstairs," she said.

She took my hand and led me up those stairs. I was embarrassed by the lump in my pants, still not sure if that was appropriate. We walked right past the master bedroom and down the hall to her son's empty bedroom; stuffed animals and action figures lined the dressers and the top of the bookshelf. There were posters of dinosaurs and superheroes taped to the walls.

"It's better here," she said, closing the door and unbuttoning her blouse. She unclasped her bra and stood there watching me stare at her breasts. I began to unbutton my shirt.

"Let me help you," she said, undoing my belt.

"Thank you," I said, but she was already kneeling to undo my pants and pulling them down so that my penis hit her in the nose.

"Uncircumcised," she said, looking up into my eyes. And with that, she took me in her mouth.

I looked down at her doing what she was doing, all the while feeling quite self-conscious, standing there wondering what I should be doing, still worrying about what would happen when she saw what was under my shirt. After a while she stopped and stood and stepped out of her slacks and led me over to the single bed.

I took off my shirt, and she didn't seem to notice my wounds.

It went on for quite some time. I was surprised how much it was like my shameful fantasies of Gloria: the ways she wanted me and couldn't get enough of me. We started out in the missionary position, but before long she'd rolled me off and was riding me until she'd come, all the while gasping my name in a way that made me feel I'd never heard my name before. I was surprised she even remembered my name. She kissed me tenderly, lying on top of me, and then she got off and turned away from me, crouching on her hands and knees, shaking her bum slowly and pleading for me to enter her that way, and so I did. Before long she wanted to change positions again—I thought maybe that would be enough, but she wanted more—and so we went back to the missionary position. In the end, when I'd collapsed on her chest, my limbs quivering, gasping for breath, she whispered into my ear, "Does it always take you this long to come?"

"To tell you the truth," I said, "I've never really done this kind of thing before."

She was silent a long time.

"I wondered if that was it," she finally said.

We lay there, listening to the sound of the birds outside the window.

"Maybe we'd better get dressed," she said, and she raised herself from the bed and did so. I watched her pull on her panties and attach her bra. "He might be awake now and waiting for you," she said, and she left the room, carrying the rest of her clothes, which she'd gathered in her arms.

I got up and started to get dressed, worried because I couldn't remember his name. The boy's name. The boy I had come there to visit. Scanning the room for clues, I spotted *Jimmy* printed in the corner of a drawing of a horse and masked rider.

When I walked out of the bedroom, I heard Mrs. Greene in the bathroom, starting the shower. I walked down the stairs and into the living room and sat down beside the bed where the pale boy lay sleeping. Or I thought he was asleep, but a moment later his eyes flickered open and he rolled his head sideways to look at me and he narrowed his eyes in a way that showed there was still life in him.

"Where's my mom?" he said, his eyes threatening. I didn't answer. "I heard her screaming. Is she upstairs? Were you upstairs with her?"

I shook my head, trying to figure out the best way to deny. "You must have heard someone outside. There was a girl screaming outside. We were having tea," I said. He turned back and stared out the window. We listened to the shower running. My ears were ringing. I reached up and felt the spot on my ear where the bullet had passed. I thought about telling him the story. A squirrel scampered through the trees, leaping from one branch to another and pausing there for an instant, looking in at us.

"I saw you on television," he said. "You shot your dad with a gun."

"Yeah."

"Cool." He looked out the window again. "Mom says you've got Jesus in you."

"I don't know about that."

"Mom's full of shit," he said.

I couldn't think what to say next, and by the time I'd thought of something, he'd gone back to sleep.

FOUR

Mrs. Greene and I agreed that Thursdays would be my day to visit Jimmy. Somewhere in the reptilian part of my brain, Thursdays are still confused with sex. My eye rests too long on the fifth column of the calendar and I begin to feel aroused. I'm not making this up. That's how deep desire hooks, and all we can do is look to God to remind us that no peace will arrive from that direction. The only other day I saw her was Sunday, when Mrs. Greene and I would face the Lord and the congregation from our separate pews. By the second week she was reporting to everyone how much better Jimmy was doing since I'd begun my visits. They all thought this was wonderful and wanted to know the details of the improvements in Jimmy's appetite and how he'd given up the wheelchair and was walking with me for short jaunts around the backyard, clinging to my arm for support, telling me knock-knock jokes.

"Knock knock."

"Who's there?"

"Screw!"

I wondered how wise it was to give him what he wanted, but seeing the fire fill those blue eyes in that skull of a face, I couldn't deny him.

"Screw who?"

"Screw you!"

His ragged laugh faded to a wheezing cough. "Tell me again about when you killed your dad."

He loved to hear that story. I knew I needed to own what I'd done, and so I tried not to make my father sound evil, but I don't think I did a good job. I always added a moral that shooting him wounded me inside and I'd only been saved by the love of Jesus Christ. It's so easy to say that kind of thing. I could say it over and over, but what would it mean in the end unless there's some truth wrapped up in the words like a tiny gift? I don't think he liked the moral, but he thought it was interesting. He was almost as fascinated by Christ as he was by the fact that I had shot my father through the head.

"You really think Jesus is watching us? Right now?"

"Of course. Jesus is here. All around us. And inside us. Jesus loves you."

He squinted those yellow eyes at me. "Really?" he said, pointing into himself. "He's in there with the cancer?" I assured him that I believed it. "Then why doesn't he get rid of it? Why doesn't Jesus cure me if He's so fucking powerful?"

I looked towards the open kitchen window to see if his mother was close enough to have heard, but she was nowhere in sight. Mrs. Greene had warned me that Jimmy might repeat the blasphemies he'd overheard from his father.

"Maybe he will," I said. "Maybe he's chosen you for saving."

It was about this time that Gloria first came to church, sitting in the same pew as I did, on the other side of her father. Her mother and Nick were there too. Very unusual. Gloria now takes Caroline to church every Sunday, but Nick never goes along. I've watched them from a bench across the street: Caroline in her Sunday dress, clutching her mother's hand, skipping up the steps to the Lord. I've never seen Nick there with them. And Mrs. Irvine would think twice about being caught dead in a church for her funeral. She and Nick are not believers.

It's not really that Gloria is a believer. She's more of a doubter, but she still goes to church every week. Mrs. Irvine and Nick are lucky enough not even to doubt. Of course, I didn't know that then. But I'd started to figure out that sometime after she'd made a gift of the Bible to me, Gloria had lost her faith. Then, all of a sudden, she appeared in the pew one Sunday morning, with Nick and her mother there beside her. Mrs. Irvine looked right through me. I did my best not to glance at Gloria while I prayed.

After the service the faithful and faithless gathered in the aisle to thank Pastor Tuttle for the passionate and inspiring words he'd borrowed from various places. Irvine cleared his throat and placed a hand on Gloria's shoulder. "I have an announcement to make."

The chatter numbed and died. Gloria smiled in a way that reminded me of when she'd won that prize for reciting her poem in grade four. Nick stared at the floor and looked like he wished he were anywhere else in the world. "Gloria, my lovely daughter, would like to be married here in this beautiful church. And she would like you to do the honour of marrying her, Pastor Tuttle."

Some of the women gasped with delight. Mrs. Irvine smiled in a stiff, proud way. For a moment I thought Irvine had offered Gloria to Pastor Tuttle, who was already married. I stared at the perfect part of Gloria's hair, and she glanced at me in a distracted way. Pastor Tuttle, who hardly knew how to smile, gave Gloria a wide grin. "Isn't that wonderful? Nick Campion, you are a lucky man." He clapped one hand on Nick's shoulder and, with the other hand, pumped his arm in an oversized handshake while Nick grimaced, trying hard to smile. "When is the big day?"

"August 25th," Gloria answered for him.

A hush descended on the congregation.

"That's less than six weeks away," Pastor Tuttle said.

Forty-one days. I did the math in my head.

"We want to be married when we go back to university in the fall," Gloria said, glancing towards Nick's bowed head. "We want to make that commitment right now because . . . we feel ready. We know we're young, but we feel ready." Nick didn't give so much as a nod to support her.

There was another moment's silence, a collective held intake of breath. From deep in the building came a single muted thump, and the entire congregation stood imagining what had made the sound until we realized it had come from the direction of the bathroom.

Mrs. Irvine snorted and said, "Well, I think it's wonderful. And Nick's family thinks so too," and Gloria rushed up and hugged her. A forced approving murmur went up and people began to add their congratulations.

"I have some wonderful news too," Mrs. Greene burst out, rescuing poor Nick from all those eyes. "Jimmy is feeling so much better since Dwight started visiting. You would just not believe the week we've had. Somehow Dwight must have put into his head that there was a lovely view from the overpass."

And now everyone, including Gloria, had turned away from Nick to look at me.

Keeping her eyes to the floor, Mrs. Greene told of how, the Thursday before, I'd mentioned to Jimmy the view I saw each day from the overpass when I was walking to their place. Right away Jimmy wanted to go there. I asked Mrs. Greene if it would be okay, but she wouldn't let him, figuring he wouldn't make it to the end of the block before he played out completely. I said I could push him in the wheelchair, but she didn't like the idea of the wheelchair on the overpass. I guess that made sense. The next day, when she took him his breakfast, he wasn't in bed. She and her husband searched the house and the yard and had already phoned the cops when they got a call from a neighbour who drove to work each morning and had seen him at the top of the overpass, staring off to the east, watching the sunrise. You're not supposed to park on the overpass, but Mr. Greene tried, resulting in lots of honking horns when Jimmy refused to get into the car. In the end, Mr. Greene had to move his car and park down below on Railway Street. He charged up the concrete steps to get Jimmy, but Jimmy wouldn't let his father carry him down the stairs. He refused even to walk down with him. He said he wanted to go home by the sidewalk, the way he'd come. It wasn't possible to change Jimmy's mind once he'd made it up, and so they walked back down the overpass and all the way home and Mr. Greene had to walk all the way back to get his car on Railway and was over an hour late for work.

Jimmy collapsed into bed and was out cold for the rest of the day, so that they began to wonder if he'd ever get out of bed again, and even though he finally woke up feeling better than ever, Mr. Greene didn't want me visiting anymore. He said I was a bad influence on Jimmy. Mrs. Greene disagreed. Jimmy had some colour in his cheeks and was sleeping through the night. Mr. Greene had even suggested moving him back to his own room since he was out of bed and getting so much exercise.

"He'd make him walk up and down those stairs," Mrs. Greene told the congregation, staring at the pointy toes of her high-heeled shoes, her hair hanging over her eyes. "Those stairs are absolutely treacherous. The hardwood is so slippery. I've asked him for carpeting on the stairs, but he says we can't afford it. I don't know how we can afford not to. It's our son. It's our *son*. It's—"

"It's wonderful, though, how much better Jimmy is doing," Pastor Tuttle interrupted her.

"Oh, yes," Mrs. Greene said, finally looking up at us as though just remembering we were there. "Three weeks ago he wasn't walking across the room. You couldn't get him out of bed. Now, thanks to Dwight, he's going outside every day."

"Praise the Lord," Pastor Tuttle said, glancing skyward.

They were all staring at me—Mrs. Morrison, who still sold real estate at seventy-six years of age, and Mr. and Mrs. Jolly, who owned a health food store in the mall, and the Schultzes, who farmed a few miles north of town, and Mr. Wells, whose wife, twenty years younger than him, had died of a heart attack just before Christmas—with a kind of warm glow about them that made me feel like blushing. They believed in the hero that the television had created. But amidst their approval I felt Mrs. Irvine's eyes digging, and I knew she was the one who really saw me, and when I finally spoke up I felt like I was offering something to her.

"It's nothing to do with me visiting. The weather's warmed up," I said, but I could already see that my denial would only make the congregation love me more. "He couldn't go out before. He can't stand the cold. It blows right through him. The sunshine's doing him some good."

"You're very modest, Dwight," Irvine said.

Gloria, standing there next to her father, was gazing at me along with all the rest of them. Since Mrs. Field's grade two class I'd been willing her to look at me like that, but she never had. And now what did it matter? She was marrying Nick Campion, who was looking at Gloria like he, too, was wondering about that gaze of hers. I thought about congratulating them, hoping that might get us off the subject of Jimmy.

"I can't say your husband's reaction surprises me," Pastor Tuttle said. "I'd like to visit Jimmy, but I'm as much a *persona non grata* as Dwight."

"He's not a believer," Mrs. Greene said. "He says that all religion amounts to voodoo, and he's not going to allow any witch doctors to bother Jimmy."

"Well!" Pastor Tuttle muttered, but, diplomatically, he didn't expand on the thought in his mind. Pastor Tuttle's wife nodded a severe nod, having understood his point even though he didn't speak. Married people are like that sometimes. I couldn't help thinking about what married people were like—Gloria was getting married to Nick Campion.

"I'd be willing to talk to him," Irvine said.

"That might help." Mrs. Greene nodded her head, her eyes aimed towards the floor again: towards my running shoes. "Gerald respects you, Andrew. He even suggested that you should start visiting Jimmy again."

"Perhaps your husband knows what's right for his son," Mrs. Irvine said. "Perhaps you should listen—"

"I've been meaning to get over to see Jimmy," Irvine interrupted her. "I've just been so busy with everything lately. But I think we can agree that Dwight's visits have been much more beneficial than mine ever were."

And so Dr. Irvine agreed to talk to Mr. Greene about the importance of my visits. Mrs. Irvine pursed her lips and said that she'd wait for her husband outside, and Nick stammered that he had to get going and left with her. Gloria was still gazing at me, so I stepped forward and congratulated her.

"Oh, thank you," she said. "It really is wonderful what you're doing for that poor little boy."

At that moment a middle-aged woman appeared from the door that led to the washroom. She was pushing an elderly woman in a wheelchair.

"Lilly!" Pastor Tuttle called out. "It's so wonderful to see you here. And your lovely mother. How is she doing?"

Everyone looked at Lilly's mother in the wheelchair. She was staring straight off into space, a slight tremble quivering her head and the wattles on her neck.

"She's doing very well," Lilly said. "She eats like she has a hollow leg, and she loves her tea. She wanted to meet the boy whose mother and father died," she said, looking straight at me.

"Hello," I said.

"It's Dwight," Irvine said. "Dwight Froese. This is Lilly Banks, Dwight. And her mother."

"I recognize you, of course," Lilly Banks said. "I was so deeply saddened by your terrible plight. You're a brave young man, and very inspiring. My mother was so excited to hear about you, weren't you, Mother? Every night she insisted on staying up to watch the news.

She's usually asleep by nine." She leaned down to yell into her mother's ear. "This is Dwight Frost, Mother. Don't you recognize him? The boy who tried to save his mother."

I nodded and bent forward to shake Old Mrs. Banks's withered hand. As I got closer, the wizened and empty face and eyes suddenly came alive.

"I know you!" she said, and she sprung out of her wheelchair and grabbed me in her arms. I was so shocked I stood up straight and stepped backwards all in one motion, but she hung on for dear life, her face only inches from mine, her mouth open wide. I wondered if she might try biting off my nose. Lilly gasped, waving her hands at me as if I was attacking her mother. Irvine and Pastor Tuttle grabbed Old Mrs. Banks and tried to coax her off me, while I tried to keep my feet firmly planted so we didn't both end up on the floor.

"Mrs. Banks!" Pastor Tuttle scolded. "Please, Mrs. Banks!"

"Mother! Let go, Mother!"

But Lilly's mother wouldn't obey. Instead, she closed her mouth and grinned at me from close up, like the year-older boys on the school bus used to grin at me.

"GET OFF!"

I didn't know I was going to say this; the words were out of my mouth before I had thought them. The old woman instantly let go. Irvine and Pastor Tuttle were as surprised as she was and let go too. Old Mrs. Banks was left standing there, unsupported, staring up at me, her mouth opening again, but this time in a look of awe.

"Thank you," she said.

And she began to walk towards the door.

"Mother?" Lilly called. "Sit down!" She pushed the wheelchair after her, catching up to her in the vestry. They argued for a minute until Old Mrs. Banks finally turned her back on her daughter, pushed through those huge wooden doors and stepped out into the sunlight. Lilly Banks glanced back at me with an accusation before she followed her mother.

Everyone stared. Gloria gaped at me with a look that made me feel like I was about to float away. Then I noticed that Mrs. Greene was looking at me with exactly the same expression she got after orgasm.

"My goodness," Pastor Tuttle said.

"Are you okay?" Irvine asked, touching my arm.

I nodded and said that I had to be going, but even as I walked away I could feel Mrs. Greene looking at me that way and the officially engaged Gloria Irvine looking at her looking at me.

Believe it or not, it never occurred to me that Gloria was pregnant. That would have meant admitting to myself that she and Nick Campion got together in that way, and I wasn't willing to imagine such a thing. I spent a lot of time avoiding the imagining of it. She was a virgin in at least one part of my mind. In other parts, I imagined her doing the same things with me that Mrs. Greene did. It was the only way I could avoid imagining her doing those things with Nick.

I hoped that getting married was about pleasing her parents. I couldn't stop thinking about the way she'd looked at me.

It was a beautiful Sunday afternoon—hot and no wind—so I drove out to the farm for a swim and to check the place out—to try to take in the news of Gloria's wedding and figure out what to do about what was happening between me and Mrs. Greene. It was this thing of sex I was having trouble with; the desiring and the doing. Once you've taken part in it, you get these unimaginable images of the taking part in it locked up in your mind, and you realize the same kind of thing is going on everywhere around you, and all of a sudden you have to spend a lot of your time avoiding the imagining of people having sex. The Irvines having sex. The Tuttles having sex. Old Mrs. Banks having sex. It was a real problem, trying to keep all that sex out of my mind. How could people look you in the eye, knowing that you knew that about them?

When I got to the farm, the door to the house was wide open. Someone had broken in and taken the television and the microwave and I'm not sure what else. They'd cooked something and eaten it at the kitchen table, right out of the cast-iron frying pan, and for some reason they'd smashed the ceramic top of the toilet tank and had pulled Mom's and Dad's clothes out of their drawers and closets and strewn them around the bedroom. I guess they'd taken what fit them and suited their style. There was at least one set of wrenches missing from the shop, and maybe other things too. I had no inventory of what was out there. I wondered if I should call the police, but the thought of facing them and telling my story made me feel tired. Instead, I decided that if there was anything there I wanted I'd better take it with me.

There wasn't much. I already had all of my books in my basement room. I took my father's only pair of dress shoes, even though my feet were one size too big for them. I took the red blouse that Mom was wearing that day I missed the bus and she had to drive me to school. She hadn't worn it for years before she died, but I liked the way it reminded me of her. I took a painting of mountains that she'd bought at a furniture store. There was a great swath of red through the middle, as though the mountains were bleeding. I took the old radio that sat on the counter in the kitchen. I thought of taking a gun, but there were none left, even in Dad's best hiding places.

I had my swim down at the creek where I'd found Mom and where Dad died. Where I'd shot my father. The water took the ache out of me. Afterwards, I looked for the spot where his body had lain looking up, wondering if there would be flowers, or if the grass would be greener, or even if there'd be a dead spot where nothing would grow, but there was nothing to show me exactly where it had happened. I knew approximately where, of course, but I couldn't tell exactly.

I walked upstream to the cutbank where I figured Mom must have fallen into the creek, and it was the same disappointment. All I could do was look down at the rocks protruding through the surface of the water and wonder which one Irvine and the cops had found her blood on.

I didn't cry that day.

When I got back to town, I tucked the blouse under the sweaters in my bottom drawer, threw the shoes in the closet, hung the painting over my bed and put the radio on the kitchen counter and plugged it in. It was good to have a voice there talking to me, and I wondered why I hadn't thought of it before.

But when I closed my eyes, I saw my father staring straight up into the sky.

This afternoon I rode the bus down from Danforth to Queen with my four bags of groceries. Grey, decaying snow, and the guy sitting next to me smelled of wet wool. After all these years and even though I'm now riding with complete strangers, I still hate the bus. The tilt and sway of the starts and stops. There's nowhere to hide and so everyone acts as though meeting your eyes might give you some power over their infected souls. Sometimes I want to reach out and touch a shoulder and say, "The Lord's looking for you." Just to jolt them out of their hiding places. They read their books and newspapers, or if they don't have anything to read, they linger on the advertisements papering the walls, memorizing the slogans as though they are actually considering whether that soap might be the one, whether it'll make their skin shine the way it makes the model's skin shine. Sometimes I think about telling them that they might as well use the Mr. Clean from under the kitchen sink: there's not that much variation in soap, aside from the perfume. I'm a janitor and I should know. I know soap. I could tell them. But I don't, because I might regret becoming involved in the state of their skin.

I shouldn't complain. It's not a long ride. A few of them talk to themselves on their cellphones. The ones reading the papers tend to skip the stories about the religious crusades and read about whatever celebrity got married or pregnant or arrested. They don't like to read about Somalia because they're too much in the middle of it. There's as much fear and boredom on a bus as in your average war. I say that having never been to any war other than the one that drags on daily between Satan, on his throne, and the battered and lonely resistance forces awaiting the Lord's return. I wish I'd asked my father for more details. He was there, cradling his rifle across the beach at Normandy, and I never spoke to him about it, and now it's all gone: everything he thought and felt. Sure, I was scared to death of him, but is that a good enough excuse? He was carrying that around with him all the years I knew him, and I never offered to share the burden. I refused to meet his eyes. I hid away in my skull, where no one could get at me. That's what I'm good for. That and cleaning.

Caroline's lucky she can walk to school so she doesn't have to take the bus. Lucky to have a nanny to walk her, since her mother and father are too damned busy. The nanny wasn't at the grocery store today. I thought I saw her reading a magazine at one of the checkouts, but when I walked up behind her, she turned and she wasn't the nanny. Caroline's lucky to have her. She's not her mother, but she's the next best thing money can buy. Cheap too. Likely makes even less than a janitor. Though I've got no education fund. That's really generous of them. I really am grateful to Nick for all the advantages Caroline has over what I'd have given her. For instance, she doesn't have to listen to the bar down the street when things get stretched thin and it starts to spill outside. She doesn't have to go to the bathroom to avoid staring at the same four walls. She doesn't have to ride a bus to school.

Here they call it transit. Any bus is a transition, and transitions are the weak link in life and love. It's not easy getting from one place to the other without exposing yourself. This particular weakness is the ideal incubator of terror. Ask any terrorist. Charon was the name of the boatman who paddled the dead across the river Styx. He was only a servant of the lord of the underworld. I don't recall what he looked like from pictures on vases or in storybooks, but I think I know what he looked like anyway. He was a stringy fellow with thin grey lips, hair like pale, dead straw, one arm, and yellowed fingertips on his one hand. He looked exactly like my father.

———

After Mr. Hahn retired to spend the endless winter playing shuffle-board in a trailer park in Arizona, my father took over as our school bus driver. The farm and his other business ventures weren't doing so well, and we needed the extra money. The year-older boys liked him right away because he allowed them to get off the bus and smoke while we waited for the Rheinfeld bus to meet us for the exchange at the Lavallee Trail. Smoking wasn't an entirely new bus diversion, but they hadn't had high hopes for Dad, seeing as he was such an old guy and that metal hand of his spooked them. But Dad surprised them. Despite being old and spooky and not the least bit interested in their conversation, he smoked too and couldn't care less if they had a cigarette while he had his. So they'd slip off the bus and huddle on the edge of the grid while Dad chewed his roll-your-owns and stared off into the early morning gloom.

One grey morning I watched Billy Newsome leave the clutch of boys at the edge of the road and shuffle over to where Dad leaned against the front fender. I could see them discussing something that made Dad kick the gravel to make his point and Billy nod his head to show he was receiving this wisdom. Dad eyed the package of tailor-mades in Billy's pocket for a while, then finally motioned to them and said something. Billy looked pleased to give him one.

All was well for a while. Dad had no rules, but he gave off a stink of danger that managed to hold the boys in check, and the bus was actually quieter than it had been under Mr. Hahn. The year-older boys stopped picking on me. Maybe they even had a new respect for me out of their new respect for Dad. Then one day I took a detour to return a book to the library after my last class, and when I got on the bus, Dad slurred into my face, "Better be on time tomorrow or you'll walk." With the words came a waft of booze and cigarettes. I got to my seat and pressed myself to the window.

At the high school, Billy Newsome got on and Dad told him to sit down in the seat behind him. "Payday. I'n pay you back for 'em cigarettes you bummed me."

Billy said not to worry, but Dad insisted he take a five. Billy took the money and offered him a cigarette. Dad took it and lit up. "Fuckin' kids," Dad said, pocketing his lighter.

Billy staggered towards the back of the bus, but when he was halfway down the aisle Dad yelled at him, "Hey, kid!"

Billy turned back to face him.

"Grow up," Dad said.

Billy nodded slowly, glancing around to see if anyone else knew what this meant. I shrugged. "Your dad's kinda cool for a stupid Mennonite," Billy said. He continued up the aisle and sat down in his spot at the back of the bus. "Grow up," one of the other high school boys said. Billy put a cigarette in his mouth and lit it. "I'm all grown up now," he said and blew a smoke ring to prove it.

Before long all the older boys were lighting up and blowing smoke rings. Ruth Giesbrecht opened her window and got a dirty look.

As we drove through town, Dad began an argument with himself about the annoying placement of stop signs. On the highway he pendulumed back and forth between centre line and ditch. From my spot in the fourth row, I craned my neck to see the speedometer hit seventy-five and watch Dad clinging to the wheel, weaving his way southward. One of the little kids kept coughing. I opened my window.

"Close the fuckin' windows, you stupid Mennonites," Billy said. "It's fuckin' cold in here." I closed my window and Ruth closed hers.

When we started down the hill into the big coulee north of Smiths', I held my breath and we avoided going over the edge: Dad managed to aim straight down the middle of the highway, straddling the centre line. I watched where the highway disappeared into the horizon, praying that no oncoming traffic would appear. As we climbed, we veered back to our own side of the road, and past it onto the shoulder. I willed the bus to stay on the highway and actually began to feel that I was keeping it there by the force of my will.

Billy and the boys thought it was hilarious. "Keep it on the road there, Jake," they called, and he shouted back at them that they should keep their mouths shut. Once we were on the grid, fighting the gravel made Dad slow down to a little more than thirty-five miles an hour, and that wasn't quite so bad. I watched for parents on the drop-offs, wondering if one of them might notice him swerving into their yards, but there was never anyone around.

The day after I found out Gloria was going to marry Nick Campion, Irvine came down to the basement to tell me he'd had his talk with the Greenes. Mr. Greene was still pretty upset but eventually admitted that my visits were good for Jimmy and that even Mrs. Greene seemed happier since I'd started visiting. I could go on Thursday as usual and he wouldn't object. I told Irvine I didn't feel very good about the whole thing and wondered how I could be sure something like the overpass wouldn't happen again. He told me I shouldn't worry; I should just do what I was doing, because what I was doing was helping this family in such a beautiful way.

How was I supposed to argue with him?

On Thursday I tried to talk Mrs. Greene out of going up to Jimmy's room. She said we could use the pullout couch in the basement, but she didn't think it would be nearly so comfortable. I told her that she was missing the point; what I was trying to say was that I didn't think we should do what we did anymore, because it wasn't right and I didn't feel good about it because of Mr. Greene. She told me not to worry about Mr. Greene because he never wanted to make love with her anymore anyway: he was making love with a woman he'd met at the Broken Head Chamber of Commerce meetings. I told her I was sorry about that but I still felt bad about it all, and she said that she understood and that both she and Mr. Greene thought it would be a good idea if I came for dinner on Sunday night and met Mr. Greene. I even suggested that Jimmy might already be wondering what was going on when Mrs. Greene and I went off by ourselves, but she told me that Jimmy was perfectly happy watching his movies while we "talked." Then she took my hand and led me up to Jimmy's room.

"What do you see out there?" she asked me after we'd finished our moaning and prodding. I'd been lying there staring out the window, running my hand up and down the ridges of her spine.

"The sky," I said.

She lifted her head and looked from the window to my eyes. "No," she said, trying to be clever. "You don't see the sky. I don't believe you. If you see the sky, what colour is it?"

"This is a test?"

"That's right. If you can tell me the colour of the sky, I'll make love to you."

"Vermilion," I said.

She turned back to the window to check. "Correct," she said, climbing on top of me.

I'd bought Jimmy a plastic model kit of a dinosaur sinking into a tar pit, and we built it in an hour. The dinosaur was doing his damnedest to keep his head above the tar, but anyone could see it wouldn't be long before he went under. It was very lifelike, with little prehistoric shrubs. Jimmy said it was the coolest model in the world. When we were finished, he wanted to take it outside and play with it in the yard.

"Let's shoot it with Dad's rifle."

"I'm not so sure that's a good idea," I said. "The bullet wouldn't stop when it hit the plastic dinosaur. It might hit something across the alley."

He nodded, seeing my point. "What about the weed whipper? It's in the garage. I bet we could totally mash it with that."

"I should have bought you a slingshot."

"That would be cool."

"We just built this. You said you liked it. Why do you want to break it?"

He shrugged and looked straight up at the clouds, bored with my question. "If there weren't any people alive when they were alive, how do we even know there were dinosaurs?"

"Because of their bones. When they died, they decomposed and left their bones. They sunk into tar pits like this one, and they died and decomposed."

He was eating a sucker he'd asked me to bring him even though he knew his mother didn't allow them. He pulled it out of his mouth and stared at it. "Decomposed. And they all died?"

"Yeah. There's none left. Have you seen any lately?"

He gave the sucker a long lick. "How come Jesus never saved *them*?"

"Because lizards don't have souls," I told him.

He thought about that. "Well, didn't your dad have a soul? How come he never saved your dad?"

I shrugged. "You can't always understand God," I said. "God has his secrets."

"Secrets." Jimmy took a kick at his dinosaur, and its head snapped off. "Maybe your dad didn't deserve to be saved."

Every payday, it was the same.

Not exactly the same: sometimes not so bad, sometimes worse. Sometimes Dad got so drunk he looked like he might tumble right out of the driver's seat, but he'd cling to the wheel and somehow manage to hold the bus on the road.

Once he crossed the centre line into the path of an oncoming car and I saw the face of the driver, mouth open in a dark circle, as he swerved into the lane we should have been in and missed us. "Did you see that? We almost creamed that car!" The year-older boys went on discussing it in an unfamiliar tone, as though some hint of their mortality had occurred to them. Even Dad was chastened enough to slow down. The younger kids went on reading their books and discussing their latest obsessions the way they always did, not noticing how little they'd lived so far.

I really thought that would be the end of it. The man with the open mouth would report what had happened, and someone would put a stop to it. That was the way of things. You couldn't get away with what Dad did.

That night Mom chattered on to me at supper, trying to get me to tell her what was going on at school. She didn't bother to wonder why Dad never came in from the shop to eat. Generally, she took this as a blessing. The phone didn't ring and no police car pulled into our driveway and the next morning Dad was up early, slurping his coffee and leading me out to the bus as usual—unshaven, looking out of his pinprick eyes like a rat peering at the putrefying bodies scattered across a battlefield.

Excuse the poetry. I've never even seen a battlefield.

The first of June it was so hot a girl passed out in gym class and had to be taken to the hospital. After school, I stood in the shade of the junior high, watching a fight between Bob Crow, the jeweller's son, and Tom Watson, who had never had a father but whose mother had tried her best to make up for the lack of the husband who'd run away in her fifth month with the man who drove the frozen food truck. I don't remember what started the fight. Probably nothing much. Tom was someone I appreciated for distracting guys like Bob from picking fights with me. He took a few tentative pokes at Bob, who stood eyeing him, looking slightly bored, until Tom strayed a shade too close. Hands stiff at his sides, Bob head-butted him and Tom went down, clutching his nose, the blood springing from between his clawed hands. The crowd cheered.

It was payday. Not that I was aware of that fact as I stood there waiting for the bus, but I do remember the fight had me feeling uncomfortable with the state of the universe. The sun was blinding when I stepped out of the shade, wondering why Dad was late. And then, as I saw the bus coming, swerving too wide as it cornered onto George Street, it occurred to me that it had been about two weeks since the last time Dad had driven drunk.

I climbed on board. Dad stared straight ahead, but I could smell alcohol mixed with the stink of cigarettes. There was a look in his eye like he was getting ready to ram the bus ahead of us. I took my seat and watched him clip the heels of Ruth Giesbrecht as he swung the doors closed behind her.

When the kids boarded at the high school, Dad asked where Billy was, and one of the boys said, "He's not on today."

"Well, whose load's he under?" Dad wanted to know. One of Billy's friends said he'd skipped the afternoon to go drinking at the Landing.

"Good on him," Dad said. "Good on him."

I'd never heard him use that expression before.

As we pulled out of town, Dad was humming a country and western song about not loving Jesus and the odour of his feet. He was in a good mood. The highway went better than usual, and I began to relax. Unfortunately, his success at manoeuvring the highway only made him more confident than usual on the grid road. Maybe it was his good mood that made him push too far. He was doing sixty on a dead straightaway and lost his back end to a fishtail. By the time we were stationary, we'd revolved 180 degrees and were facing exactly the opposite direction, as if it were morning and we were on our way to town. Even the little kids had noticed something was wrong, and some of them were crying.

"Stop the racket," Dad said. "I can't hear myself stink." He laughed at himself. I'd never seen him in such a good mood.

He drove a quarter-mile back towards the highway until he could get turned around on the approach to someone's field. We continued through the route, more slowly at first, but before long he was doing better than fifty again.

At the Geisbrechts, Ruth got off and Dad managed to clip her heels one last time.

As we approached the draw at the head of the spring that ran below our house, Dad lost control. He braked, and the bus skidded one way and then, when he corrected, the other, towards the edge of the road, which was a sharp incline to the draw. We teetered for a moment, everyone holding their breath, before we slid over the edge. No one screamed as we went. Not even the little kids. The balance slowly shifted and the world lurched, kids starting to shriek as the ones on the high side began to slide from their seats, grabbing for handholds, falling against other kids. I found myself on my back, lying on the window I'd been looking out, gazing straight up through the windows across the aisle at the blue of the sky. I rolled my head and saw crested wheat pressed against my window. The Harvey girl, who'd been sitting across the aisle, was lying next to me, bleeding from her forehead. Her window was broken and there was glass in her hair. I didn't want her to see me looking at the blood, so I glanced down at her breasts. Then I felt bad about looking at her breasts.

"Are you okay?" I asked, and she nodded blankly. I touched her forehead and studied her blood on my fingertips, and she started to cry.

I don't remember getting to my feet, but I must have. Randy Fox, nine years old, had been sitting across the aisle in the row in front of me, but was now draped over the edge of a seat, moaning. He didn't seem to be bleeding. I lifted him to help him down onto the windows, and he squealed in terrible pain. Once he was lying down, he cringed into a ball. "Don't touch me. Don't touch me. Don't touch me. Don't touch me," he said.

I looked at my hands and saw the Harvey girl's blood.

There was crying and moaning coming from all sides. Dad was crumpled in a heap on the doors. For a moment I wondered if he was dead, but no sooner had I made this wish than he opened his eyes and rubbed his head.

"Whoops," he said.

A couple of high school boys at the back of the bus were on their feet, looking around with wide eyes. "Fuck me," one of them said. They tried opening the emergency door at the back, but it was jammed. Aside from Randy Fox and the Harvey girl, everyone started picking themselves up and looking around, some of them whimpering but most of them too much in shock to cry. There was the smell of urine, and I wondered who'd peed their pants before I saw the evidence: Jenny Leifson was showing her older brother where her hand was bleeding, screaming at the top of her lungs as he tried to calm her. She might not have been the only one who'd peed.

Dad got to his feet, and the kids who'd been sitting at the front shrank away from him, moving towards the back of the bus. I stepped back too. Glass crunched under my feet when I took that step. One of the high school boys kicked at the emergency door until it finally gave, and he and his friend climbed outside. I made my way to the back and helped lift the younger kids out to the boys outside. Dad stepped over Randy Fox and was banging at the emergency side window, which was now at the top of the bus. Us kids had the only exit blocked, and he was in a hurry to get out of there. He managed to force it open and climbed out, using the seats for a ladder.

"Help me," the Harvey girl said, and I gave her a hand getting up and walked her to the door at the back, trying not to touch where I shouldn't as I helped her climb out. Randy Fox was still moaning behind me, but I wanted to escape, and so I kicked my leg over the edge and dropped to the grass. Kids were sitting or standing in small clusters behind the bus. Jenny Leifson was being tended to by her brother: he was using his shirt to bandage her wounded hand. The Harvey girl curled up in the grass while her sister tried to make her sit up. In the distance, I could see Dad staggering down the grid towards the creek.

"Oh my God! Oh my God! Oh my God!" My mother was suddenly there beside me, straining to see inside the bus.

She must have walked straight across the pasture from the house. I hadn't seen her coming. I guess I was staring at her with a funny expression, because she asked me, "You okay, Dwight?" I started to cry and she put her arms around me, holding my head against her breasts and stroking my ear with her fingertips the way she did. All of a sudden, I remembered that the high school boys were there and I pulled away from her, wiping my eyes. They hadn't even noticed. Mom started tending to the other kids, kneeling to check on the Harvey girl.

"Are you okay? Let's get something on that." What was left of the Leifson boy's torn shirt was lying on the ground, and she started winding it around the Harvey girl's head.

"What happened?" she asked me.

Inside the bus, Randy Fox was on his feet, whimpering and crying out at each new pain.

"We went off the road," I told her.

Randy screamed, clutching his own arm to protect his chest, but took another step.

"No kidding? *Where's* your dad?"

I pointed, though he was no longer visible. "Heading towards the creek."

She nodded as though she already knew the answer and turned her attention to the other kids.

The police arrived ten minutes later, and an officer assessed the situation and made a speech about an ambulance and another bus being on its way.

"Are you the driver?" one of them asked my mother, and she explained that Jacob Froese was the driver. She didn't tell them he was her husband.

"Where is he?"

Mom looked in my direction and I told them which way he'd gone. They asked if I could help one of them find him while the other stayed with Mom and the other kids, and Mom said she guessed that would be okay, so I got in the front of the car like I was a cop myself and told the guy which way to drive. He spoke into the radio while he steered the car with one hand, and I watched the lights blinking and scanned the dashboard, wondering which button made the siren work. The speedometer only went up to 120 miles per hour.

It wasn't long before we spotted Dad: he'd left the road and was stumbling through the pasture down the trail towards the creek. I pointed out to the cop where the gate was and started to get out to open it, but he told me to stay put and rushed off to do it himself.

It took him about a minute to get it open—I could have done it in two seconds—and then he rushed back to the driver's seat. We wheeled off towards Dad, hitting plenty of bumps because the cop didn't have much sense about driving across a pasture—he ignored the trail and so hit holes and ruts and rocks. His idea was to go straight towards Dad, as if that were the best way of getting there, even though it seemed to me that it should be clear enough that it was not. Dad was trying to run, and when he fell he just lay there, maybe hoping he hadn't been seen and might not be noticed. The cop stopped the car a few feet away and got out.

Dad rolled over and looked up at him. "Whaddaya want?" he yelled, trying to give the impression he'd been taking a nap and was annoyed about being so rudely awakened.

"We'd like to give you a ride into town, sir. It looks like you've been drinking."

"I wasn't drivin' no fuckin' bus. Did he tell you that?" He pointed at me through the driver's open door. "My wife was drivin' it. I wasn't drivin' no fuckin' bus."

"You're going to have to get in the car, sir," the officer said.

"I know my rights. I'm not gettin' in no fuckin' car."

The officer didn't discuss the situation for long. He handcuffed Dad without much resistance and hauled him to his feet, but found that Dad's reluctant compliance made it necessary to force him into the car. He wrestled him to the door, told him to watch himself as he smashed his head against the top of the door, and booted him in the hind end to get him the rest of the way inside. Dad collapsed across the back seat, coughing. He lay there, making a funny sound that I eventually realized was crying.

The officer dropped me off in my yard, shaking my hand and thanking me for my help.

"Aren't you the hero?" My mother met me at the door. I didn't answer her. "Did you make a new friend?"

"We found him," I said.

"How many times has he been drunk before?"

"I don't know."

"He could have killed you. All of you. If you'd told me, I could have put a stop to it and none of this would have happened. Do you realize what this'll mean? How are we going to live? They'll probably throw him in jail and throw away the key. What the fuck are we going to do? Do you not have the sense to save your own life?"

I was looking into the eyes of a stuffed moose hanging from the wall. I'd heard Dad tell Chandler the story of when he shot the moose: the bullet entered the moose's heart and the moose dropped to the ground. It wasn't really much of a story.

"You didn't know he was driving drunk?" I said to the moose.

Mom turned and looked over her shoulder at the moose. "Hello?" she said. "Of course I didn't know." She turned back to me, shook her head and walked into the house, saying, "God knows what'll happen to us now."

FIVE

I finally relented and went for a coffee with the nanny after yoga. I can't drink coffee in the afternoon or I won't sleep all night, so I had a cup of herbal tea that smelled like flowers in the dark. She hadn't been at the grocery store last week because she'd been away with her foster family for Christmas and New Year's and she wanted to know what I'd done for the holidays.

"I got a thousand-piece puzzle and built that," I told her. "I've been doing some writing."

"Who'd you spend Christmas with?"

"Nobody. I don't have any family."

"You spent Christmas alone?"

I gave a philosophical shrug. "Everybody's busy with families at Christmas."

I figured maybe it would sound like I had a whole bunch of friends who might normally have invited me over. She looked sad, picking at the foam on her latte with a spoon. I insisted on buying her the coffee. She made a big deal of it, but in the end she let me.

"That's terrible. You have no family at all?"

"None. My parents died a few years ago."

She leaned back into her chair, and I felt her knees brush against mine under the table. I drew back my chair to give her room.

"That's sad," she said.

I kept shrugging. "Your parents died too."

"No. They didn't. What gave you that idea? My mom just gave me up. I have no idea about my father. Maybe he is dead. He could be the prime minister for all I know."

"That's even sadder. At least I know what happened to my father."

"What happened?"

"He died. He's dead. I know."

"How? How did your parents die?"

She was sitting there on the other side of the table, telling me that she wanted to know me. It's been a long time since I let anyone know me. When I was living in Vancouver, there was a girl, but that didn't end very well. When I told her about my parents, she listened to the story like she thought it was interesting enough, but afterwards she never returned my calls. Finally I got her on the line, and she said she didn't want to see me. She said she was scared of me and if I didn't stop bothering her she'd call the police.

I scanned the neighbouring tables to make sure no one else was listening. "My mother drowned. In the creek. On the farm where I grew up."

She was waiting for more. I took a drink of my tea.

"That's terrible. I'm sorry. What happened to your father?"

"Bullet through the brain. I shot him."

She sat considering me, a twist of disappointment in her eyes. "Do you not want to talk about it?"

"About what?"

"About how your father died."

"He was killed in the war."

"Really? Which war?"

"World War Two."

For a second she looked puzzled, and then she frowned. "Well, you've got my sense of humour. I'll say that for you. You might even have a weirder sense of humour than me, if that's possible."

"You're not so weird," I said.

She looked at me like I'd insulted her. "If you don't want to talk about your father, just say so."

"I don't want to talk about my father."

She crossed her arms and sat up straighter. "So you spent Christmas writing. What are you writing?"

"Nothing," I said.

She stood and picked up her coat from the back of her chair. "I gotta get going," she said.

"I'm sorry," I said. "When I talk about my dad, it always ends up ugly. Like this."

"At least you had a father you could talk about if you wanted to," she said.

"That's true. I should count my blessings. That's true. I'm sorry."

She took a deep breath and sat down again. She took a sip of her coffee. "What was the thousand-piece puzzle?"

"The *Mona Lisa*."

And she smiled that little smile.

Choppy saw the nanny talking to me after school by the playground set while Caroline was running around playing tag and going down the slide, and the next morning he cornered me in the little room with the red door under the stairs.

"She's in my yoga class, so we got to know each other a little bit. We've gone for coffee once or twice."

"Yoga? Coffee? You gotta be careful with this kind of thing, Johnny. It's ticklish. You need to keep in mind that you've got a professional relationship to keep in mind."

I laughed at him a little too heartily, and he looked hurt. I started to feel bad. "Sorry, Choppy. But it wasn't that long ago you were telling me to make love to the principal."

He looked at his boot, sat down and untied the lace, then tied it again. "Don't play stupid, Johnny. This is different. Stoufing the principal's not gonna make any difference to anyone in the end, but the bitch you've lit on'll stick like shit to a blanket. You're so young and sweet you don't understand these things. You still got that new-boy smell, and she's got you deep in the sinuses, even with that spike through her nose."

"That's the problem? The pierced nose?"

"She's an Injun, Johnny. Doesn't matter what end of her you happen to be sniffin'. I know this might be considered racist, but I've had more than enough of Injuns and their land claims."

"I don't think she has any land claims, Choppy."

"That's what I figured. Stinks of that new-boy smell."

He left, slamming the red door behind him.

One Saturday in Broken Head, I'd got home from work a little after five in the morning, as usual, and turned on the radio while I made my breakfast before bed. I was eating the last of my Hutterite eggs when the six o'clock news came on and the anchor told me something that made me set down my fork.

"A genuine human tragedy occurred yesterday in Pittsburgh when a future hockey great, former Broken Head Rhino star Marty Sunaski, collapsed while doing wind sprints at the Pittsburgh Penguins rookie camp. Doctors pronounced Sunaski dead on arrival at hospital. A hospital spokesman said Sunaski had suffered a heart attack due to a congenital condition that had gone undetected."

The reporter actually said "future hockey great." There's a grave danger in newsmen's attempts to report on the future. In this case, his pronouncement was even more hollow than usual: it should have been clear even to a sports journalist that Marty Sunaski's career was no longer a subject for prophecy.

After breakfast I went to bed but couldn't sleep because when I closed my eyes I kept imagining Chandler and Marty Sunaski lying side by side in corpse pose, glassy eyes open, watching clouds moving like the hand of God across the sky. Two years before, I had wished

Marty Sunaski dead. We'd had a run-in at school. He was a nasty piece of work, and I thought the world would be just as well off without him. In fact, it was Marty Sunaski I'd first imagined challenging to a duel with my father's antique pistols. It was a daydream I enjoyed for a while: me in a black cape like a St. Petersburg aristocrat, peeling off my white gloves and slapping him across the face with them. Shooting him through the forehead in our pasture at dawn. I think I mentioned that I wanted to be Russian. His name almost sounded Russian, and I resented him for that probably as much as anything else. Who was he to steal my name and have it written all over the papers as the name of his glory? He could not have been more different from Chandler, but when you looked into their eyes, you could see something not quite human in both of them. Or maybe all too human. And now they were both dead. If I was guilty of my father's death, why should I be any less guilty of these two acts of God? What did He want from me in exchange for granting my wishes?

I got up and went out for a walk and found that, even in the midst of the drought, it was a gorgeous morning in Broken Head. The birds sang the glory of the day in the shade of the old elms that arched over the Irvines' street. Their roots went deep down into the sticky black of the water table, quenching their thirst in the subterranean world. Everything down there has its own being that needs nothing of us, except those trees that reach all the way up into our world and wait for us to die.

As I was coming back to the house and walking towards my entrance, Gloria intercepted me. She must have seen me go out for a walk and been waiting for me to come back, but that didn't occur to me until later. I thought she'd just happened to be passing my door. Seeing her made my heart palpitate, and I frantically tried to think of the right thing to say. I couldn't conceive that she might be there because she wanted to see me. I stopped and nodded to her, and she looked in both directions like she was checking to make sure we were alone before she whispered, "Did you hear? Marty Sunaski is dead."

I had to lean closer to hear because she was whispering.

"I didn't do it," I said.

She looked at me wide-eyed for a moment, a serious stare, before she clapped her hands to her face and let out a peal of laughter that harmonized perfectly with the birdsong.

"Of course not. He had a heart attack," she said. No cause of death has ever been announced with such pure and innocent joy. "I think it's eerie. Isn't it eerie? I don't know if I should be saying this to you, but the weird thing is—I hope you're not offended by this—but when I heard about you and your mom and dad last year, the first thing I thought of was Marty Sunaski. And when Dad brought you here and told us you were going to be living in the basement, the first thing I thought of was Marty Sunaski. And then today, what do I hear on the news but that Marty Sunaski is dead? I got these chills. Really. Actual chills running up and down my spine. Just hearing his name again. Because he's absolutely the only connection between the two of us. You know what I mean? And all of a sudden, here you are living in our basement. And all of a sudden, I hear that Marty Sunaski is dead. Isn't it eerie?"

"Well, there was the choir," I said.

Her hands covered her blue eyes. "I never thanked you properly for standing up to him. That was very brave of you. When I told Nick about it, he thought it was very brave too. He had no idea that Marty Sunaski was such a thug. You know, everybody who likes hockey thinks he's a hero just because he can score goals. But he's really such a thug. He's just the biggest pig imaginable. Don't you think? Or he was. Shouldn't speak ill of the dead. I'm sure he had all his own problems and everything. I'm sure his parents must feel awful."

"You thanked me fine."

"No, I didn't. You stood up to him for *me.* It was so noble of you. And they arrested you. And I didn't say a word in your defence. I could have said something . . ."

"They didn't arrest me. The police came and talked to me, but they didn't arrest me."

"I'm sorry. I'm glad they didn't arrest you, but I still think

I should have said something. It was just that—my friends told me it would be better not to get involved. Not Nick. My girlfriends. I didn't even tell Nick at the time. He was away at university. I didn't tell him until we saw you in the newspapers last year. I was just so embarrassed. Marty Sunaski had done that before, you know, but he never did it after that, because of you. I wanted the whole thing to be over and done with, and so I listened to my friends and didn't say anything. I'm so, so sorry."

"You don't have anything to be sorry for. You want some tea?"

"Tea?"

"Yeah. I could make you some tea."

"Tea would be very nice."

I led her through the door, across the basement and into my room, and she followed so innocently I was almost afraid for her. Didn't she know what went on in basement rooms between the bodies of men and women?

I made tea. There has never been a stranger and more momentous occasion for me than having her there in my room for the first time while I ran the water in the kettle and set it on the burner. I felt like I was floating two feet above the floor. She sat at the table, looking at a pen I'd dropped in the corner and left there.

"I shouldn't be saying this to you, but I'm going to," she said. "I just feel like I can trust you, and so I want you to know every little thing, because I feel like you'll understand." She was still looking at the pen. "Part of the reason I didn't say anything to the police was because . . . it was the look in your eyes and part of what I think I heard you say to him. I couldn't hear it that well, but . . . that's what I remembered when you were in the news last year. I thought that maybe if I told them, it wouldn't help you with the police. It scared me. Not that I blamed you. I wished I could kill him too."

She got an expression on her face like a child who'd stolen a cookie.

"No, you didn't," I said.

That made her look at me. "I did! He was such a pig. I really did wish he was dead."

"Well, he is," I said. "Maybe wishing got it done."

She gave this a thought and shook her head. "He had a heart attack. I feel terrible for his parents."

The kettle whistled and I made the tea.

After neither of us had spoken for a long time, she asked me, "Do you actually believe in Jesus? I mean that He was God and He died for all our sins and everything."

"Of course I do."

"I don't know if I really do. I wish I believed, but I don't think I can. I bet it's because you really do believe that you can help that little boy. Sometimes I even wonder if my dad really believes, but I have no doubt that you do. I can see it in your eyes."

She said all this to me in a voice that made my stomach flop like a fish dying in the bottom of a boat.

"You're the one who gave me the Bible," I said.

"Pardon?"

"In grade four. You gave me the Bible. I'd never even seen one before that."

"I'm sorry? I'm not sure what you mean."

"When you won the contest for reciting the twenty-third Psalm, I asked you what book it was from, and the next day you brought me a Bible."

She sat there looking at me, her mouth slightly open. "You went to Fairview?"

"Yeah."

"Isn't that funny? I don't remember you. I remember winning that contest, but I don't remember giving anyone a Bible. Are you sure?"

I went to the bookshelf, got the Bible and set it on the table in front of her. "There it is."

She sat looking at the cover as if she were trying hard to recognize herself. A strip of grey duct tape held the torn binding together. "Isn't that funny? You were a grade ahead of me?"

"No. We were in the same class. Well, not always. There were two teachers for each grade, so sometimes you were in the other room."

"Yeah," she said. "You must have usually been in the other room."

"Sometimes," I said. I set the teapot, sugar and milk in the middle of the table and brought us both cups. She pushed the Bible aside so as not to spill on it, and took milk and a couple of spoonfuls of sugar.

"Nick and I are going to a movie tonight. Do you want to come along?" I opened my mouth to speak, but nothing came out. "I'd really like you to come."

"I'm not working," I said.

"Well, that settles it. If you ask me—not that you are asking me, but—I think you spend too much time alone. I said that to Nick, and he told me to mind my own business. That's what Nick always tells me, even though he knows I never will."

I agreed to come around to the front door to meet her at six thirty that evening, which was about the time Nick was to show up as well. After that, she talked some more while we drank the tea. It doesn't really matter what she talked about. I sat there and listened, amazed that she could be talking to me like she really wanted to be there. She could pretty much hold up both sides of a conversation. It wasn't like she seemed to be in any hurry to leave.

After a while she said she had to go, and I walked her back out my door into the basement and she started up the stairs.

"And use the pool," she added before she climbed out of sight, waving her hand to indicate the direction of the backyard. "Any time you feel like it."

In early May of my grade twelve year, the choir was scheduled to do a special performance in the Broken Head Comprehensive High School Auditorium. "Spring Magic," it was called, and there were posters up all over town. The show was sold out, which wasn't surprising because there are a lot of Mennonites in Broken Head and Mennonites love choirs. We had a final lunchtime rehearsal the day of the performance. Everything went without a hitch, and Mr. Whiteside, the choir director, was happy. I'd moved my lips spectacularly. He reminded us to be sure to arrive half an hour early that evening. I walked out of the music room, following Gloria and a couple of her friends. I confess that I was watching her bum, but not only her bum: I loved the way her hair fell over her shoulders; I loved the freckle on her left shoulder blade, beside the strap of her halter top; I loved the skin at the back of her knees; I loved the lilt of her walk.

The Broken Head Rhinos were the local Major Junior A hockey team, and the players who went to Broken Head Comprehensive High School had claimed a bench outside the door of the school library, owing to the fact that it had the best view of the girls who passed the most highly trafficked junction of hallways in the entire school, and not owing to how close it was to the library. A couple of the guys who had made the Rhinos used to terrorize me in gym class in junior high. This group had been joined by young men of their kind from across the country, come to Broken Head to pursue fame and wealth. Physical geniuses all of them, most had been pushed their entire lives by hungry and desperate parents in pursuit of glory, even vicariously, and wealth. Now, having crushed thousands of rivals to get so far, they'd arrived at the second-last step of their journey, the cruellest plank, from which most of them would fall and find themselves rolling the rest of their unhappy lives towards oblivion. They would become real estate agents who'd almost made it to the NHL. For the moment, though, they were the gods of Broken Head, the gods of desperate citizens in pursuit of civic glory. There were no laws for them: they could assault, steal, vandalize and rape, and their crimes would be overlooked. "We were all young once," the business leaders of Broken Head told each other at Chamber of Commerce meetings.

As I mentioned, Gloria was walking with a couple of friends of hers about twenty feet in front of me. One of the Rhinos, Marty

Sunaski, spotted her and called out, "Gloria! I love you, Gloria! I have an English exam with Stuart this afternoon, and I haven't studied. Can you give me a kiss for luck?" Gloria kept walking, not making eye contact, but Sunaski got such a good response from the other Rhinos that he kept it up: "Gloria, couldn't you give me just one little kiss? Maybe a little tongue? I'm crazy for girls with big . . . brains!"

Gloria and her friends were about to escape through the door ahead when I heard my own voice shouting, "Shut your filthy mouth, you moron!"

The Rhinos were so surprised that for a second they didn't know what to do. Everyone froze, a hush falling over that noisy hallway, and everyone turned to stare at me. The second passed and, seeing that he was skating towards an empty net, Sunaski smiled. He told the other Rhinos that he could smell the cow shit on me from a mile away.

"Oh, farmer boy, are you in love with Gloria too? Did you try giving her a bottle of Corral #5?"

I did my best to sneer at him and started walking again, hoping he might let me pass, but he stood up and stepped in front of me, and I had to stop. "Well, you're just gonna have to fight me for her then, aren't you?" His hands were raised. Not in fists: the fingers spread and wiggling to coax me into an attack. Forty-seven students had paused in their goings to watch. Gloria was one of them. I could hear the shrill pitch of the fluorescent lights over forty-seven held breaths. Sunaski's fingers clenched to become the necessary weapons, and he smiled sideways, winking to his Rhino friends.

"Shut your mouth, Sunaski," I murmured from between my teeth, "or I'll kill you."

Sunaski slowly lowered his fists. "What's that?" he said. "I can't hardly hear you."

The young gladiator smiled stupidly out of the left side of his mouth. The bridge of his nose was humped where it had been broken on four separate occasions, once by a puck, once by a stick and twice by fists. (I read this later in a newspaper article). He'd grown up in a suburb of Vancouver, where he survived an unfortunate early talent for figure skating, encouraged by his mother and his Russian coach. He was saved when his father put his foot down after an older bully at school broke his nose for the first time. Now, here he was in a little prairie town, waiting for the draft he expected to blow him into immortality.

I leaned in closer, so that my nose almost touched his four-times-broken nose, breathing my words into his crooked face. "I'll kill you," I whispered. "I'll get a gun—my father has plenty of guns—and I'll blow your brains out and leave you for the magpies to peck. You deserve to be dead. You're scum. It would be a pleasure to kill you."

It was wish-fulfillment, but I survived on wishes and fears, and so all of it was out of my mouth before I could stop the saying of it.

Sunaski stepped back.

I glanced over to where Gloria stood watching and saw her staring at me, but when my eyes met hers, she looked at the floor. And I did too. I kept my eyes on those scuffed tiles as I rushed through the set of doors in front of me.

It's difficult to describe what went through my mind after Gloria came to my room for tea. I couldn't imagine what it meant. It was like I'd been standing at a door for years, waiting for it to open but never daring to touch the knob, and now the door had opened and I was being told it had been unlocked all along and she'd been waiting for me to come inside.

No. That's not right. It wasn't like that at all.

I got no sleep that afternoon and was in a deep fog when the evening rolled around. But at the same time, I was ecstatic that she'd come to tell me about Sunaski and invited me on her date. It was one of those mixtures of fatigue and adrenaline that keep you going even when something tells you you should stop. I put on my brown corduroy pants and a button-up blue shirt my mother'd given me our last Christmas and squeezed into my father's dress shoes and stood in front of the mirror, posing and examining every pimple on my face. It was only a quarter after six, but I couldn't wait another minute. I wanted to be first. I walked out my door and around the house and pressed the doorbell. The door opened, and there was Irvine.

"Dwight. Come on in. Gloria's still getting ready, but you can sit and watch the news with us."

I followed him into the living room, where Mrs. Irvine was curled in a corner of the couch, a glass of wine in her hand, watching a politician talk about acid rain. She looked up at me and stared, as though an elephant had just entered her living room and she couldn't believe the nerve of the elephant's owner.

"Emily, Dwight's here to pick up Gloria. They're going to a movie."

"They are?" she said.

Irvine nodded.

"Nick's coming too," I said.

"Sit down, sit down," Irvine urged me, and I perched myself in the chair farthest from Mrs. Irvine.

"Well, isn't that nice of Nick and Gloria, taking you on their date?" Mrs. Irvine asked.

I nodded, already feeling the place on my foot where the blister would form. Nobody said anything else, and we watched the news. The weather came on and Irvine said something about what a beautiful day it was and I agreed. The sports came on and the lead story was about Marty Sunaski.

"I guess he went to school with you and Gloria, didn't he?" Irvine asked, and I said he had. "Tragic," Irvine said. "So much talent."

I looked over towards Mrs. Irvine. She gazed on numbly at the television, a hand in her hair massaging her scalp.

We sat in silence until the doorbell rang. When Irvine got up to answer it, I followed him out to greet Nick, who shook my hand and asked me, "How you doing, Dwight?" in a way that made it sound like he was pleased I was coming along. Gloria still hadn't appeared, so Irvine led us back to the living room. Mrs. Irvine got up when Nick came in, and they hugged. It wasn't until then that I realized how ridiculous I'd looked getting up to follow Irvine to the door. I settled back into my spot farthest from Mrs. Irvine, while Nick sat down on the couch next to her.

"I was just saying what a nice idea that was, taking Dwight on your date," Mrs. Irvine said, patting Nick on the knee.

Nick glanced at Irvine and then at me. "Yes," he said, and offered nothing else. He wore a shirt that advertised some product I didn't recognize. The Clash. I guessed it was a musical group of some description. His running shoes were four different colours and would have cost more than I made in two days of janitoring.

"It's really *so* generous," she continued. "Don't you think, Dwight?"

"Yes," I said.

Irvine studied the three of us and finally said, "I'm sure they're glad to have Dwight along. Aren't you, Nick?"

Nick smiled and said, "Yeah. It'll be great." There was another awkward silence before Nick said, "Hey, Dwight, did you hear about Marty Sunaski?" I coughed and concentrated on relieving the pressure points on my feet. "Gloria told me you had a bit of a dust-up with him one time, didn't you?" He lifted his eyebrows as he asked the question.

"A fight?" Mrs. Irvine said. "Is that right?"

"Oh, it was nothing," I said.

"What was it about?" she wanted to know.

"Nothing," I said. "He was being a little rude. To some girls."

"To Gloria," Nick said. "Wasn't he was being rude to Gloria?"

"Probably," I said. "He was rude to a lot of girls."

"And you told him to stop?" Irvine asked.

I nodded.

"Really? How gallant," Mrs. Irvine said.

And Gloria entered. "Who's gallant? Weren't you just saying yesterday, Mother, that there wasn't a gallant man left on the face of the earth? So I guess you're talking about a woman."

She wore jeans and a plain white cotton blouse, but she'd put on makeup and some dangly earrings and white nail polish that made me look at her beautiful fingers. Nick stood up. I wondered what to do and decided this time that it would be safer to stay in my chair. Nick gave her a hug and she kissed him on the cheek. Finally, she acknowledged me with a smile and a hello.

"Well, we'd better get going or we'll be late," she said.

"Dwight was just telling us that he once got in a fight with this dead hockey player, Marty Sunaski, in defence of your honour," Mrs. Irvine said. Gloria glared at Nick, who gave her back his impression of confused innocence. "The hockey player who passed away today," her mother elaborated.

"Yes, Mother. Dwight was very gallant that day, wasn't he? And a man, too."

"It wasn't a big deal," I said, getting to my feet.

"I thought you were arrested," Nick said.

"Nick!" Gloria said.

"No," I said. "I wasn't arrested. That's not what happened. Not for fighting with Marty Sunaski."

"Arrested! That was just a stupid rumour," Gloria scolded Nick. "Do you really have to go around repeating every stupid rumour you hear?"

Irvine sat up and waited to hear more. So did Mrs. Irvine, still perched in her corner of the couch. The anchorman blared on like one of those guests who never know when to stop talking. I shuffled and shrugged my shoulders three times. At last Nick shrugged too and said, "I guess I heard wrong."

Irvine walked us to the door and said to have a good time, and we filed to Nick's yellow sports car. He moved the seat forward for me and I got in back. There was so little leg room that I stretched out lengthwise, with my back against the side window, so that I was looking directly at Gloria's profile and that dangling tusk-shaped earring. Why was she wearing tusks? She turned to me and said, "I'm really sorry about that, Dwight. And I'm sure Nick's sorry too."

"Whatever. It was you who told me he was arrested," Nick said.

"Shut up, Nick," Gloria said. Lips pursed, she looked straight ahead.

"Better put on your seat belt," Nick told me, so I strapped it around me, still sitting sideways. "We're late," he continued. "Grant and Mary will be waiting."

"Grant and Mary?" Gloria asked.

"Yeah. They were going to a movie anyway, so I told them to meet us there."

"Oh?" she said.

Nick shrugged. "I figured the more the merrier."

Gloria nodded blankly and stared at the dashboard. I tried to catch her eye to tell her it was okay, but she stared straight out the windshield until we were at the theatre.

I'd joined the school choir for the single solitary reason of keeping my eyes and ears on soprano Gloria Irvine. She had a voice like spring water bubbling from the earth to tumble over shiny white pebbles. Maybe she still does. I was in the second row of tenors, where I had a good view of her profile in the front row. I could always hear her, somehow, over the boom of fifteen basses, ten tenors, eighteen altos and twenty other sopranos.

The eleventh tenor only moved his lips, which was fine as far as Mr. Whiteside was concerned. I'd tried to join the choir the year before and was one of only three boys who didn't survive the cuts. There's a certain humiliation in coming that low on a list that I couldn't have entirely expressed without the aid of a grenade launcher, but it didn't stop me from trying out the next year, and Mr. Whiteside didn't have the heart or stomach to humiliate me two years in a row.

Never mind singing, even speaking I had to control a voice dropping steadily towards bass. It was just one more way my body was revolting against me as I finally arrived at puberty at sixteen. Revolting and erupting. The acne on my face wasn't any worse than the average teenager's, but on my neck and my back and my chest I was exploding. My shirts were stained with blood, so I had to wear undershirts, no matter how hot the weather. Mom figured it was what I was eating. She made me follow one of her diets and cut out pretty much everything but fruit and vegetables and plain bread. But the diet made no difference to the acne, and the lack of protein made me feel weak. My joints ached.

I was like Job with his boils, wondering why God was afflicting him.

Nick's friends Grant and Mary were waiting for us outside the Twin Cinema. Mary had graduated the same year as Gloria and I. She was a one of the general group you'd see Gloria with, but otherwise I don't remember much about her from high school, except for one story, which I won't repeat, about something she was supposed to have done at a house party. It probably wasn't true. Grant Robinson was Nick's age and was pretty famous around town for being the son of Mayor Robinson. He'd been the president of the student council when I was in grade ten, and managed to carry it off as though he were the monarch of some tiny European state, which I'd admired him for in a distant, peasant-like way. He was a smart guy and the sort of hand-some that made everyone like him, unlike Nick, who had a chin that made you feel inadequate. Grant and Mary had gone off to univer-sity together, like Gloria and Nick, only they'd gone to some other down-east university. They were both from well-off families and, like Nick, Grant was home to work for his father, who had a legal prac-tice as well as being the mayor. They said hello in a way that surprised me and made me nervous—as though I was a kind of a celebrity, but also as though they'd just as soon have kept a screen between us. Grant asked how the crops were, and I told him I thought we could use some rain but that I was not farming.

"Oh? What are you doing now?"

"Janitor," I said.

He nodded blankly and turned to Nick. "So, what are we gonna see?"

Nick voted for the action film over the romantic comedy, and Mary went along, and Grant said it didn't matter to him because it was all bottomless commercial trash. I shrugged.

"Who am I to force romance on everyone if they prefer action," Gloria said, and so it was decided.

I sat next to Nick, Gloria on the other side of him, next to Mary and Grant. The film had many explosions as the hero battled a villain who was trying to take over the world for no apparent reason. I suppose that running the world has its advantages. Grant and Mary spent a lot of time necking, which made Gloria look very uncomfortable. It made me feel uncomfortable too. The most uncomfortable part was the scene where the hero seduces a beautiful foreign agent. The actress moaned in a way that made me think of Mrs. Greene.

At some point I nodded off and woke up during the credits. I was so very tired. I don't think anyone noticed.

When it was over, Nick suggested we go for a drink, but Gloria said she didn't feel like drinking and I said I didn't drink, so he suggested we drive to a restaurant at the mall for coffee. There are actually two malls out by the highway in Broken Head. We went to the newer of the two, where most of the high school kids still went for coffee. I suppose it was kind of nostalgic for the four of them. It was my first time there. We took a table in the window, in the orange glow of the evening sun, and there was some chat about how they'd managed to end up back in the middle of nowhere, and how they wouldn't allow it to happen again next summer, before Gloria asked Grant if he'd decided which of his poems he'd recite at the wedding.

"Grant's promised us one of his love poems," she told me. "I know which one I want, but because I've asked for it he keeps threatening to recite something else."

"I'm working on a new one especially for the big event. A sestina. It's an obsessive form, and weddings are fairly obsessive occasions."

Nick and Mary laughed. "It's all about a very young man who can't run fast enough to get away, and so gets caught." Mary laughed again, but Nick didn't this time.

Gloria puffed up her cheeks and let out a breath of air. "I wish you could be a little more respectful."

"I didn't know you wrote poetry," I said, wanting to smooth over the silence even though Grant didn't look the least bit unnerved. "I'd like to read some."

"I don't write them down," Grant said.

"Pardon?"

"My poems are all in my head. I don't believe in writing them down. Poetry—all literature—comes out of an oral tradition. I'm trying to recover the magic and mystery that was lost when we lost that tradition."

"Oh," I said. "Well, I'd like to hear one."

He licked his lips. "I'm flattered, but I don't do requests over coffee at the mall. You're coming to the wedding?"

I looked at Gloria.

"Of course! Of course you are, aren't you?"

"Gloria," Nick said. "I think you'd better talk to your mother. Didn't she say the guest list was . . . fixed?"

"Is it my mother's wedding or is it my wedding?"

"Well, getting married when you're nineteen's at least a generation out of fashion," Grant winked at Mary, "so I think it must be your mother's wedding."

Mary smiled and blushed and looked at the table.

"To Grant Robinson, everything's about fashion," Gloria said. "He's not aware that getting married isn't about fashion."

"No. Apparently it's about reproduction. And that never goes out of fashion."

Gloria gave him a look that was meant to melt his brain and other vital organs.

"Shut up, Grant," Nick said.

"I'm sorry. My apologies for being such a boor. I'll be happy to recite whatever you wish, Gloria my dear." He grabbed her hand and tried to kiss it, but she yanked it away from him.

Mary, who was staring across the parking lot at the cars going by on the service road, said, "God, this town is a hole," and we were instantly back on the safer subject of all the inadequacies of Broken Head. Nick picked it up and ran, telling about the idiot his father had him reporting to at his summer job in the oil patch. Gloria peered into her coffee cup. My feet ached and I wanted to lay my head down on the table and sleep. I wished I hadn't come. During one of the silences I turned to look out the window at the parking lot, where I could see a group of Hutterite women gathering at their van, waiting for the men to come and drive them back to the colony. I wondered what they were doing in town on a Saturday night.

"Oh, look," Grant said. "Sale at Zellers tonight. What is the world coming to? First they strike down the store-hours bylaw, unleashing an utter chaos of uncontrolled shopping, and now even the Hutterites are coming to town on Saturday nights. It's getting so you can't find a good Commie anywhere."

"I'm thinking about joining a Hutterite colony," I said.

We sunk under an even more oppressive silence. At the next table a teenage girl was talking about the smell of her boyfriend's breath. It was at least twenty seconds before Nick dared to say, "Really?"

"Yeah," I said. "Their lives are so pure and simple. They have purpose."

All three of them looked at Gloria, as if it were her talking, and she looked back at them defiantly. "I think that's really interesting," she said. "I think the Hutterites are fascinating."

No one said anything else for so long that I thought they would let it drop and move onto something else, but Grant wasn't satisfied. "You know how they get new blood into the colony?" he said, stirring his coffee loudly. "They pay young bucks, like Dwight here, fifty bucks to have sex with their young women."

Mary giggled and Nick smiled until Gloria's look warned the smile off his face.

"That's a myth," I said.

"Is it?" Grant said. "What makes you so sure? I knew a guy who knew a guy . . ."

"It's a myth," Gloria repeated.

Grant shrugged. "Obviously you two know better."

The girl at the next table was describing her boyfriend's general body odour.

"Remember that girl who gave us the tour of the colony last summer?" Mary piped in. She turned and spoke directly to me. "She was trying to teach Gloria and me how to catch a husband."

"What do you mean?" Gloria protested. "She let us see her hope chest."

"Makes sense," Grant said. "Women often show their chests when they're trying to catch a husband."

"Fuck you, Grant," Gloria said.

Mary tried half-heartedly to stifle her laugh. Grant grinned slyly at me and looked out the window. "Don't you think you should watch your language in front of Dwight, Gloria?"

The girl at the next table was describing the colour of the walls of her boyfriend's bedroom. Mary started talking again: "Her hope chest had all these advertising buttons pinned to the crinoline on the inside of the lid, like 'Budweiser, King of Beer' and that kind of thing, and there was this plastic rose in a liqueur bottle and a bunch of romance novels with tall, dark men and women with heaving bosoms on the cover."

"She was gracious enough to invite us right into her home," Gloria interrupted her, "and she showed us things you don't usually ever get to see." She was speaking directly to me. "She had this beautiful linen table-cloth that she was embroidering herself. Absolutely gorgeous."

"She really took Gloria under her wing," Mary said. "She was giving her advice on matters sex-u-al."

"Shut up, Mary," Gloria said.

"She told her, 'Milk drinkers make better lovers.'" Grant let out a long oooooh, and Mary leaned towards me. "I'll bet you're a milk drinker, aren't you, Dwight?"

I blushed and held my breath and picked up my spoon and stirred my coffee.

"You two are so ignorant," Gloria said. She'd crossed her arms on her chest and was speaking to the table. "You go around putting down everything you can't understand."

Mary look mortified over what she'd set off, but Grant sighed and rolled his eyes.

"Gloria!" Nick put a hand on her arm to try and calm her. "Lighten up. They're just joking around."

"All they do is joke around, and they think they're so smart, but they're really so ignorant. They're making fun of you too, you know. Trapped into getting married by your slut of a girlfriend. Why doesn't she just get an abortion like everybody else?"

"I apologize, Gloria," Grant said. "We got a little carried away, and I definitely stepped over the line."

"This baby could be another Mozart. He could be another Einstein. And you'd just kill him without even a second thought."

"Nobody's talking about killing . . ." Nick said.

"I really don't want to debate you about your beliefs, Gloria," Grant said.

"No, you just want to make fun of anybody who believes anything."

I stared into my coffee cup in the same way that Mary was staring into hers.

"I don't think this is the time to talk about it," Nick said.

"Oh, really? And if it ever were the time to talk about it, what would you have to say? Whose side would you be on, Nick? Why don't you tell everybody about how you'd like to kill this baby too?"

Nick made the face of a man who had died in a swamp with a rope around his neck a thousand years ago. "I love you, Gloria," he said. "You want this baby and so I want this baby, and I'm marrying you because I love you. We'll talk later. Not now."

"Why not now?" Gloria said. "The more the merrier."

She rose and walked towards the washroom. Nick took a deep breath and got up to go after her. The girl at the next table was laughing at the top of her lungs, laughing so hysterically that I wondered if she might not begin to cry. We were drowning in our silence. Mary bit her lip and looked out the window so intently she might have been watching souls ascend into the deepening orange of the clouds. Grant Robinson tattooed a rhythm on the table, craned his head back to peer into the ceiling and said, "Sooooo, did you hear that Marty Sunaski dropped dead?"

I took a long sip from my coffee. "God's will," I said.

It wasn't the greatest first date in history. I said I had to be going, thanked Grant and Mary for their company, walked home and stumbled down to my room. I don't remember pulling my shoes from my aching feet and taking off my clothes and falling into bed. But when I woke the next morning, I was naked, so I must have undressed before I crawled in. Naked and alone on Sunday morning.

If there was solace in Christ, I hoped He might come and visit me in my room that day. I didn't want to go to church. I only wanted to lie there. The conversation the evening before had made it difficult for me to avoid thinking about Gloria and Nick getting together in a way I didn't want to think about. It was pretty much all I could think about. Jealousy is the devil at work in your soul. He hooks you with desire and reels you to his bidding through the workings of your jealous heart.

I prayed and prayed to God for forgiveness and to let Nick Campion and his baby live.

And then I remembered that I was supposed to go to supper at the Greenes'. If I was so sick I couldn't make it to church, they couldn't be offended if I didn't come to supper. I tried to fall back to sleep, but it didn't happen. Christ was looking down on me, urging me to throw back the covers and clothe my nakedness and make my way to the house of the Lord.

Our Lord lived in an austere house up by the highway, not so far from the old mall. Sometimes I wished it was like other churches I'd visited for choir recitals when I was in high school: the light falling through stained glass in shafts that carved visions of peace directly on the soul. Hard to accept that God could have a bone to pick with stained glass, but our Lord has no time for show-offs, aside from Mother Nature, and I have to admit that I can see His point. When man tries to compete with nature, he's competing with God, and there are certainly more productive ways to spend your life. Like cleaning toilets.

I arrived early and took my place in the fourth row, alone except for the pastor (who nodded) and the members of the tiny choir, who were helping him prepare for his flock. Luckily, Christ had no argument with the beauty of the human voice, though I sometimes wondered if He'd considered how singing was only an overly refined imitation of what the birds do every day.

When Irvine arrived and slipped into the pew beside me, he was alone. I asked about Gloria, and he whispered that she wasn't feeling well that morning. He didn't look so well himself, but he claimed to feel fine. Mrs. Greene gave me a faint smile as she walked to her pew. Lilly Banks was there without her mother, and she glanced back at Irvine and me with an expression I couldn't identify. I was wearing my running shoes, but my feet still hurt.

Pastor Tuttle's service was about Christ's parable of the brides who hadn't prepared by buying enough oil to ready themselves for the coming of the bridegroom. There were ten brides, and five had enough oil and five didn't, and when the five realized they weren't prepared, they asked the other five to lend them some oil, but the other five wouldn't, saying that if they did they might run out of oil too and not be able to see the glorious bridegroom when he arrived. So the other five silly brides ran off to the market to buy oil, but by the time they got back, the bridegroom had already arrived and taken the five brides with the oil into the house and locked the gate behind him. The five abandoned brides beat at the gate and asked to be let in, but the bridegroom came and peered out through the gate at them and told them they were too late. He was only interested in the five brides who had come prepared. He told them to go away.

It's one of those nasty little stories where no one comes out looking very good in the end.

After the service I said goodbye to Irvine and headed for the door, but Mrs. Greene intercepted me to remind me that I was expected at six. I told her I'd be there. Shuffling my feet and staring at her high-heeled shoes, I asked if she wanted me to bring anything, but she said all I needed to do was show "my perfect self." When she'd floated off, I glanced over my shoulder and saw that Irvine was watching. He lifted his hand in a wave, and I waved back before grasping the brass handle and pushing through the heavy wooden doors.

Having slept so well the night before, I was too wide awake for my afternoon nap. Worrying about the Greenes didn't help. I needed the sleep or I knew I'd be tired out by the time I showed up for work on Monday night. I lay in my bed, reading Dostoevsky, hoping I'd lose consciousness.

The thing I love about Dostoevsky is the way he knows you, even though he lived so long before you were even born. When you read him, you can feel him reading you right back. And it's strange, because even though you're expecting the world to be so different before all our technology, it's so much the same that you wouldn't really be all that surprised if one of his characters flagged down a cab and it was a Chevy, or even if he got a call on a cellphone. Hard to believe that people were every bit as messed up back then, but apparently they were, and they were basically worrying about and arguing about all the same things they're still worrying about today.

I think I mentioned that I wanted be Russian. I know it was silly, but I was particularly connected to Dostoevsky. I used to imagine I was my great-grandfather Froese, wandering the steppes, hobbling along, clinging to the handles of a plow pulled by horses or mules or oxen, the blade peeling back the rich black soil. I glanced up from my furrow and saw a carriage driving by on the road, heading west. Dostoevsky was inside that carriage, on his way to some spa and gambling table in Germany or Prussia or Austria-Hungary. The great writer was so close I could have run over and leapt in beside him and rode into some vastly alternative yesterday and today and tomorrow. But instead, I trod on behind the plow.

That's how close I was to Dostoevsky.

A knock came at the door.

An image of Gloria standing there flashed through my mind, and I called out that it was open. The door came towards me and it was Irvine, looking pale and sickly. I jumped to my feet to meet him and ducked under the beam.

"How are you doing?" he said.

"Fine. Are *you* okay?"

"I'm fine. I just wondered how things went with you and Gloria and Nick last night."

"Good. Very good," I mumbled.

He looked at me, and I knew that he knew I was lying.

"That's great," he said. "Her friends are such privileged children, and sometimes those privileges are not well reflected in their behaviour."

I told him everyone was charming. "I didn't know Grant Robinson was a poet."

"Apparently." He nodded, but kept staring at the fern in the metal pot stand. I'd never watered it, and the fern was dead. "Gloria and Nick seem to have the idea that he's an artist of some sort. I haven't seen any evidence."

"He doesn't write them down," I said. "He doesn't believe in writing them down."

He nodded again. "So I understand." He sat down on one of my kitchen chairs, and I sat on another. "Feeling tired," he said.

"You look sick. You should see a doctor."

After I said it, I realized that he was a doctor, and I wondered if doctors went to doctors.

"I'm wondering about this disagreement you had with the hockey player. Can you tell me more about that?"

I shrugged. "It wasn't anything, really."

"I understand that you threatened to shoot him. Is that true?" He was looking into my eyes so that I couldn't look away.

"Yes."

"You consider a death threat to be nothing?"

It was the first time he'd ever spoken harshly to me. I shrugged again. "I shouldn't have done that. But I didn't really mean I was going to kill him. People say that kind of thing all the time: 'Stop that or I'll kill you.'"

Again he studied my face all too intensely, but after a moment he seemed to accept what I'd said, and he nodded. "How's the job going?"

As soon as he'd asked, he turned away and stared at the dead fern.

"Good. It's . . . interesting."

He turned back and glared at me. "Interesting?"

I looked at the ceiling and nodded, not wanting at that moment to have to explain how janitorial work was interesting.

"What I do is interesting too," he said. "I deal with the dead. Tag them and declare the means of their death and give them back to their families. It's not everyone's cup of tea, but it needs to be done. You clean toilets. People take for granted that a toilet should be clean. But somebody has to get in there with a brush and scrub."

"Yes," I nodded vigorously. "That's what I mean. That's what I mean by interesting."

"I'll bet you sometimes wish they'd clean up their own messes."

I stopped nodding. "No," I said. "It's my job."

He was looking at the fern again. "If that bullet that hit your ear had gone through your head, I'd have had to clean up that mess."

I touched my ear. "It could have. Or it could have left you a vegetable. They'd have put you in a hospital where the nurses would have had to clean up your messes."

He stood and ducked neatly under the beam. He lifted the fern from the stand. A hail of dead fronds floated to the carpet.

"Sorry about that," I said.

He stared at me. "A little water would have satisfied it," he said.

"I didn't kill Marty Sunaski. Or Chandler," I said.

The fern balanced in his arms, he stood looking down at me for a long moment. "Of course you didn't. And your father didn't kill your mother either. It was an accident."

And he walked out the door, the plant raining down fronds so that he left a trail across the room and into the laundry room.

I've never been good with plants. With houseplants, you can never count on rain.

No sleep came my way, and by evening I was wobbly and a little nauseated as I walked across the overpass to the Greenes'. Mr. Greene opened the door and shook my already shaking hand, welcoming me into his home with thanks and best regards so that I felt as if I were already leaving. He was short and had a hairline that receded all the way to the crown of his head. His eyes were blue like Jimmy's. He led me into the living room, where Jimmy was watching a science fiction adventure story on videotape. He was excited to see me because they'd been on a Sunday afternoon expedition to the Saskatchewan River and he'd found a tiny bird's egg, which he handed to me in a jewellery store box, the egg cradled on a bit of cotton fluff.

"Feel how light it is," he demanded, and so I rolled the egg into my left hand with my right, but my hands were shaking. The egg slipped between my middle and index fingers and, trying to stop it from falling, I squeezed my fingers together and the egg collapsed like a soap bubble.

"I'm sorry!" I said to Mr. Greene instead of to Jimmy.

"Yes. They're very fragile," he said.

Jimmy grimaced and shrugged that it didn't matter, and he really didn't look upset. In a second he was back inside his movie, and you couldn't have distracted him from it if you'd passed a hand in front of his eyes.

Mr. Greene sent me to wash my hands: "I guess you know where the bathroom is."

I rinsed off the shell and yolk and white from my hands, watching the flecks of shell spin counter-clockwise down the drain. It was a bird's egg. Nothing but a bird's egg.

The dinner, a roast chicken with roast potatoes and carrots, was more elaborate than I was used to, and I had trouble getting it down. The Greenes sat at either end of the table, and Jimmy, who wanted to get back to his movie, sat across from me. He kept complaining that he was tired and wasn't hungry, and he picked away at the tiny offering of food on his plate. Mrs. Greene was worried he was losing his appetite again and kept insisting that he had to finish his dinner before he could go back to bed and finish his movie.

Mr. Greene asked me about my job and was excited when he found out that I cleaned his building. "Do you hear that, Jimmy?" he said. "Dwight cleans your father's office."

"Whoop-dee-doo," Jimmy said, and his mother scolded him for being rude.

"I never see the cleaners," Mr. Greene said. "I always wondered when it was cleaned."

"We usually get to your building around four in the morning."

"Really? That must be strange. Hanging around office buildings in the middle of the night."

"Kind of," I said. No one spoke, and I felt I was supposed to say more. "You start imagining the people who work there by the things on their desks. It's like living in a ghost world. There's evidence of life, but there's no one there. And it's always dark outside."

Mr. Greene chewed on as he took all of this in, but didn't say anything.

"Ghost world," Mrs. Greene repeated.

"BOOOO!" said Jimmy.

At which point Mr. Greene asked Jimmy to leave the table, and he got up and went. Mrs. Greene complained that this wasn't wise, because Jimmy hadn't eaten enough and Mr. Greene was teaching him that if he wanted to get his way all he need do was misbehave. Mr. Greene shrugged, and she sprang up and stomped off to the kitchen.

Mr. Greene looked at me and smiled. "So, you're going to save our Jimmy, are you?"

"I—I can't save anyone."

"Really? Well, it's always refreshing to hear some honesty. Especially from a religious man. But saving Jimmy's not why you visit us, is it? You have other reasons for visiting."

"Pardon?"

"The young stud," he said. "I can smell cunt all over you."

He smiled wider and asked me if I'd like more wine.

"No, thank you," I said. I stood and said I had to be going.

"Oh? Well, thanks for coming," he said. "I guess you know where the door is."

I walked to the living room and said goodbye to Jimmy, who didn't even hear me because he was watching the movie; touched his shoulder, but that didn't get his attention either, so I walked out the door.

I wandered over to Southside Park and sat under a tree, where I watched the creek flowing by. Lying on my back, gazing into the leaves fluttering in the breeze, I must have actually drifted off to sleep, and when I woke up, the light had fallen to grey. I wondered if the Greenes were fighting as I was sleeping there. Would he hit her? He didn't seem the type. He was having sex with the woman from the Chamber of Commerce, she'd said, and none of it mattered much to him. I can still see his crooked smile as he savoured the word "cunt." Such a hard word, not the least bit appropriate for what it signifies. It was all a big joke to him. All he cared about was being in control of the situation.

I prayed to God that Mr. Greene would not die that night.

The sun was just going down as I crossed the overpass. I stopped for a few minutes, watching the great orange ball sink into the new subdivision behind the mall. The sunset lit a full half of the sky in reds and pinks that slowly faded in the direction of yellow. I went on back to my basement and collapsed into bed, finally feeling exhausted enough to sleep.

SIX

On Thursday, I was lying in bed with Dostoevsky when I heard voices in the basement: Gloria and Mrs. Greene. I got up and took a step across the room, smashing my head on the beam so hard it crumpled me to my knees and I blacked out. When the knock came, I was crouching on the floor, rubbing at the lump that was already growing on my skull, the ring of my father's bullet back in my ears.

"I'll be right there," I said, pushing up to my feet and stumbling towards the door. As I turned the knob, I was still massaging my wounded head. Gloria stood between Mrs. Greene and me.

"Somebody here to see you," she said.

I squinted out at them.

"Jimmy's expecting you," Mrs. Greene said.

"Oh, yeah," I said. "I'll get my things." As if I were a country doctor going off to deliver a baby. I sat down and pulled on my running shoes.

"All right, I guess I'll . . ." Gloria said, pointing straight up as she began to retreat.

"Thank you, Gloria," Mrs. Greene said.

"Thanks, Gloria," I said.

She nodded and walked up the basement stairs directly into the house. I hoped Mrs. Greene wouldn't start talking the second the door closed, and she didn't. She stood there looking up at the ceiling, waiting for me to get ready. When my shoes were tied, I stood and led her out my private entrance.

Once we were in her car and pulling away from the house, she launched right in. "What happened to you on Sunday? Why did you leave that way?"

"Listen, Mrs. Greene, I don't think it's a good idea that I visit anymore."

"Gerry told me what he said. Don't worry about Gerry. I told him it was none of his business."

"But it is his business, Mrs. Greene. He's your husband. How can it not be his business?"

She started to cry, but kept driving, dabbing at her eyes with her right hand as she steered with her left. "You just don't understand, Dwight. You're so young. How can you possibly understand?"

"I do understand. And it's wrong, what we do. It can't help but be wrong. How can we do what we do and still go to church every Sunday? It's a joke, Mrs. Greene. The Lord must be blushing at us."

Her weeping was too much and she pulled the car over. As she cried, she glanced at me through her tears, and I knew she wanted me to comfort her. I wanted to touch her, but I wouldn't let myself. A woman was walking on the sidewalk on the far side of the street, making her way up the hill towards the hospital. She wasn't looking at us, but she might have already seen our predicament—the weeping adulteress, spurned, beside the insensitive young stud—and was perhaps looking the other way only out of embarrassment.

"What about Jimmy, then?" Mrs. Greene said when she got a handle on herself. I didn't answer. "Don't you care about Jimmy either?"

I looked over my shoulder and saw that the woman was just about out of sight. "I can't help Jimmy," I said. "What you and I do is only hurting Jimmy. We have to deny our desire, or God will turn away from Jimmy."

I opened the door and got out of the car and followed the woman up the hill. I did not glance back at Mrs. Greene's car until I got to the top of the hill, but when I did, the car was still sitting there, as if she were waiting for me to come back and get in and ride away with her.

I kept putting one foot in front of the other.

On Sunday morning I didn't go to church. Not an hour after the service was over, the knock came at the door. I was already sitting at the table, waiting for him. I had even made tea, and it was hot and steeped and ready.

"Come in," I said.

Irvine opened the door and peered in at me.

"Would you like tea?" I said.

He stepped up into the room and sat down across from me at the table. "Tea?" he said. "Tea would be fine."

I poured some into the cup I'd set there for him. He watched me pour, sitting back, sideways, leaning against the wall, his arm draped across the back of the chair. He sighed deeply. "Mrs. Greene says you've told her you won't see Jimmy any longer."

"That's right," I said.

He picked up his teacup and held it under his nose for a moment before he sipped. "He asks for you," he said.

I coughed. "Jimmy?"

"Yes. He's not doing well. He hasn't been out of bed in the last two days. He's very weak. Dr. Botha can't explain the sudden decline. They want to do some tests, but his mother wants to keep him home until he's feeling stronger. He keeps asking for you."

I nodded as coldly as I could manage. "He'll get over it," I said.

"The cancer?"

"Over me. My visits."

He nodded as though he understood, but said nothing.

"I think it's time I went back to the farm," I said. "Thanks for allowing me to stay here for so long."

"You don't need to leave," he said.

"I think it'd be best."

"The same way stopping your visits to Jimmy is best?"

He sipped again from his cup.

"I can't really explain it properly," I said. "I just know the Lord wouldn't be happy with what I was doing there. I was making things worse, even though they might have seemed better."

He set down his cup and turned and looked me in the eye to see that I was telling the truth. "I see," he said. "But Jimmy was getting better. How could that be worse?"

"I didn't have anything to do with making Jimmy better. If he was better, he was just better. And he obviously wasn't better if he's worse now. Was he? And I was making things worse for his parents. There are . . . divisions between them that my visits were only making . . . wider."

He nodded his most serious nod. "But couldn't you still visit Jimmy without making love to Mrs. Greene?"

It was a question I didn't know how to answer, so I could only stare at him, waiting for him to answer the question for me, and finally he did.

"I suppose Mrs. Greene would make that difficult."

I nodded, my heart beating too fast, my hands shaking. How had he known? Had she told him? How else could he possibly know? Did everyone know? Did even Gloria know? Was it written all over my face?

"It would be impossible," I said.

He considered this for a moment. "Anything's possible," he said.

I shook my head. "I don't think so."

He sighed and stared into his teacup. They were cups his mother had used when she lived in that room, and he was probably recognizing some stain he had seen down there at the bottom many times before.

"I understand," he said. "I respect that you don't want to go back into that house, considering what's happened, and I recognize that, while you do hold some responsibility, Mrs. Greene is ultimately much more responsible."

"No," I said.

"Of course," he said. "Though you're perfectly right not to let yourself off the hook. You do hold some responsibility. And so do I, for sending you into that house."

"How could you have known?"

"That's the way of the world," he said. "That we become responsible for things we are unwilling to foresee. But we are still responsible, and we must recognize that responsibility and forgive ourselves, and thus allow Christ to forgive us."

"I didn't have to make love to her," I said. "She didn't force me."

"I understand," he said. "It's all very sordid, and I'm sorry it's happened to Jimmy and to all of us. And I realize how difficult it would be for you to go back there. But you don't need to think about leaving. We're happy to have you here. And you don't need to stop going to church. You need the Lord more than ever. And He aches for you to come to Him."

"I liked it," I said. "I liked making love to Mrs. Greene."

He nodded slowly, but avoided looking at me. "Making love is very pleasurable," he said.

"If I went back there, I'd do it again."

"I understand," he said. "You can't go back. It's very unfortunate." He leaned against the wall again and drummed his fingers on the table, gazing off into space. "Unless someone went with you." His fingers stopped drumming.

"Pardon? No. I wouldn't want you to be involved."

"Not me," he said. "She'd see immediately that I knew, and that wouldn't do. She's suffering so much, and we must allow her her dignity. I was thinking that maybe Gloria could go with you. She'd perhaps see Gloria's presence differently and allow both of you to visit for Jimmy's sake. She'd know that you wouldn't have told Gloria."

"Gloria?"

"Yes. Gloria went to church with me today. Mrs. Greene told us that Jimmy was not doing well, and on the way home Gloria asked me where you were today and why you'd stopped visiting Jimmy."

"She did?"

"Absolutely. She's very worried about Jimmy. Perhaps because of her own circumstances. You see, Gloria is pregnant. That's why she's decided to get married so suddenly. You may have already guessed. It's given her a different perspective on this kind of thing. On Mrs. Greene and Jimmy. She's about to become a mother herself. I'm sure she'd be willing to go with you if you thought that would allow you to go."

I poured more tea into my cup, slopped some on the table and wiped it up with a tissue I found in my pocket.

"I'm not . . . I guess we could try that, if Gloria . . ."

"Wonderful," Irvine said, already standing. "I'll speak to her. You could probably go this afternoon. I don't think Gloria's doing anything. I always wondered why you didn't go to Mrs. Greene's on Sunday anyway."

"Mr. Greene's home on Sunday," I said.

"Oh, yes, of course. Well, maybe that would be best. If you and Gloria were to go when both Mr. and Mrs. Greene were home, that might be best. I'll speak to her right away."

And he walked out, closing the door behind him.

I took a shower, washed my hair and stood staring at myself in the mirror, studying my pimples and other imperfections. I shaved my face and cut myself three times.

Twice I was about to go out for a walk but decided against it because I worried Gloria might come looking for me while I was gone. I stayed in my room, reading Dostoevsky, waiting for her, listening to the sounds of the house above me.

I heard Caroline upstairs with Gloria this very evening. I'm sure it was Caroline and even more sure it was Gloria. I recognized the fall of her footsteps from a decade ago when I was living in her basement.

Her nanny had gone to the bathroom, and I was slouching there at the table with the red Arborite they have for her down there, listening to the water running in the bathroom and the house settling around me, and I heard Caroline's footsteps and her mother's.

I was wearing my sweatpants, long johns and the same cotton T-shirt I always use for yoga. It's cold enough that I need the long johns. I'm still wearing them as I write this.

The nanny asked me to her place for a drink, and I couldn't say no. Her whiskey glass was waiting for her on the other side of the table while she went to the bathroom.

I was in Caroline's basement.

Her nanny came out of the bathroom, gave me a long inspection and took her seat across the table from me. "What's wrong?" she said.

"Nothing," I said. "There's nothing wrong."

"You look like a ghost just bit your balls."

She's very beautiful, the nanny, with those flecks of gold in her brown eyes, but she often has a reckless way with words.

"I was thinking about my mother," I said. "I was sitting here listening to all the noises in the house, and for some reason I started thinking about my mother."

It was the only way to tell her the truth without telling her.

"Your mother?" she said. "Tell me about your mother."

But I couldn't tell her, because there was too much to say, and so I said, "I can hear Caroline up there."

"Yeah. She should be in bed by now. I hope her mom doesn't come down here and ask me to put her to bed. It's supposed to be my night off, but she'll do that, and try to make me feel guilty. 'Are you busy with something? I have to finish a report for work tomorrow. I'd appreciate your help, if you're not busy with anything.' She probably wants to get a look at you. She's probably got a cup pressed to the floor and is listening to us right now."

"You think?" I whispered.

"Oh, she hates it when I have men over. If you said that to her, she'd deny it to the moon, but she'll go out of her way to fuck up any kind of relationship I get into. I'm her best friend, and she doesn't want to share me with anyone. Even other women. I don't know. She's pretty lonely. She's mostly good to me. I shouldn't complain. I'm such an ungrateful little dirtbag."

"You think she might come down?"

"Don't worry about it. I have a right to have you here. She doesn't own me."

I said I had to go, even though I hadn't finished my beer.

"You haven't even finished your beer," she said.

"I'm sorry," I said. "It's really good beer. I just remembered something I forgot to do. I really need to go."

She walked me out the door at the side of the house and stood and waved as I walked away.

After Dad lost his driver's licence, he lost control of Mom. If he needed to go anywhere, she had to take him or, once I had my licence, I had to take him. Unless he tried driving himself and risked getting thrown in jail. That was the end of his business trips. There wasn't much for him to do but drink and make guns on his lathes and have shouting matches with Mom or me. She'd taken to working for a couple of charities in Broken Head because, so she said, his attempt to murder so many neighbour children had made us all pariahs in the eyes of the world and she needed to do something to try to redeem our name.

He turned the farming over to me. After the bus had delivered me home, I'd change my clothes and head out to summerfallow. Aiming down the line of the furrow, perched on the rusty metal seat of our '53 LA Case tractor, I practised for the choir—belting out the tenor part for Bach's "Jesu, Joy of Man's Desiring," singing at the top of my lungs but only hearing my voice inside my head because of the noise of the tractor and the earmuffs I wore to stop me from going deaf. When I looked across the field, I sometimes saw Mom jogging down the grid road, the border collie she'd adopted from the SPCA running along beside her. She'd named him Prince, because she said she'd always wanted a prince to sniff her crotch.

The vibrations of the tractor made me imagine Gloria. It really was beyond hormonal, towards mechanical, the way the constant vibration would set off arousal, which would set off images of her in my head. There she was, before me, spread out on the front of his tractor, completely naked. We're too much like machines, and it's the devil who operates us.

Afterwards, I was always left in a depression of terrible shame, vowing never to indulge in such disgusting behaviour again. But the next day, or even the next hour, she might appear to me again. I knew she wasn't really Gloria. I'd been reading the Bible she gave me, which I still kept hidden in my sock drawer, and I knew the devil was at work in this world. I knew who it was I was consorting with, but I continued to consort, hoping that God wouldn't see. But He did see. As punishment for my sins, He made my skin boil and fester and stick to my shirt.

One evening, as the sun was setting, I got into the truck to drive home from the field, and Gloria was there, in the passenger seat, wearing a diaphanous white negligee, her foot up on the dashboard. She was painting her toenails.

"It's a little frightening to consider that accident and not design is the most important force shaping history, isn't it?" she asked, and then, "Do you like them red?"

I took a deep breath, trying hard to keep my eyes off her. I knew it wasn't really Gloria, but I couldn't stop myself from wanting her there.

"I don't know what you're talking about," I said.

"Sure you do. It's all an accident. The entire universe. It's all random. People die by accident. Like your father. There's no design."

"My father's not dead."

"Not yet. And there's no such thing as true love and soul partners and happily ever after and all that bullshit. It's all flesh and longing. Flesh and longing. A man fucks a girl and the girl gets pregnant and so they get married and have a little baby that nobody wants. Where's the love in that?"

I needed to tell her that I didn't believe she was there, but I honestly didn't want to be rid of her. "I don't believe in you," I said.

"Of course not. You don't believe in anything. Lapsed Mennonites are always interesting. Lapsed fanatics of any kind."

"I'm Russian, not Mennonite. I've never been a Mennonite."

"Is that so?"

"And it's my dad who doesn't believe in anything. I do believe in things. I believe in God and truth and beauty. And I'm not a pacifist. I believe in fighting back."

"Oh, really? How quaint. I understood you didn't believe in anything. I understood that nobody believed in anything anymore."

I started the truck and put it into gear. "I'm imagining you. You're not real."

She dabbed a spot of red on the tiny nail of her baby toe, smiling at me even though she was not looking at me. "Then why are you talking to me?" she said.

I ignored her for the mile home, staring into the blush of light as the sun sank deeper below the horizon, but when I turned in the driveway, she was still sitting there beside me, still working on her toenails.

"You're nothing like Gloria Irvine," I told her.

"Thank you," she said. "Prissy little virgin. Afraid of her own body." She yanked up her negligee and peered at her breasts. "Not much of a body, either."

I almost drove off the road.

"But you're afraid of your body too, aren't you, Dwight Froese?"

I ordered myself not to answer. I didn't look at her. I parked in front of the garage and tried to open the door and get out, but she actually reached out and took hold of my arm. I could feel her cool fingers on my wrist.

"I'm not afraid of my body," I said.

"Then why don't you touch me?" she asked.

I turned and looked at her. The negligee was still pulled up over her breasts. I could see the hair between her legs. I raised my hand and reached towards her.

Of course, there was no one there.

The knock that roused me was so soft you'd have thought the person was afraid of hurting the door. At first I imagined it was my mother, wondering if I was awake, and I knew that if it was her she'd come in even if I didn't answer, and so I waited for her to sit on the side of my bed, kiss me on the forehead, rub my shoulders and tell me it was time to get up. Then I realized I was in Dr. Irvine's basement and that my mother was dead. I listened for a moment, trying to distinguish any noise that might reveal who was on the other side of the door. Now that the knock had finally come, I couldn't really believe that it might actually be her. I said I was coming and waited another moment for a response, but there wasn't a sound to give me a clue, so I staggered groggily to my feet, crossed the room, ducking under the beam, and turned the knob.

It was Gloria.

"Hello," she said. "Dad said you were looking for someone to visit Jimmy with you, and I'd be so pleased to do that. When did you want to go?"

"Any time," I said.

She nodded and said, "Well, what about now? Or are you busy right now?"

"No, now is good. Would you like to come in?"

"That's all right," she said. "I'll wait out by the pool until you're ready to go." She smiled and turned and walked away, leaving the basement by my private entrance. Worrying what it was that made her think I wasn't ready to go, I brushed my teeth and combed my hair again. I sat around for five minutes, staring at the walls, because I didn't want it to seem I was ready too soon. I wondered if that's what the bridesmaids were thinking when they didn't buy enough oil.

Gloria sat on one of the patio chairs by the pool, reading a drugstore bestseller.

"Is that good?" I said.

"Kills time," she said.

"Oh? Sorry I kept you waiting."

"No. I just sat down. You were quick. Amazingly quick. Just like lightning." I nodded, embarrassed for us both, knowing I was nothing like lightning. "Dad said we could use his car." She dangled the keys before me.

"Sure. We can do that. I usually walk. It's not a bad walk."

"Walk? Would you rather walk?"

"It's up to you. We don't have to."

"That's a great idea. I'd love to walk."

"We don't have to. We could take the car."

"No. Walking is fabulous. I really would prefer to walk." To demonstrate how willing she was, she took a step. "I'll just take Dad back his keys," she said over her shoulder, disappearing into the house. Thirty seconds later she was back, and we set off. "I don't do enough walking. I don't even have a car—Nick's always driving me everywhere. In Montreal we did a lot more walking. Around the neighbourhood where we live."

"You and Nick?"

"Yeah. But Nick and I didn't live together," she said, and I blushed and shook my head to show that I hadn't suspected it was so. "We lived in the same neighbourhood. I had an apartment with another woman. From Winnipeg. She's in med school. She's studying genetics. Nick and I will get a place together in the fall."

I tried to imagine her former apartment in Montreal and saw a sunny room filled with frilly things, Nick slouching on the couch, waiting for her to emerge from the bedroom.

"You like Montreal?"

"Yeah. There's a lot to do there," she said.

"Must be."

"There is," she said, and she spent the next five minutes telling me all the things there were to do in Montreal.

When she paused for a breath, I said, "I meant to congratulate you on the baby," even though there'd been no adequate transition from the things to do in Montreal.

She did not look at me. "Thank you," she said.

As soon as I'd said it, I wished I hadn't, but I'd felt so uncomfortable not saying anything. To change the subject, she mentioned the weather and the beautiful flowers in one woman's garden: old Mrs. Grange. She remembered her giving many treats at Halloween. I tried to think of things to say, but I really didn't have to say much, because Gloria kept up a steady stream of chatter.

As we reached the overpass, she said, "You know what's crazy? I've lived here my entire life, but I've never walked across the overpass before."

"Really? It's a great view from the top."

"Fantastic!" she said. "I can't wait. I remember Mrs. Greene telling us about Jimmy running off to see it after you told him about it."

As we got close to the apex, we were both looking down, and for the first time Gloria seemed to have nothing to say. A plump man in greasy overalls trudged beside a graffiti-covered freight train, the dozens of horizontal lines of rusty rails running off towards the horizon, and I wondered what it was that had impressed me so much. I could tell from her expression that Gloria was wondering too.

"A long way down," she said as we began our descent.

We were a couple of blocks from the Greenes' when it occurred to me to worry about how Mrs. Greene would react to the sight of me standing at her door with Gloria by my side, and how Jimmy might behave. You could never tell with Jimmy. And what would Mr. Greene do if he was home? I figured they'd both behave themselves with Gloria there, but I wondered what she'd read into the silences. Until that moment, I'd been so overwhelmed by the idea of doing anything with

Gloria and without Nick that I hadn't considered the consequences of showing up at the door unannounced.

"Maybe we should have phoned first," I said, interrupting something Gloria was saying. She actually stopped walking. We were standing there in the full blaze of the sun, as there wasn't much shade on the south side, it being the newer side of town, where, if there were trees on the lawns at all, they were only the size of shrubs. For the first time, I saw a hint of her mother in her eyes: I guess she wasn't used to being interrupted. But in the next moment she must have found an excuse for my rudeness, because she smiled.

"Dad called. They know we're coming."

I nodded. "Oh. That's good. Sorry for interrupting."

She nodded and we started walking again, neither of us saying anything for a quarter of a block.

"I really want to thank you for coming with me," I said when I couldn't stand the silence any longer.

"No, that's silly. I should be thanking you. I'm happy to do whatever I can. It's just so unfair that a little boy . . ."

"Yeah. I know. It doesn't seem fair."

"That's one of the big reasons I have trouble with God. If there's a God, then how can life be so unfair?"

She looked at me as though she expected me to have the answer, and that made me feel like I had to give one. It wouldn't surprise me if more than one religion got started that way.

"I don't know. Maybe God's where we get our idea of what fair would be if things were fair."

For some reason, she licked her lips. Maybe they were dry. "You should write that down. I wish I had a pen. Do you ever write things down?"

I could feel myself blushing. "I've been thinking of writing something about my mom and dad. My dad actually claimed to have met God."

She was looking at me, her eyes wide, the pinprick of her pupils drowning in the blue of her irises. There was a kind of uneasiness in her look that made me wish I hadn't mentioned my father. "I'm glad to hear you talking about your father," she finally said.

"Maybe I shouldn't write any of it down, though."

"You should. Why not?"

"I wouldn't want to destroy the magic and mystery."

She looked puzzled for a second before she gave a nervous laugh. "Oh, Grant Robinson. He's such a pretentious pig. I'm sorry about all that."

"No, no. No reason for you to be sorry."

"I'm glad you came," she said. "It was good to have you there."

"Really?"

"It was," she insisted.

I couldn't think what else to say, and she seemed to be having the same problem. "Don't they live right up here?" she finally asked.

We went on without saying another word until we were at the door. Gloria pushed the tiny glowing orange button that rang the bell. Mrs. Greene opened the door and looked at both of us in a way that made even Gloria hesitate to offer a greeting. She managed a timid hello.

"Gloria," Mrs. Greene said, after a long silence. "What are you doing here? Very nice to see you."

"Nice to see you too, Mrs. Greene. Dwight asked me if I'd come along with him to visit Jimmy. Didn't Dad tell you I was coming?"

"Did he? Oh, what a nice idea," Mrs. Greene said. "Jimmy hasn't been feeling well at all today, and he's been sleeping for the last couple of hours. I hate to wake him up, but he'll be so glad that Dwight and you are here. He'd hate me if I sent you away." We stood staring at her staring back at us. No one said anything for a very long time. "Come on in," she finally said.

"Are you sure?" I said. "He probably needs his rest."

"Perfectly certain," she said. "Jimmy wouldn't have it any other way."

She turned and walked into the living room, leaving the door wide open, and leaving us with no alternative but to follow her. I looked at Gloria and took the first step into the house.

"Oh my God!" Mrs. Greene screamed.

She was standing in the doorway to the living room, her hands covering her mouth. I have this strange recollection of having seen the full image of what she was seeing before I rushed into the room. Jimmy lay in his bed, his eyes wide open and staring up at the ceiling, his face contorted as if he'd been gasping for air. By comparison, my mother had looked very peaceful. Even my father had looked more peaceful, despite the blood and gore. There had been a look of resolution in my father's eyes, as though he had watched the bullet approaching and accepted its entry into his skull, through his brain and out the other side. Welcome and come again, his eyes had told the world.

Gloria was pale, terrified by Jimmy's expression, afraid the horseman was still there in the room, looking around for other victims. I stepped forward and laid my ear on Jimmy's chest. There was nothing, but he was still warm. I grabbed his wrists and started pressing them hard on his chest, trying to remember how to do CPR.

"Call 911," I told Mrs. Greene, but she only gazed at me dully, shaking her head to rattle loose something inside, and she didn't respond.

"I'll call my father," Gloria said, struggling to control her weeping as she walked towards the phone. I kept working on Jimmy. With his eyes open, his face looked so frightening. When I glanced over my shoulder, I saw that Mrs. Greene was standing there watching while Gloria dialled and waited; both of them were watching, waiting for Jimmy to giggle and sit up in bed and stick out his tongue and laugh at all our silliness.

Jimmy did not sit up. I kept pushing at his chest, but I knew he was already gone.

Gloria couldn't get her father and dialled 911. "An ambulance will be here soon," she said when she'd finished speaking to the operator.

"An ambulance," Mrs. Greene said, nodding.

I stopped what I was doing, closed Jimmy's eyes and pulled the blanket up over his face.

"Where's Mr. Greene?" I asked.

She only shook her head.

"We'll stay with you as long as you want," I said.

"That would be nice. I'll make some tea," she said, and went immediately to the kitchen.

Gloria stared at me, her mouth half-open as if she was about to speak but couldn't think what to say. I walked over to her and touched her shoulder, and she threw her arms around me, weeping into my shoulder. I held her until Mrs. Greene came back and saw us standing there, embracing in her living room beside her dead son.

"The tea will be ready in a minute," she said. "Why don't we have it in the kitchen?"

"We'll be right there," I said. Gloria had already released me, embarrassed. Mrs. Greene turned and went away.

"I'm sorry," Gloria said, and I told her she had nothing to apologize for. We heard the kettle whistling, and I led her to the kitchen.

Mrs. Greene motioned us to the table. She brought the pot of tea and we silently waited for it to steep.

"Beautiful day," Mrs. Greene said, gazing blankly out the window. "Why did he have to die on such a beautiful day?" Gloria gulped some air and started crying again. Mrs. Greene poured the tea. I wished she'd cry too. "Not that it would have helped if he'd died on some dismal day. It wouldn't have made any difference, would it? Except that it wouldn't be today."

"God chose today," I said.

She looked me squarely in the eye, and it was the most focused look she'd ever given me. "He did. Jimmy so enjoyed Dwight's visits," Mrs. Greene told Gloria, and Gloria nodded.

Somewhere in the house a clock chimed twice.

"You should call Mr. Greene," I said.

She considered my statement, looking from the table to me to the table to Gloria. "He's gone fishing. But I could call his motel."

"You should call him," I said.

"But he hates it when I do."

"He'd want you to call him. Call him," I said.

She went to the other room to make the phone call while Gloria and I drank our tea. When she came back and sat down, she put her hand on Gloria's, and Gloria clasped her hand with her own and started crying.

"I couldn't get him. But I left a message for him at the desk."

Gloria and I both nodded.

"Is there someone who can come and be with you?" Gloria asked.

Mrs. Greene smiled joyously. "He's already here. Jimmy so enjoyed Dwight's visits, and Dwight is here." Tears began running down her face. Gloria smiled weakly at her and reached out to squeeze her hand. "Dwight was so good to both of us. Did he tell you about his visits?"

"Mrs. Greene," I said.

Gloria turned to look at me. I sat there gawking at them both, and finally Gloria turned to Mrs. Greene and said, "You told us every week at church. They meant so much to Jimmy."

"They did. And to me, too. But Dwight stopped visiting, and now Jimmy's gone and it's all my fault. It's all because of me."

I pushed back my chair to stand. Gloria and Mrs. Green sat looking up at me through tear-filled eyes.

"That's not true," Gloria said. "Tell her it's not true, Dwight."

"Yes, it is true," Mrs. Greene answered when I couldn't make my tongue work. "I know it was wrong, Dwight. I just want you to know that I know it was wrong. I know you were right that I made God turn away from Jimmy."

"It wasn't your fault," I said. "It was cancer. You can't blame yourself for Jimmy's cancer."

"It was my fault. I needed you too much. I needed you more

than God would allow. I think Gloria understands. I can see that she needs you too."

Under any other circumstances, Gloria could have and would have interpreted this "need" Mrs. Greene was describing as being of a spiritual nature, but the combination of her grief and maybe our grief and the way Mrs. Greene said the word made it impossible for either of us to pretend we didn't know exactly what she was saying. Or maybe it was the expression on my face that made Gloria's go a shade of pale I'd never seen before.

"It was my fault," Mrs. Greene said. "It was all my fault."

"No, Mrs. Greene," I said, even though it was obvious that nothing I said was going to make much difference. She reached over and placed her hand on Gloria's hand again, and it was as though she shocked Gloria with a jolt of electricity that made her rise immediately to her feet.

"I think I'd better go and get my father," Gloria said. "I'm so sorry for your loss, Mrs. Greene." She didn't look at me as she bolted from the room.

I caught up to her as she opened the front door. "Gloria," I said, and she stopped to hear what I'd say. I didn't know what to say.

"I'd better go," she said.

"I'll come with you," I said.

"No. You need to stay with her until the ambulance comes."

She stood there shaking her head, pale and gasping for breath like she'd just run a few miles to get away from me.

"Of course. You're right. Someone needs to stay with her," I said and she fled, shutting the door in my face.

I didn't know what to do, so I went into the living room and sat down next to Jimmy on the straight-backed chair that had been placed beside the bed for visitors. Jimmy was dead, and I sat there grieving my loss of Gloria, who had never been mine. I prayed and asked the Lord for forgiveness for what I'd said three days before in Mrs. Greene's car. I tried to convince myself that I'd cared about

Jimmy and that God had not taken him because I had not cared enough; asked Him to shelter Jimmy in His arms; pulled down the blanket and looked at his contorted face. I wondered where he was and what he was doing there. A few minutes later Mrs. Greene came in and sat down on the sofa. For a while I was able to hope that she might not speak. Until she did.

"She's so young and beautiful," she said. "Her breasts must be very firm." I thought it best not to answer. "I'm sorry. I hope I haven't ruined things for you. With her. I hope not. I didn't mean to ruin things, like I did with Jimmy."

"You haven't ruined anything," I said. "Gloria is getting married to Nick Campion in a month."

"Yes," she said, "but she's in love with you. Jimmy was in love with you too. And I drove you away from Jimmy, and now I've driven Gloria away from you. I'm so sorry. I'm so, so sorry."

She went on weeping softly. I saw the squirrel sprint along the branch outside the window and disappear.

"It isn't your fault that Jimmy died," I said. "Jimmy had cancer."

"You tried to warn me. I turned God away from him."

"No. It doesn't mean anything that Jimmy died, except that he was sick. God's not punishing anybody for anything. Jimmy was sick. I wasn't making him better. He just felt better for a while. That happens. God wasn't making him better, and God didn't take him away." She kept shaking her head at me. I could see that she wasn't believing me and I would have to go further. "If you want to know the truth, there is no God. None of it means anything. Jimmy had cancer and he died of the cancer. Maybe it's some pesticide company's fault, but it's not your fault. It's a terrible thing. Do you hear me? There is no God. It's just a terrible, terrible thing that happened to Jimmy and to you and to your family."

She actually stopped crying. She sat there staring at me with great wonder, and I could see that she believed me, just like she used to believe me when we were making love. We didn't speak again until

166

the ambulance arrived. I opened the door to two young paramedics and they rushed around frantically, thumping Jimmy's chest while asking Mrs. Greene a series of questions, which she answered slowly and deliberately. While all of this was happening, Mr. Greene rushed in the door (wearing his business suit, so that for a moment I wondered where his hip waders were) and asked what was going on.

"Jimmy's dead," I said.

The paramedics went on trying to shock him back to life.

One weekend, when Mom was in town canvassing for one of her charities, not long before I threatened to kill Marty Sunaski, Dad caught me reading my Bible in my bedroom.

"This figures. This figures entirely. There's cattle having calves out there that need checking, and you're hiding in here, reading crap and corruption." He yanked the book from my hands and tore open the binding so that he was holding half of the book in each hand. Then he tossed both halves in the corner. "Where did you find it? Where did you find such a nasty piece of shit to be reading? Don't you care about your eyes? Come with me if you're so interested, and I'll show you what it's like to be crucified."

He grabbed me by the arm and dragged me out of the room and out to the shop, where he found a hammer and a rusty four-inch spike and prepared to drive the spike through my hand. But when I placed my hand on a creosote blackened old railway tie and waited for him to do it, he dropped the hammer and walked silently away.

Not long after that, I was summerfallowing one day and an RCMP car stopped at the edge of the grid road. Two officers got out, climbed through the fence and started walking across the field towards me. I pulled the clutch lever, throttled down, jumped to the ground and began walking towards them. We met at no spot in particular. Just a place where there was a large, round, white fieldstone that should have been picked. The frost pushed them up. I rolled it over with my toe and the officers noted my action as though the stone might reveal some important clue, but there was only dirt and a large beetle underneath.

"Dwight Froese?" one of the officers asked, staring into my eyes.

I looked down at the beetle scurrying for new cover and nodded, but didn't speak.

"We have a report that you uttered a death threat against Marty Sunaski." The officer looked grim, as if he hoped it wasn't true and I'd tell him so and we could all go back to what we'd been doing and forget the whole thing. "We'd like to hear your side of the story," the officer continued.

I didn't answer. I didn't want to lie, but I couldn't help feeling it would be rude to tell them the truth.

"We'd like you to come with us so that we can ask you a few questions," the other officer said.

"I'll have to shut off the tractor," I finally said.

They escorted me back to the tractor, and I twisted the cock that turned off the gasoline and then allowed them to escort me back to their car. When we got to the fence, the tractor started sputtering, and by the time they'd opened the door to the back seat for me, the engine had finally starved.

They drove me into town and to the city detachment station and took me into a funny little office with acoustic panels and a desk with only a telephone on it. They asked me many questions. Sometimes the same question in many different ways. My response was always the same: I wouldn't say a word. They explained to me that what I'd done was very serious and that I was going to be charged with uttering threats, and the best thing I could do for myself was to cooperate, but I didn't see their logic. To me, the most sensible response was to make no more utterances. Perhaps they would even see the irony if I let them work it over without my help. I knew that Marty Sunaski boarded with a cop, and I guessed they went to all of the games and sometimes drank beer with him in their colleague's basement, discussing the win or loss and the blood on the ice. Their young friend was a hockey player and had made similar threats a thousand times without ever being questioned by them. Hadn't he been threatening to beat me and humiliate me? Of course, he hadn't uttered the threat, only implied it in the wiggling of those blunt fingers with the scarred knuckles. It was the power of words that interested them at the moment, not scars and wiggling flesh. It didn't matter if words were only breath, and fists were skin and bone and muscle and ligament and blood. It was the breath that made the fists flesh.

I thought these things but didn't say them.

They uttered their threats to me. I was afraid.

"Dwight! Are you listening to us, Dwight? Because I don't appreciate not being listened to. Some cooperation here might do you a lot of good, you know?"

One of the officers needed to use mouthwash. I didn't tell him. He didn't want to know the truth.

They finally became frustrated that they couldn't make me speak, and they left me alone, hoping some time on my own might change my mind and make me want to talk. But when they left, Gloria joined me. There she was, sitting backwards in the chair across the desk—facing me, the back of the chair towards me, the same way one of the officers had been sitting during the questioning. I was glad to see her. She wore her white negligee, her legs straddling the chair. Her chin rested on her arms, which rested on the back on the chair.

"Somebody oughta use that guy's penis to test electrical outlets," she said. I wasn't sure if she was talking about Marty Sunaski or the officer with bad breath, who had paced around the room instead of sitting on his chair. I didn't ask her to elaborate.

"I prefer a policy of passive resistance," I said.

"Mennonite."

"Up yours."

"Ooooooh. I love it when you talk dirty."

I realized they were watching through the improbable mirror above the desk and recording my words, but I wanted to talk to Gloria and so I did.

"I thought you said you believed in fighting back," she said.

"You were right. I don't believe in anything."

"No. I see now you were right. You're a fraud. You're just a stupid romantic like that guy in the book you're reading. Pechorin. You really believe in love, don't you? But she's with that Nick guy. Slight problem, Nick. He's probably fucking her right now. If she fucks. If she's not too scared of being too much like the animals. I must admit, it was a grand gesture. Even a cold little fish like Gloria would have to be impressed that you'd kill somebody for her. Might even warm her up a little."

"I don't believe in anything. I don't even believe in love."

She shrugged. "Is that so?"

I thought about it a little longer and changed my mind, because it seemed to me that I ought to get it right. "I guess I do believe in chaos. I invented you, didn't I?" She didn't answer. "You can't say anything new to me."

"Tell them to call my father."

"What?"

"Tell them to call Dr. Andrew Irvine."

I looked her in the eye and wondered where those eyes led. "Your father? I know who you are. I know you're not really Gloria Irvine."

"Oh, so you do believe in me after all. How quaint and nineteenth century of you. Don't say anything except that they should call Dr. Andrew Irvine. He's Gloria's father, and you were only defending Gloria. That's your way of wiggling your fingers. He's an influential figure in Broken Head, and they're afraid of him. They don't want their hockey star in any trouble. You have that, and you need to use it. That's the fear you see in their eyes. Use it."

She leaned towards me and tried to kiss me, and I turned away to avoid her lips. When I turned back, she was gone.

A few minutes later the two officers came back into the room. They asked me four or five more questions about my relationship with my father. Finally, I tested the sentence on my tongue: "Call Dr. Andrew Irvine."

They looked at each other. "What's that? Did you speak, Dwight? So you do know how to talk? I was asking you whether your father ever hit you or threatened to kill you the way you threatened Marty Sunaski."

"Call Dr. Irvine," I said again.

The roving officer with bad breath pulled his chair over beside the other and sat down for the first time. "Why? What does Dr. Irvine have to do with this?" He shrugged. "Tell us, Dwight. We're listening."

But I said nothing else, and twenty minutes later they gave up again and left, and an hour after that they came back and told me to come with them. They escorted me back to the police car and drove me home.

When we pulled into the driveway, the light was on in the kitchen and Mom stood in the window like a worried woman in a picture. The officer who had sat backwards in the interrogation room opened the car door to let me out.

"We're continuing the investigation," he said. "We'll be talking to you soon. In the meantime, stay clear of Marty Sunaski."

"No problem," I said.

Mom was waiting for me at the door, her arms crossed, leaning on her leg the way she leaned on her leg.

"How was the concert?" I asked her. "Spring Magic?"

"Just glorious. Tenor section was a bit weak, though." I was supposed to be moving my lips that night, but I didn't feel like it after telling Marty Sunaski I was going to kill him and so I'd refused to go with Mom, who had a ticket, of course. I told her I had to summerfallow. "Did you get much work done?" she asked.

"I was doing okay until the cops came to take me for a ride."

"And what did they want, Eisenhower?"

"I don't know. They asked me a lot of questions about Dad and the guns he sells to Chandler."

I brushed past her and walked through the living room. The television was on, tuned to some stupid horror movie (there were only two channels), and I stopped to watch one of the characters scream as a monster attacked.

"I'd like to know what goes on inside your head," she said.

"Your movie's more entertaining."

"What kind of trouble are you in, Dwight?"

She only called me Dwight when she was really upset.

"I don't know what you mean. I live in this house. Is that trouble?"

Her face fell, and I could see I'd hit a sore spot. "We've gotta talk, Dwight. What have I done wrong? What can I do different?"

"Different*ly*?" I pretended to think, scratching my head. "You could have kept your legs crossed. But that would have been too difficult, wouldn't it? You just had to feel that metal hand on you. Was that it? Was that what turned you on?"

She slapped my cheek. I could feel the imprint of her hand burning there, and I'd never felt anything better in my entire life. I turned away and walked to the bathroom. Having sat so long in their little office with the acoustic tiles, I needed to relieve myself.

"I'm your mother, and I will not be talked to that way!" she shouted through the door. Any second my father would be up from his lair, and we'd all be into something serious and grim. "You come out of there right now and apologize!"

"I'm taking a piss. Can you give me some privacy?"

I sat on the toilet, head resting on my fist like *The Thinker* on his rock. I'd always sat down to pee because she complained so much about the mess my father made of the seat.

"I've put up with enough of that kind of talk from your father for an entire lifetime, and I'm not going to put up with it from you. You're turning out exactly like him, you know?"

I stood and zipped myself and flushed the toilet and rinsed my face, staring into my empty eyes in the mirror. I could see that what she said was true: the line of my eyebrows and my mouth were his. No doubt, I was the son of Jacob Froese. Some of us are not fortunate enough to be ignorant of our paternity.

"What about your father? Am I just like him, too?"

"Shut up, Dwight."

"Why don't you tell me what he did to you? I'd like to know. I'd like to know what twisted you so far."

"I think you know. You aren't so different from him. I think you know."

I pushed the door open fast and it hit something solid and she cried out. She staggered back, clutching her nose, and when she took her hand away, she saw the blood there and I saw it trickle down over her upper lip. She stared at me accusingly, but neither of us spoke.

"It was an accident," I said.

Still she didn't respond, except to walk to the sink and turn on the tap and wash the blood from her hands.

"I'm sorry," I said.

Instead of forgiving me, she rubbed some soap onto her hands.

"The police say they're going to charge me with uttering death threats," I said.

She turned to look at me, pinching her nostrils to staunch the bleeding. "Did you tell somebody you were gonna kill me?"

A drop of blood formed at the end of her nose, and I wanted to wipe it away but didn't dare take a step towards her.

"Of course not. I love you."

"Oh? Well, who then? Your father?"

"A hockey player. Marty Sunaski. From the Rhinos."

She stood there, holding her nose, looking at me. "I've heard of him. He's supposed to be good, isn't he? One of their best players. Why do you want to kill him?"

I shrugged, watching her blood as though it were a drop of water ballooning on the end of a faucet, waiting for it to fall.

"I question his goodness."

Mom flinched. Still holding her nose with her right hand, she touched it with her left hand and peered at her fingertips. "This is pretty serious trouble you're in, then, isn't it?"

"I didn't really mean that I was actually going to kill him."

"Of course not," she said. "You just want an accident to happen to him, don't you, Beelzebub? A happy little accident." I looked at the floor. "Go to bed," she said. "Bus comes early."

She had turned back to the sink. I nodded and did as I was told.

We did the moon salutations tonight, from mountain to half-moon and eventually around to triangle. I can never remember it all without the instructor to tell us what's next. At the end, we lay there in corpse pose, our palms cupped at our sides as my mother's were when I found her, and the instructor told us she hoped we might lose track of where our bodies ended and the rest of the universe began. But I thought about things I wasn't supposed to be thinking about. I always do. There's no hope that I'll ever empty out my head. There's too much in here, crammed up in spaces where I once stashed it for the time being and never got around to putting it properly away.

After class, the nanny asked me to come back to her place for a drink, and I said I didn't think I could, and so she wondered if I wanted to go for a coffee on Queen Street where we usually went, and I thought that would be okay.

"You're not much good with the balancing poses," she told me.

I sipped my herbal tea and agreed. "Standing on one foot is a problem for me."

"You need to find a spot on the wall or the floor and focus on that and forget about falling over."

"I know," I said, "but I can never find the right spot."

"There is no right spot. Any spot. The spot doesn't matter. It's the focus that's your problem."

"You're right. I was thinking that in the relaxation. I can't quite focus."

"You're not supposed to be thinking in relaxation."

Nothing to do but nod.

"Why did you leave the other night?" she asked.

"I can't remember. What's Caroline's father like?"

She gave me a suspicious look and shrugged. "Who knows? I have no idea. He seems nice enough. I don't know him very well. He's always at the office or away on business. Why do you care?" She leaned in a little closer.

"I don't. Just wondered. Her mother sounds sad. From what you said."

"Sad? Angry, I think. She's mostly angry."

"Afraid," I said.

"Yeah, that's true. Afraid. I think maybe he's got some other secret family somewhere. That's what she's afraid of. Not that they ever fight. She does all her fighting with me. I worked my ass off cleaning today, and she walks in the door from work and wonders why supper's not on the table. Starts yelling at me that she can't trust me because I'm such a lazy little bitch. The whole house is gleaming, but she doesn't even notice. I'm lazy. All she cares about is that I'm a few minutes late with supper."

"That's . . . that's terrible. Cleaning's important. People don't realize how important cleaning is. They take it for granted."

"I'm not gonna put up with it much longer. I'd be gone now if it weren't for Caroline."

"You like Caroline."

"Of course. I love Caroline. That's why you left the other night, isn't it? Because of Gloria listening. Caroline's mom."

"No. No. No."

"I would have liked you to stay."

I twisted my neck to look across the room at the window to the street. A woman was pulled past by an anxious Doberman. The woman was talking on her cellphone. The dog wanted to get somewhere the woman had never been, and the person the woman was talking to would not tell her.

"I've given it up," I said.

The nanny thought about that for a while. "What have you given up?"

"Desire," I said.

That made her sit back in her chair. "Oh, my," she said. "How big of you."

I didn't bother to defend or explain myself.

"What else have you given up?" she asked.

"My daughter."

"Oh," she said.

We sat there a long while, listening to the murmurings of others drinking their steeped liquids.

"What do you mean by that? Tell me about your daughter."

"I have a daughter. I don't have a daughter. I have a daughter out there in the world I can't be with. A beautiful little girl."

"Speaking as a daughter who was given up," she finally said, "I think you should find her."

"Have," I said.

"You have? Where is she?"

"Not so far away."

That gave her pause, and she leaned towards me again. "I'm not your daughter," she said. "I'm too old to be your daughter."

"You're not my daughter. Not my daughter, not my mother."

She reached up and fingered the ring in her nose. "A father should spend time with his daughter."

"Yes. Her mother doesn't think so."

"She can't be kept from you entirely if you're her father. There are laws."

"She'll deny it. She'll deny I'm the father, and they'll have me arrested if I go near my daughter."

"Sounds pretty messy," she said.

"It's a nasty little story. I think I'd better go," I said, and I did go, even though she tried to stop me.

I walked all the way home along Queen Street. Five Queen streetcars passed me.

———

Jimmy's funeral was three days after he died, on what turned out to be the hottest day of 1984. I got home from work and could not sleep and so spent a few hours swatting flies. When I thought I'd killed them all, there was always another.

I didn't want to go to the funeral, but who ever really wanted to go to a funeral unless their feelings were less than honourable? Funerals are a duty and I'd already missed my parents', and having denied the existence of God to Mrs. Greene only made me feel all the more in need of some sort of repentance.

The Irvines sat in their usual pew near the pulpit. Mrs. Irvine and Nick Campion were there with Gloria and Irvine, so I sat near the back and shook my head calmly when Irvine motioned me to come forward. The heat made my head swim, and all I wanted to do was sleep. I had not slept in days.

Jimmy had a silver coffin, by which I do not mean it was precious metal, but only that there was some kind of silver finish covering the wood. It made the box look like some sort of curious machine—perhaps a missile or spaceship. I imagined Jimmy rocketing off towards some other galaxy. Pastor Tuttle spoke about lost innocence and Christ's special love for children. Many wept, while others, such as me, felt all the more empty for our lack of tears. Mr. Greene, tearless, held Mrs. Greene while she hid her face to make us think she was crying. Probably she was crying. One might have guessed they were deeply in love, and I hoped that maybe it was true. As it turned out, it was only a last public display of love and grief. Two years later, the last time I visited my parents' graves, I saw something in the Broken Head paper that made it clear Mr. Greene had remarried: he and his new wife were pictured giving a cheque on behalf of the Broken Head Chamber of Commerce to a cancer charity. I have no idea what happened to Mrs. Greene.

After the funeral, while most went to the graveyard to see Jimmy lowered into the ground, I went home to try to catch a few hours of sleep before I had to go back to the scrub brush and urinals and the little white cakes of dichlorobenzene. The air conditioning was on in the Irvine house, which had made the flies disappear, looking for warmer parts. The basement was so cool that I was thinking I would need a sweater as I put my key in the door and found that it was already unlocked. When I stepped inside, I found Gloria sitting at my table, still in her little black dress, her legs crossed and her hands cupping her knee, as though she was waiting for her name to be called.

"Gloria?" I said.

She had not switched on the light and was sitting in the dull glow of the sunlight that squinted through the two tiny windows.

"Hello," she said. "Sorry for intruding."

She didn't look at me. There was a dead fly lying on the table where I'd killed it that morning, and she was staring at it.

"No problem," I said.

"I needed to talk to you."

"Okay."

"I wanted to apologize to you for that night we went to the movie. Well, not just for that. For the things Nick says about you all the time. And my mother, too. They like to make fun of you. Nick has this routine he goes into about how you're visiting from another planet to kill all the evil fathers on earth, and Mom laughs so much that it encourages him. Maybe you've even heard them. You can hear a lot from down here, can't you? I've just been sitting here listening to all the things you can hear. I'm sorry."

"You've got nothing to be sorry for."

"My mother—"

"You can't be sorry for your mother."

"I'm sorry that you—"

"I don't want you to be sorry for me."

"I'm sorry."

She could not bear to look at me and so was studying her hands in her lap. I reached up and flicked the light switch.

"Turn it off," she said.

178

I did. She still didn't look at me and wouldn't speak. I wondered if I should make some tea or should sit down across from her.

"What is it between you and my father?" she asked.

I decided to sit down. "Nothing."

"What do you talk about when he visits?"

"Nothing. God. Can I make you some tea?" I flicked the dead fly off the table and onto the floor.

She looked up at me. "No. It's too hot."

She hugged herself for warmth because of the air-conditioned cold. I wanted to tell her how the chilled air shrunk and sank through the house until it was all down here, enveloping her beautiful body. She ran her hands over her face and her fingers through her hair, massaging her scalp in exactly the way her mother had done that day I was waiting for her to get ready for the movie. The day Marty Sunaski died. I wanted to tell her that Marty and Chandler and Jimmy were all gone and we were still here and it wasn't anyone's fault but God's.

"Are you okay?" I asked instead.

"I lost the baby," she said.

"Pardon?"

"I had these terrible cramps and I went to the bathroom. When I got off the toilet, the baby was there. In the toilet bowl. I didn't know what to do. I just flushed it down. What else could I do?"

"Today?"

"About a week ago. I can't seem to tell anyone. Until you. I think Mrs. Greene was right about my needing you," she said, staring at the dead fly on the floor.

"No," I said.

Her eyes found me out for an instant before she went back to studying the fly.

"I don't think I do," she said. "Love Nick."

"No," I said. "No, no."

"You can see I don't love him?"

It didn't feel fair for her to ask. I felt cornered, and at the same time I'd spent my whole life wishing I was in that corner. I knew it was cold, but I wasn't feeling the cold. It was only air. I hated God for answering my wishes and killing that unborn child. Of all my crimes, this was the worst. This was the wish I could never forgive myself for.

"I don't know," I said.

"I—I think maybe I am in love with you," she said.

"Oh," I said.

I couldn't look at her.

Finally I heard her stand and approach me, and a moment later I felt her lips touch my forehead. I still didn't look up. She kissed my nose. I looked up. Her lips touched my lips and she put her arms around me the way she had when she was weeping at Jimmy's. She embraced me and held me, and I felt her bones through her skin and her heart beating in her chest. I returned her kiss, and a moment later she began to unbutton her blouse. I watched her fingers clasping the tiny discs of her buttons and working them through the slots in the cloth until her blouse was open and I could see that her white bra had tiny flowers printed on it. Her pale skin was freckled and her breathing so ragged I thought she might hyperventilate. I kissed her neck and her breasts.

"Oh my God," she whispered. "Oh my God."

SEVEN

Gloria picked up Caroline from school today. When I opened the door to go out and deal with the afternoon snow, she was standing talking to another mother, and for a second I thought she'd seen me, but she looked right through me like I was invisible and went on with her conversation. One of her mitts was off, and she bit the end of her finger. I ducked back inside.

Every day I ask Gloria's forgiveness for the young man she once knew—every which variety of forgiveness. Forgive his ignorance. Forgive his naïveté. Forgive his thoughtlessness. Forgive his thoughts. Forgive his best intentions. Forgive his awkward tongue. Forgive his back. Forgive his skin in general. Forgive his black and wounded heart. Forgive his rage and stupid pride. Forgive his endless capacity for hatred. Forgive his inability to distinguish love from terrible and aching need. Forgive his defensiveness. Forgive his faulty hearing. Forgive his bodily emissions. Forgive his blisters. Forgive his bandages. Forgive his scars. Forgive all the unforgivable in him. Forgive his being.

I can't stop thinking about what the nanny said at the coffee place. That I should find Caroline. That *she* wants to be found. That Caroline wants to know who I am. I keep thinking about what the nanny's words mean for me, and what they mean for her. The difference is that Caroline doesn't know she's been given up. And the difference is that I had no choice but to give her up. I keep telling myself that: I had no choice. I had no choice. I had no choice. It is a difference. I wouldn't have given her up if I'd had a choice. But if I give her this writing in ten years or twenty years or thirty years, she'll think I'm a terrible man for not having told her who I was. I am. I should tell her, and we should be together, but I know that if I tell her, that's not what will happen. We should spend March break together. That's why I asked her yesterday, "What are you doing for March break?" And her friends laughed. And she blushed and didn't answer. It's not cool to talk to the janitor, and it's even less cool when he talks to you. Maybe she'll hate me for giving her this and letting her know that she was forsaken. Why would she want to know that she was forsaken? By a janitor. What would she care for choices? I had a choice. It was her who had no choice. She'll probably think it was better not to know about that particular choice she didn't have.

Gloria needs to hate me. She's wished me right out of existence. But if things are to be tidy, there needs to be a janitor hiding out with his mops and pails in a little room with a red door under the stairs. I truly believe Gloria would understand that. She has a reliance on order that means she needs to trust a professional to do what he or she is expected to do. She probably trusts the janitor hiding under the stairs more than she trusted the janitor she allowed to lie between her legs.

Gloria was a woman of perfect parts. Her hair, her lips and her voice, her eyes, her cheeks, her throat and shoulders, her arms, her hands and fingers, her breasts. I could go on, but I'd only be further dismembering and misleading. She wasn't perfect. She had a thing about frills. Every piece of clothing she wore had to have a frill. I know I haven't mentioned this before. I wonder if she still wears frills. Her black overcoat, at least, has no frills, and that's all I ever see of her now. It's not something I'm judging, but I can't help but believe that she'd have been better off and happier with fewer frills. It was her way of being in the world; her way of suggesting her lack of importance, so that she couldn't be taken too seriously and held accountable. It was her way of suggesting she was a frill. Which she was not.

She had more potential than Antarctica.

Once she fell asleep in my bed, and I lay there and watched her, felt her breath on my face and tried to imagine what she dreamt.

She had a terrible fear that chaos was encroaching, and it was, in the form of me. She had a mania for order and tidiness that she claimed to have inherited from her parents. It's possible that's where it came from. The scalpels and scrapers and saws and other stainless steel instruments all sterilized and lying in a row. The wedding invitation list I wasn't on. She was mostly her father's child, but every now and then I'd catch sight of her mother: in her chin; in her glance; in the way she ran her fingers through her hair, massaged her scalp, comforting herself with her own touch as though she wore some loving parent's hands. She was so terribly afraid. Afraid of lightning. Afraid of flying, heights, germs, strong winds. Afraid of poverty. Afraid of nuclear attacks against small towns in Saskatchewan. She told me that one of her earliest memories was how she had huddled outside her parents' bedroom door, afraid of the dark, crying as quietly as she could because she knew she'd get into trouble if she disturbed them. Her father told me that when she was a baby she used to clutch the side of her crib and bang her head against the wall until one of them would come and rescue her.

She found the red blouse in my drawer and wondered what I was doing with another woman's clothes. God knows why she was going through my drawers. I can see her sniffing the blouse and testing the texture of the material between her fingers. I wonder if it was silk. I don't have it anymore, and I don't remember.

"Is this yours?" she asked, when I came home from work. She was waiting there in my room for me.

She knew it wasn't mine.

"It's my mother's. It *was* my mother's. You can have it. Try it on," I told her.

She was afraid of me. I could see she was afraid of me. "Why?" she asked. "It won't fit. Your mother was . . . she was bigger than me."

"You're right. I missed the bus."

"Pardon?"

I took the blouse from her, folded it and put it back into the drawer.

"Tell me about your mother," she said. "I need you to tell me about the day your mother died."

She sat down at my table and waited.

In my eighteenth summer I graduated. With school over, there was barely any need at all to go to town, and I began what was meant to be a complete withdrawal from the world. I was to spend the rest of my life running the farm and looking after my mother. It had been decreed—or so I thought.

Halfway through the second sweep of summerfallowing, on a hot dry July night, I was standing while I drove—standing because my bum was sore—and singing an enthusiastic Vivaldi, which I'd learned from my time in the choir (I know that down east here they doubt we have any knowledge of cultured things at all out west, but I can assure you that our high school choir was remarkably cultured). I was singing at the top of my lungs, even though the song was entirely drowned out by the noise of the tractor. That was when I saw my mother alive for the last time.

My whole life was ahead of me until I reached the fence at the edge of the field, where I etched my turn and headed back the way I'd come. The heat of the engine made me sweat, and the wind had shifted a couple of hours before sunset so that when I was heading northeast I was driving along in the drift of my own dust: eating it and breathing it and wearing it on my skin. I knew I should set a new course, but I couldn't be bothered. I'd marked this path when I'd begun the field and why change now to avoid a little dust? It was my dust. There is a certain beauty in being left in your own dust.

My mother jogged by on the road, not bothering to wave, Prince running along beside her in the ditch. She jogged and went swimming every day. Getting a life, she called it. Went along with the charity work she was doing. She specialized in fighting pestilence. She wanted to do some good in the world, and so she was involved in the campaigns raising money to fight cancer and multiple sclerosis and heart disease. The slight bulge of her midriff that had started all this exercise had long ago disappeared. She was styling her hair differently: still long, as always, but more layered, as though the person cutting it actually knew what she was doing. Her skin shone, and she claimed it was some new cream she'd discovered.

When I was finished, I'd go swimming too, and I'd wash away all the sweat and the dust and the last eighteen years and be left clean.

Later, I noticed my father's Fargo pass, heading down towards the pasture. He still drove around the farm when he felt like it. I didn't notice any other cars.

When the sun had sunk through the horizon, I kept summer-fallowing because I was so close to finished. In half an hour I was done except for working out the corners: the turns left weedy triangles of uncultivated soil that still needed to be worked under. Once I was through with that, I lifted the cultivator with the hydraulics, pulled out onto the approach and stopped to lock the drawbar by dropping a heavy pin on either side. Then I pulled out onto the grid, put it in high gear and headed down to the creek.

Wind on my face and grit in my eyeballs.

The gate to the pasture was open. I figured it must have been Dad who left it open. There were no cows in sight. They were all up at the north end of the pasture, but they had a way of finding an open gate, and I didn't like the idea of spending tomorrow chasing them down, so I closed it.

I parked at the swimming hole, picked up the bottle of shampoo from the rusty old pesticide bucket Mom had placed there as a receptacle for just this purpose, and walked out of my dusty clothes.

The night air felt good on my testicles. The water was shiny black and dappled with light like a river of oil. Downstream, I could see the half-moon reflected. There were no clouds, a million stars.

I always walked into the creek to let my body adjust gradually to the temperature. Not that it was cold that day: it was like bathwater. The muck and weeds on the bottom curled between my toes. Once I was up to my chest, I dove in and swam underwater forty feet upstream before I turned and let myself drift downstream until I couldn't hold my breath any longer and had to come up for air. There's something more real than symbolism about baptism: my whole being was hauled back from some dark underworld when I dove into the creek. Singing Vivaldi's *Gloria* at the top of my lungs, I opened the shampoo, lathered my hair, hurled the bottle to the shore and ducked under to rinse. "Gloria, Gloria!" Coming up again, I shook the excess water from my hair and rubbed my eyes. "In excelsis Deo!" When I opened my eyes again, I saw a dark shape floating gently by on the slow current.

The shape had legs and arms. It was a body, floating on its back, the hands open and cupping the water at its sides. The face was just below the surface, and there were no bubbles.

"Jesus," I said.

"Oh my God. I can't begin to imagine what that must have felt like," Gloria said. "It's no wonder you're so—different from other people. None of us can fathom what you've been through. I think I'd have just slipped under the water right there and drowned myself. But you've come out of it with faith. Believing in goodness. You amaze me more than any person I've ever met. You're real and none of the rest of us are. I don't think you know how much you amaze me. And what happened next?"

"How are the wedding plans coming along?" I asked her.

She began to examine her nails, and then she bit the end of her finger. It was a strategy she'd developed to avoid actually biting her nails: she'd bite herself hard as a way of reminding herself of the ravages of chewed-up fingernails.

"There's not going to be any wedding."

"I'm gonna go. I'm gonna get in the truck in an hour and drive away from here."

"You can't go, Dwight. I can't face them all alone. I need you here."

My idea, based on my experience with Mrs. Greene, was that all we needed to do was to keep it a secret. No one had to know. I wanted to protect her from being associated with me. My plan was that I'd move away, and a few weeks later, so that no one would make the connection in a hundred million years, she'd tell Nick that she didn't love him and tell her parents that the wedding was off. She'd tell them that because of the embarrassment of calling off the wedding, she had to leave home and move away from Broken Head, and we would meet in some city where no one knew us. In that strange and exotic place, we'd walk out together and face the world.

It could all have come straight out of some silly romance novel, but for some reason I didn't notice at the time. Desire made me stupid—made me the devil's plaything. She stood up and kissed me and I put my hand on her leg and under her skirt, and we were making love in the kitchen, five feet from the bed.

She didn't agree with my plan—she pretended to have some sentimental attachment to the quaint idea that truth could set you free. She kept insisting, day after day, that any minute she would tell everyone. I didn't think she could do it, but she claimed she was tired of living with lies. She loved her father. She hated her mother for hating her father. I wondered why she thought her mother hated her father, and instead of explaining she told me she hated her mother for the glasses of mineral water she drank all day long. Those tall, sweating glasses tinkling with two cubes of ice and garnished with a slice of lemon. The mineral water, Gloria explained to me, was spiked with vodka. It had been going on as long as she could remember. Irvine was ashamed of his wife's drinking. How could he take her out in the world when he had no idea how she'd act. She was a bomb ticking. Gloria had the same fears that her mother would embarrass her, along with a fear of her temper when she was drunk. She never hit Gloria, but she had a wicked tongue.

"Your mother scares me a bit, with those eyes of hers. When she looks at me, it's like she's sticking pins in a doll. But I've never seen her drunk," I told her, thinking of my dad.

"You've never seen her sober."

She hated her mother and she hated her parents' marriage, and she insisted that I'd somehow made her see that staying with Nick would be carrying on the same terrible lie in her own life. She only had one life. She was obsessed with that fact: she had one solitary life to live, and she had realized through me and through Christ that she wasn't allowed to waste it. I told her we had to make a run for it if we were going to survive. I begged her not to tell anyone about us.

But I had these long, elaborate fantasies about her telling Nick.

He was in the kitchen. She had come downstairs when he called her and found him in the kitchen, getting a beer from the fridge, and because her mother was in the garden watering, she took advantage of the privacy and launched right in. He stood there listening, astonished by her words. He couldn't believe it, but obviously it wasn't a joke. Gloria didn't joke. Those few words changed the way he saw the world. Afraid of chaos, she did it in her calm, ordered way. By the time she'd finished speaking, he'd hid his shock and pain behind an expression of utter contempt. Gloria took off the ring he'd given her and placed it on the table. He picked it up, rolled it between his fingertips and casually tossed it across the room. She watched it roll into the corner and come to rest against the baseboard.

"I can't believe this. Do you hear yourself? The guy murdered his own father. Think, Gloria. You don't know what you want."

"Yes," she responded. "I do. I want love."

He nodded slowly. "Love. Yes, I guess he can love you like Jesus, which I could never do. Does he fuck you like Jesus?"

"Yes. Exactly like Jesus."

He held his silence for a moment, considering the appropriate response, before he leaned forward and screamed at her so loud that I could have heard him from the basement, where I would have been reading the King James.

"You don't know what love is! You have no idea what love is!" Pacing back and forth across the room, he gave her a few breaths to recover, but she didn't try to answer. "You like your killers born again? You want me to kill somebody for you? Is that it? Okay. Maybe I'll kill him and then get born again. Or maybe I'll kill you to save you from him. Is that what you want? You want me to kill someone?"

"No," she said. "That's not what I want."

"Then what the fuck do you want from me?"

"Nothing," she said, studying her clasped hands. "Nothing at all. I don't want anything from you anymore, Nick. I want you to go away and be happy without me."

He stood there without speaking for many seconds, becoming strangely self-conscious of his final moments in the kitchen of that house where he had spent so much of the preceding four years. Even at moments of great pain (especially at moments of great pain), he found himself turning over the moments and examining them for their significance, and in doing so he'd discovered the possibility, before he'd even left the Irvine house, that he'd never stand there in that kitchen again. It seemed to him that he'd lived half his life in that house. She was the most beautiful girl in the world, and she had been his. In grade twelve she had finally agreed to make love to him. His friends kidded him about throwing away his freedom, but they had already kidded him for two years about the fact that he and Gloria had never done it—Grant told him that love meant never having to say you're horny.

He blamed it on her father. He hated her self-righteous father, so full of his bloated god. "Fine," he said, calmly, quietly. "I hope you're very happy. I hope you get exactly what you deserve."

He walked out of the room and out the front door and got into his yellow sports car and drove swiftly away. Gloria sat down for a moment at the kitchen table. After a few minutes she struggled to her feet, walked over and picked the ring up off the floor. She took it to the sink, dropped it down the drain and turned on the garbage disposal. It made a terrible noise.

Even though only that single yellow car carried the news away, it spread like a prairie fire ignited from a single tossed cigarette. Gloria's mother heard Nick yelling from the garden, but the air conditioning was on and all the doors and windows closed, so she couldn't actually hear the words. When she heard Nick's car speed away, she knew something was wrong. She dropped the hose and went straight in to ask Gloria, but Gloria, standing at the sink where she'd just thrown her ring away, wasn't ready to tell her about me. All she said was that she and Nick had broken up and the wedding was off, and she ran up to her bedroom when her mother demanded an explanation.

Mrs. Irvine poured herself another glass of mineral water and added a couple of ounces of vodka. She was devastated. Mrs. Irvine loved Nick. Nick was the husband Irvine had turned out not to be: a good man, but without the taint of sanctimonious religion. Sometimes when Nick walked in the door, he would kneel and kiss her hand. She imagined Nick making love to Gloria and had fantasies about making love to him herself. She could see the way he looked at her sometimes.

Irvine wasn't yet home from the hospital when the phone rang. Her friend Sally Bendall, who was at the very top of the wedding list, and who lived next door to the Campions, was calling because she'd already heard the story from Nick's mother, Ruth, and wanted to hear from Emily Irvine if it was actually true.

Mrs. Irvine went straight up to Gloria's bedroom and found the door locked. She began knocking somewhat calmly, calling to her little girl, desperate for Gloria to tell her it was only a misunderstanding, but when Gloria wouldn't answer, she realized that the story Mrs. Campion had told Sally Bendall must have had at least a filament of truth. She screamed at her daughter as she hammered at the door, wondering what she could possibly have been thinking. Did she understand that she had thrown away her future when she gave Nick Campion back his ring? Had she gone insane, rejecting a wealthy and sophisticated young man for a psychopath who had murdered his own parents? How could any Irvine possibly face anyone in Broken Head ever again?

When she'd given up on Gloria, she came down and knocked at my door. Hoping it was Gloria, I immediately opened it to her.

"Mrs. Irvine?" I said when I saw her standing there, glaring at me.

"I know what you've done," she said. "You've assaulted my daughter. You've raped my daughter, and you're going to pay for it. You may have got away with killing your parents, but you're not going to get away with this. I'm calling the police. Get out of my house!"

And she turned and walked away.

She called her husband at the hospital, but he wasn't there. She blamed him for what had happened, for inviting the lunatic into her basement, but he was still her last hope. He would have to make things right. She believed he could. It was what he did. His charitable acts, saving destitute families, were what he lived for, and charity begins at home. She met him in the doorway as he was taking off his hat. She told him what had happened, and he listened, saying nothing until she was finished.

"Where is she?" he said.

"Upstairs. In her room."

She followed him up the stairs and watched him knock at the door.

"Gloria?" he said.

The door opened and he disappeared inside, the door closing between Mrs. Irvine and the rest of her family.

That was my fantasy. It's all terribly embarrassing and contrived, but I still like to imagine it would have happened that way if

Gloria'd had the guts to tell Nick. I imagined Irvine betraying me, ordering me out of his house. The whole thing finishes up with Gloria and me leaving Broken Head and her family behind. I sell the farm and we drive away in the same pickup truck my parents drove north from Denver; we go to Calgary and rent a little apartment and have Caroline nine months later, and we're all happy together for the rest of our lives.

"We're having a family meeting about the wedding preparations after dinner tonight," Gloria said. "Nick will be here. I'm going to tell them all at once. It's going to be over and done with tonight."

I begged her not to tell them. I begged her and begged her until she promised she wouldn't. We would just run away. I'd go first and she'd follow. We made love again. We made love like we believed we'd invented the practice. Afterwards, I made her tea, and she sat down at my table, wearing only one of my white T-shirts.

"I used to imagine you looking something like you do now," I confessed. "Visiting me on the farm. Before my parents died."

She nodded as though she understood and she didn't want to talk about it.

"What happened after you found your mother?"

Her eyes were wide open. She wore her jogging suit. For a few moments I watched as she floated past, waiting for her to turn over and swim a stroke towards the shore; waiting for a hand to rise and splash water up into the starlight; waiting for a leg to kick. She floated on peacefully.

I swam to catch her and grabbed her arm. The cold of her flesh confirmed what her eyes had already told me, but I dragged her to the shore and lifted her and carried her up the bank, where I lowered her to the ground and performed mouth-to-mouth resuscitation. Her lips were cold and rubbery, and there was water inside her. I twisted her head to dump the water out and tried again.

Prince ran up and sniffed us, and I stopped the mouth-to-mouth. He whimpered and walked over and peed on the tractor tire.

I looked upstream, the direction he'd come from. He stood watching me watching him, whimpering, his tail twitching.

She was grimacing, not peaceful at all, really, as though someone had told her a particularly bad joke. There was blood on the back of her head. Something had hit her hard—hard enough to knock herself out of her and leave a hollow shell. I knew instantly that my father had done it. It was as though I had been expecting it for years; standing by, just waiting for it to happen. I stood looking down at her and thought I should cry, but I couldn't. All I could think was that I could leave now and never come back, because there was no longer anything keeping me there. The world was waiting for me in some other place. Maybe she was there too, waiting, a drink with an umbrella on the table before her, checking her watch because I should have already arrived. It wasn't like me to be late. It was like her. She was always late. An hour, at least, just out of principle.

So why was she all of a sudden leaving so early?

She stared up into the stars. I wondered if she was looking at herself out there, sipping from her umbrella cocktail, but couldn't believe it, no matter how hard I tried. The heavens had long closed, and we were alone under empty skies marked only by sparks of wasted light.

I knelt before her and tried to close her eyes.

The dog barked and I saw headlights approaching. My father's old pickup truck: the same one they'd left Denver in almost two decades before. I rose and stepped over Mother's body, wanting to put myself between them; I crossed my arms and stood there waiting. The truck creaked to a stop and my father stepped out and looked us over. The dog rushed up and jumped on my father, and he patted its head. Animals liked him. What was that about? The innocence of animals. He touched them. He was not interested in reaching out to other humans, but animals were no threat.

"Is she okay?"

"No." I shook my head. "She's not okay."

He walked up beside me and knelt and touched her arm with his real hand. "He killed her," he said.

I stared down at him, still kneeling there. "*He* did?"

He got to his feet. "Her father."

"*Her* father?"

He looked around, and I thought maybe he was about to point out her father's hiding place in the rose bushes.

"Or maybe your cop friends. They want to blame me. They've been trying to find a way to put me away for years. This is how they decided to get me. They'll blame me and try to lock me up. We'll have to bury her somewhere."

He didn't look at me as he spoke, but continued to study something off in the distance, imagining the right place to dig the hole. He might have been giving orders on how we'd deal with a cow that needed a shot of antibiotics. I stared at him, not speaking, until he finally met my eyes. With my eyes I tried to tell him everything I'd always been too afraid to say to him.

I bent down, lifted my mother from the ground, carried her to the truck, managed to grab the handle of the passenger door and open it without setting her down, and placed her on the seat. Prince jumped in the back of the truck. While I was arranging her body so that I could get the door closed, my father opened the driver's door and slid behind the wheel.

"Get out of the truck," I said.

He turned and looked at me again and began to read the message in my eyes. "What do you mean?"

"I'll take her."

"Where you gonna take her?"

"The hospital."

"The hospital? She's dead."

"I know. I'm taking her to the hospital."

He shook his head. "They'll blame me."

I nodded. "Amen."

"That's what you want? You want them to blame me?"

"I don't give a fuck about *them*."

194

Dad nodded. "Oh. I see."

He waited for more, but there wasn't anything else I wanted to give him. "All right, then." He got out of the truck and stood there looking at me, rubbing his jaw with his hand. "That suits me fine. You go and you tell them your lies."

I walked around to the driver's side. "Stay here," I told Prince, and the dog shrank lower in the box, hoping I would change my mind. "Prince! Get out! Stay here!" He flattened his ears against his head, shuffled to the tailgate, dragging his hind end, and jumped down to the ground. I got in and closed the door, but it was such a warm evening that of course the window was open, and Dad was still standing there, with his nose practically in my ear.

"Coward," he said. "You go ahead and let them do your dirty work for you. But you'd better warn them to watch out when they come for me. I'll be waiting for them."

I leaned out the window and spat at his feet. There was still dust from his field in my mouth. I didn't have the courage to look him in the eye. "Wait for *me*," I said. "I'll be the one who comes for you. Tomorrow at sunrise. Bring those duelling pistols you bought from Chandler. I'll meet you right here."

I put the truck in gear and pulled away. When I glanced in the mirror, Dad was reaching down to touch the dog's nose.

I know it's all contrived from Russian novels, but I'd been dreaming about it for so long that I felt an awful delight in making it come true. My revenge fantasy was more important than grieving, which I didn't really know how to go about. I couldn't quite believe that what was happening was real and she was actually gone, even as her body was lying there on the seat beside me, so I made it all into a romantic story. I would face him with a pistol for what he'd done, just the way they did in those novels. It wasn't only a stupid hockey player like Marty Sunaski, it was my father, and the justice of it was beautiful. He had killed my mother, the way I had always known he would.

His perfect aim meant I was committing suicide, and that was exactly what I wanted.

Gloria was also delighted. When I'd told her that much, she wanted to hear more, but I leaned over and kissed her and we made love again. I made love more in those three weeks than I have in all the rest of my life put together.

After she left, not ten minutes had passed before I heard her father's familiar knock at my door. I opened it to see him hunched before me, pale and tired. But he smiled as he extended his hand to me. "Good to see you," he said.

"Why?" I said, not immediately taking his hand.

"We haven't talked since the funeral. You've been spending a lot of time with Gloria, haven't you?"

"Not really. A little bit. She likes to talk. She visits."

His hand was still there, the fingers extended towards me, perfectly steady as a surgeon's ought to be, even if the surgeon operated only on the dead. Though his hand was flesh, it made me think of my father's prosthetic. It looked like some kind of cunning mechanical trap. I grabbed hold of his fingers and squeezed.

"That's nice. I'm really pleased you two are getting to know one another."

I stood back and he entered and sat at the table.

"I was just about to pack," I said.

"Why would you do that?"

"I've got to go away. There's nothing for me here. In Broken Head. I think I'll sell the farm and go away somewhere and start over."

He shook his head. "You're welcome to stay here."

"I think I should go. I'm gonna go."

"Don't worry about Mrs. Irvine. She doesn't understand the situation."

He lifted his eyebrows, waited for a response. Wondering whether I understood the situation, I scratched my nose and found it was still there, in the middle of my face.

"Would you like some tea?" I asked him.

"Tea would be good. What about Gloria's wedding? All the people from the congregation will be there. You can't leave until after that."

I stood at the sink with my back to him, filling the kettle. "I didn't think I was invited."

"Of course you're invited. What made you think that? You and Gloria are getting to be so close. Of course you're invited."

I placed the kettle on the stove and switched on the burner.

"Have you thought about a career, Dwight? A man your age needs to think about a career. Perhaps you'd be interested in apprenticing under my friend, Mr. Bantam. I know he was very disappointed that his son wasn't interested in keeping up the family business. I could talk to him for you."

"The funeral guy?"

"Funeral director. Yes."

I ran the hot water and rinsed out the teapot. "I'm thinking of going to the city."

He considered this for a moment before he cleared his throat. "What city?"

I shrugged.

"The city's a tough life. Rents are high. It takes a great deal of money to make ends meet in a city. You'll still need a career, and you have more connections here. The funeral business is a lucrative one. It'll be a challenge. More exciting than you'd think. Plenty of trade secrets. Not because they want to keep things secret, but because nobody wants to know. For best results, you need to start embalming while the cells are still alive. Did you know that?"

Shaking my head, I threw two tea bags into the pot.

"You know how everyone always says that a corpse looks peaceful? Well, that's done with sutures. And pins. They sew the mouth shut and pin the lips in place so that they're just slightly parted." An image of Jimmy's face gasping appeared in my mind's eye. "Sometimes they use staples now, but Mr. Bantam still does it the old-fashioned way, with a needle and thread. Sutures."

My father, I remembered, had looked at peace with the bullet. I stood watching the kettle, waiting for it to boil.

"I had another fellow today who died of smoke inhalation. Like Chandler. He was from a town down near the border. They think there must have been something wrong with the wiring. It was an old house. I find smoke inhalation victims particularly interesting. They don't need much makeup. Smoke inhalation always gives a nice pink look that even Mr. Bantam can't match."

He paused and I tried to train my eye into the spout of the kettle, but there was no light in there.

"Smoke is God's undertaker," he said.

The kettle began making that sighing noise it makes on its way to a boil. I lifted it, gave it a quick shake and set it back on the burner.

"That's the kind of thing you'd be learning. It really is quite fascinating. It's an art in its own right."

I took a deep breath. "Doesn't sound like it's for me," I said.

He was silent for a while and the kettle began to boil. Maybe his words had kept it from boiling. I poured the water over the tea bags, brought the pot to the table and set it before him, only then realizing that we both still needed cups. I went to the cupboard for them.

"Do you have any milk?" he asked. "I've sworn off sugar, but I still like a drop of milk in my tea."

I brought the carton, set it on the table and sat down across from him.

"So, you don't think the funeral business is for you," he said, adding the milk to his tea and looking around for a stirring instrument.

"I don't think so," I said, fetching him a spoon.

"Maybe you should think about it a little more. It's a very good business."

"There are always customers," I said.

"Yes. There are. Why don't you think about it for a few days before you reject the idea completely? I could take you over to talk to Mr. Bantam any time."

"I don't think I can stay here," I said. "In Broken Head. People think funny things about me because I killed my father."

He considered this statement, his eyes on me. "That's ridiculous," he said. "People admire you. That's not a problem at all."

"I think it is. I think it's a problem that I'm only admired for killing my father."

"No, no, no," he said. "You've got to give people a chance. There will be all kinds of talk, of course, but once you let them know you, it will blow over. You have plenty of friends. The people in the congregation admire what you did for Jimmy."

We both sipped our tea.

"Jimmy died," I pointed out.

"Everyone dies," he said. "You tried to help him. People respect you, Dwight. They can see you're no ordinary person. Hasn't Gloria told you that? They can see you're special. You've been chosen. I believe that the Lord has touched you." He took another sip of his tea. "Everything will be fine," he said. "God willing."

That night I went to work and told Mrs. Spalding I was leaving Broken Head. Told her right in front of the others. Mrs. Spalding was upset. She said she'd invested so much training in me and I should have been honest with her if I was thinking about taking off all of a sudden. All I could do was apologize and promise to stay two more weeks so that she'd have a chance to find somebody to replace me. The older women looked awkwardly away, but Patty smirked at no one in particular, as though enjoying some private joke.

While we were having coffee at three o'clock in the morning, Patty out of the blue asked me, "Isn't Gloria Irvine going to miss you when you go away?"

I said I didn't know what she meant, and she shrugged and smiled and took another drag on her cigarette. The older women smoked their cigarettes, sipped their coffee and stared at the ceiling.

Gloria was more than a little upset when I told her. "Why would she say that? Did you talk about me to her?"

"No. I might have mentioned your name."

"Why? Why were you mentioning my name to her?"

"I don't know. She was bugging me to go to that movie we saw, and I told her I'd already seen it with you and your friends."

"So she wanted to go out with you?"

"Yeah. But I never did."

"So she's jealous. And you go using me as an excuse for not going out with her. Perfect, Dwight. Do you want everyone in town talking about us?"

"Are you ashamed of being mentioned in connection with me?"

"Dwight. I'm engaged."

"You said you were going to call off the wedding last night."

"You told me not to. You *begged* me not to."

"I told you not to tell them about us. That doesn't mean you couldn't call off the wedding."

"What? That's not what you said last night. You said you were going to quit your job and go away, and then I should call off the wedding after you were gone. And now you tell me you're going to work for another two weeks. That takes us to—a week before my wedding. You expect me to call it off at the altar?"

"I thought you said you didn't want me to go at all."

"I don't want you to go, Dwight. But that's the way it has to be, isn't it? Isn't that the plan?"

"I guess."

"What did my father say when he came for his visit?"

"He wants me to be an undertaker."

"He what?"

"He wants me to apprentice as an undertaker with Mr. Bantam. He says it'd make a good career."

She shrugged and shook her head. "He didn't say anything about me?"

"He said he was glad we were getting to be so close."

She put a finger in her mouth and bit, and then examined the tooth marks. "I don't think Dad would care. I don't think he likes Nick anyway. Why does he like you so much?"

"I don't know. Why do you like me so much?"

"Not for the same reasons," she said, and she put her arms around me and kissed me. "Oh, you're all prickly."

"It's a Mennonite thing," I said, kissing her neck. "We grow beards when we marry to symbolize our union with God and woman."

"Is that true?" she whispered into my ear.

"Yes, it's true. Or it is with the Hutterites, anyway. And they're Anabaptists like Mennonites."

I unbuttoned her blouse and kissed her breasts.

"I'm worried," she said. "I'm worried that people are talking."

"Patty's just one person."

She sighed a heavy sigh. "I'm worried about Mom."

Mrs. Irvine was drinking even more than usual and telling everyone who would listen that she wanted me out of her basement. The Irvine family had become entwined in the horrible shame of the Froeses. Broken Head listened. You could feel it listening and watching. In the middle of the night I'd walk the empty streets, because it was the only time no eyes followed me as I passed. But still the houses listened. Sometimes the trail of the glow of a cigarette on a front veranda would reveal someone watching, and I'd hunch my shoulders against the night air and walk faster. Other times a car would drift by, the eyes of the driver drilling through my skull and into my brain. I'd walk to the graveyard and stand over my parents' graves, trying to catch what they were saying about me and Gloria Irvine.

———

The last dry August weekend before I was supposed to leave Broken Head, Gloria asked if I would take her to see the farm. We snuck away at night, after everyone thought she was asleep.

The windows had all been smashed. When we went inside, shining around with our flashlights, I half expected to see messages scrawled on the walls, but there was nothing of the kind. I couldn't see anything missing, but what was there that anyone would have wanted? The pigeons had moved in; there was bird shit on the floor. For the first and last time, Gloria walked through the house where I had grown up. She lifted a fork lying in the middle of the living-room floor and studied it, as though looking for evidence of something. I picked up a stone that had come through one of the windows and threw it at the clock on the stove, but I missed and smashed a salt shaker. I looked around for something else to throw, but Gloria put her arms around me and calmed me down. She asked to see my bedroom and I showed her. The window there was not broken. She stood pointing her beam out it into the dark passageway my father had built.

"Let's go," I said, and she nodded and followed me out the door.

I took her down to the swimming hole and told her that was where I'd found my mother but didn't tell her that it was where I'd shot my father and she didn't ask. We stripped off and went skinny-dipping in the moonlight as though we were kids. The horseflies hovered over us, waiting for a chance to bite. We made love in the water to avoid them.

In the truck on the way home, she asked me what it was like to see my home that way. I shrugged and she asked, "Does it hurt?" When I shrugged again, she turned away.

When we got back to my room in her basement, we made some tea and drank the tea and went back to bed and made love again. She was straddling me with her arms on either side of me, her breasts swaying over me. She told me she was coming and I saw that she was. She began to cry. "Don't ever leave me," she said.

I lay there holding her, telling her that she would join me soon in Calgary and we'd be happy there. I told her that everything was going to be okay.

The police wanted a statement. My mother was dead and they asked me, the boy who uttered death threats, for a statement. An officer took me to the same pinhole-lined room they'd taken me to before, but this time I talked. I knew I should cry for them, but it all seemed too theatrical, and so I just sat there, numb, and talked.

"What blood?" he interrupted me.

"On the back of her head. There's blood. There's a bad cut. Didn't you see it? Go have a look."

"How did that happen?"

"I don't know. It was there when I found her floating. Maybe she fell in the creek and hit her head on a rock."

"You think so? But you just said you didn't notice the blood until after you did your mouth-to-mouth."

"No. But it had to have been."

"Had to have been what?"

"Already there. When I found her."

"Are you sure you didn't bump her head when you threw her down?"

"I didn't throw her down."

"Laid her down, I meant. You said you laid her down. On the ground. After you found her and pulled her out of the creek."

The cop leaned back in his chair, crossed his legs and waited for my answer. It was a different cop from either of the last ones. I found out later that it was the colleague who boarded Marty Sunaski. He wasn't much older than me and had the eyes of a lizard.

"Yeah," I finally said. "I'm sure."

He nodded grimly, but I could tell he was enjoying himself. He leaned forward, resting his elbows on the table. "So what did you do then?"

"I carried her to the truck and drove her to the hospital."

"Uh-huh. The truck? You said you drove the tractor down to the creek."

I looked up at him for an instant before I looked away. "Yeah. She drove the truck down. That's how she got there."

"I thought you said you saw her jogging down there."

"Yeah. I don't know. She must have gone home first and got the truck and drove down there to go for a swim. She left the truck there."

"So you noticed the truck when you first drove down there?"

I took my time, felt my front teeth with the tip of my tongue. Looked him in the eyes. "No. It was dark and the truck was a bit upstream. I didn't see it at first. Then I saw the dog come from that direction."

"And then you saw the truck and you carried her to it."

I shook my head. "I went and got the truck and drove it over to her and put her in the truck. And I drove her to the hospital. Even though she was dead. She was already dead. She's dead."

The officer nodded and wrote something in his notebook.

When we were finished, he said they'd need to take at look at where I'd found her, and I agreed to lead them there. When I opened the door to the truck, the interior light came on, shining through yellowed plastic. There was blood on the passenger seat.

I led them to the swimming hole. They looked around with their flashlights for a while, but it was too dark to see much. They asked me if I was okay and said they'd be back the next morning.

It was still very warm, though it was the middle of the night, so I drove with the window open to let in the breeze. When I came back to the truck after closing the gate to the pasture, Gloria was there, wearing her white negligee, both knees against the dashboard, her heels swinging.

"God," she said. "Look at the stars. I love looking up at the stars. It makes me feel like I'm flying. Just look at them. They're all right up there, shining."

"Leave me alone," I said.

"You are alone," she told me. "There's no one more alone than you are. I just wanted to say goodbye."

"Goodbye. Write if you get work."

It had become clear to me that this was an improper haunting. If the devil had to come to me, why couldn't he come in the form of my mother? Why couldn't it be her telling me about the stars? It wasn't right to be haunted by the living.

"You're in a bad mood tonight, aren't you? Lighten up. Look at the stars. I love the stars. Infinite stars, infinite space. There's enough room for everyone. There's places out there that even God's never seen."

"Please go away."

"Don't worry so much about God. This is a just killing. I think it's very brave what you're doing. Shoot him right between the eyes. You won't miss."

When I turned to see what expression she'd lend her words, there was no one there.

I didn't tell Gloria about Gloria being there that night. I wasn't sure she'd understand.

I got home, stumbled into the house and went to bed, but I couldn't sleep and before long a knock came on my bedroom door.

"Time to get up," my father called. "The bus is coming."

My bedroom was pitch black. There was a window, but no light came through that window. The red numbers on the digital alarm clock read 4:52. I'd wished for the end of the bus for most of my life, and now the end had come and I wished the bus would pull into the yard and the door would open and I could climb aboard.

By the time I'd pulled on a clean T-shirt and my jeans and walked to the kitchen, the Fargo was already pulling out of the yard. The horizon to the east glowed pink. The refrigerator chugged to life, but I didn't feel hungry. I walked out into the yard, and the birds were singing a song of great joy. Each was answering the other with its own beautifully articulated melody, and the answer revealed not one single bird but a great, glorious chorus of song. It was the origin of music, and you can hear it any morning, but for some reason I'd never noticed before. I couldn't help crying, and I was relieved to finally cry, even if it wasn't entirely for my mother.

Mom's car started, so Dad must have put in a new battery, because the day before she had been complaining that the alternator wasn't working. The day before she'd been complaining, leaning on one leg. Perhaps he'd even changed the brushes in the alternator. He could do things like that if he wanted to. It was one of his strange powers that I wasn't able to understand.

He'd left the gate open. I didn't bother to close it.

The truck was parked by the swimming hole in roughly the same spot he'd parked the night before. The case with the duelling pistols was open on the hood, and Jacob Froese leaned there, watching the creek flow by. The dog was wandering around the flat, chasing after birds. I heard a meadowlark.

"Never seen you up so early," he said.

He hefted a pistol and began to dump the powder down the barrel; pushed in a wad of cotton and tamped it with a metal plunger; held up the lead ball like a waiter presenting a cork before he dropped it down the barrel and tamped it again with the plunger. Finally, he placed the pistol back in its velvet case. He lifted out the other pistol and repeated the process.

"These things aren't very accurate," he said. "Aim for the heart, not the head. Right dead centre of the chest." He pointed to the correct spot. "That's your widest target. Besides, the ball would likely bounce off my head." He handed me the pistol.

"I might not get to shoot," I told him. "I challenged you, so you get first shot."

"What are you talking about? We draw and fire."

"Not with these pistols. You're talking about a cowboy duel. We're fighting a Russian duel."

His expression turned sour. "Russian? That's where you hold it up to your own head and pull the trigger? Be my guest. There's only one chamber."

I switched the pistol from my right hand to my left, testing the weight, trying to calm my shaking. "We stand twenty paces apart, and the man who was challenged fires first. Then, if he's not already dead, the other fires."

Dad listened and his face slowly curled into a smile. "Really? 'Bout the same difference as pointing it at your own head. I don't miss. Where did you learn so much about commie duels?"

My entire body was shaking, and I don't think I'd ever seen him look calmer. He looked happy. It was the first time I'd ever seen him look happy.

"Books," I said.

"Yeah. You like to learn from books. But you don't learn to shoot from a book. I took my schooling overseas. I was a sniper. I was good at it. I could kill a man from half a mile away. Until I lost the arm. But I can still shoot pretty good."

He never talked to me about the war, and it almost made me want to ask him more. But why? Wasn't that what his telling was meant for? He was pleading his case by bragging. *I murdered your mother because I was trained to be a killer, and the world did that to me. It wasn't my fault.*

I paced off twenty steps, turned back to face him and waited, the gun hanging at my side.

He looked around. "So you really want me to stand here and fire away at you?"

"Those are the rules."

"Rules? Uh-huh. And why would we be fighting a Russian duel?"

"You have to match your tools to the rules," I said.

He looked at the pistol. "They're pretty tools."

"Shoot," I said.

207

In one motion he raised the pistol. I saw a flash and at the same instant felt something burn my ear. An instant later, I heard the whistle of the lead ball, which was already behind me, still flying. I reached up and touched my ear, looked at my fingers and saw my mother's blood. My ear burned like it had been touched by a branding iron, and there was a ringing sound that I thought might go on for the rest of my life. I felt queasy and knelt down on my hands and knees and vomited. There was not much in my stomach, but the dog, only a little frightened by the shot, came over to investigate and, holding my forehead in my bloody hands, I let him eat.

I'd set the gun down, so now I picked it up again and stood. My father was watching me, smiling. "Boy. These things really aren't very accurate, are they?" he said, raising the pistol to his forehead as though in salute. "I was aiming for the other ear."

The world spun a slow loop, leaning towards the equator.

"Are you okay?" he asked. "I guess it's your turn."

I raised the pistol and aimed it at my father's head, my hand shaking as though I was freezing to death.

"For Chrissakes, grab it with the other hand." He was smiling a grin that lit up his entire face. You couldn't fire at a man with that grin.

I lowered the pistol. "That would be against the rules."

"Two hands are against the rules?"

I nodded.

"Well, that's one I won't likely break," he said.

I touched my ear again. The pain had begun to numb, but the ringing had grown even louder—so loud that it had started to drown out what I could hear with the other ear. I felt like I was floating, the world far below me, Dad looking up at me. I was a kite and he was flying me. I looked away from him, down at the creek, and saw my mother floating by and floating by and floating by.

"Let's get this over with," he called.

I raised the pistol again, my hand shaking as badly as before.

"Oh, just a second. Let me put the dog in the truck. I wouldn't want you to hit him by accident." And he did, the dog whimpering. When that was done, he returned to his mark.

I raised the gun again.

"That's too high. Remember. The heart." He touched his metal finger to the centre of his chest.

I pulled the trigger.

The mark bloomed there in the centre of the forehead where I had imagined it would appear. He stood for what seemed like ten or twenty or maybe thirty seconds, his expression changing slowly to a look of delighted surprise (which gave me a fleeting sense of pleasure), before he finally dropped straight backwards like a falling tree.

He lay staring up at the sky. I don't remember walking towards him, but I do remember standing over him and saying, "When you bleed onto the earth, you're a piece of the sky. The world drinks up your blood and makes flowers." It was the eulogy I'd planned for him the night before, even though I knew I couldn't win. Something else I'd stolen from Dostoevsky.

I heard a siren announcing an arrival and looked around, only to realize it was my ears ringing. Dad's pistol was still clutched in his hand, so I pried it from his fingers and replaced both pistols in the velvet case. Prince jumped out of the truck when I opened the door. He rushed over and sniffed Dad's body, whimpering. When I started the truck, he jumped in the back.

Caroline's nanny has returned.

When I saw her waiting for Caroline after school, she mouthed the words, "See you tonight at yoga."

I followed the instructor, but as usual, I couldn't empty my head. I'm too tied up in the past to ever be in the moment. That's exactly what I told the nanny afterwards at the coffee shop.

"I can see that. You're barely even here," she agreed. "Where exactly are you?"

"I'm in Saskatchewan," I said. "I'll always be in Saskatchewan. I'll never really be here."

"Is it nice there?"

"Nice? What's nice? Where were you?"

She shook her head and had a drink of her coffee and finally said, "We had a fight and I left."

"Who had a fight?"

"Gloria and I. Caroline's mother."

"What happened?"

"Nothing."

"Tell me what happened."

"You don't want to know."

"I do. You can tell me."

She shook her head and crossed her arms. "I was cleaning the floor, down on my hands and knees working on this spot on the hardwood where the cat had barfed and it had been left to dry, and she wanted me to help her with something, and I told her she'd have to wait until I was finished. She doesn't like to be told to wait. When she wants something, she wants it right now, and she started screaming at me about how lazy and useless I am or the cat's barf would have been cleaned up before it dried on but instead I was off fucking some man all afternoon, and I was just so pissed off because I wished I'd been off fucking some man all afternoon that I told her she had one hell of a sense of entitlement. And she grabbed me by the hair and smashed my head on the floor."

"Oh, shit."

"It didn't hurt that much. It's only my head." She laughed. "But I got up and walked out the door, and she was screaming at me that if I didn't come back 'right this moment' I should never come back, and I told her that was just fine with me."

She looked out the window while she told me.

"So why are you back?"

She shrugged. "Don't make it into such a fucking catastrophe.

It wasn't that big a deal. I shouldn't have told you. She loses her temper, but she's always sorry after. And I have my part in it all. I push her buttons. I know exactly what to say to push her over the edge. I kind of like to see her lose control."

"Have you ever talked to your parents about this?"

"They're not really my parents. It's not that bad. She's good to me most of the time. Did my parents have any education fund for me?"

"Why don't you use your education fund? Why don't you go away to school?"

"It's nine o'clock," she said, looking at her wristwatch. "Do you know where your daughter is?"

"Yes."

"Where is she?"

"At home."

"Where's home?"

"That's a good question. That's always a good question."

"I'd like to hear the answer."

"Home is the house on the hill. Home is inside you. Home is at the end of a hallway above Queen Street."

"Let's go there," she said, and she stood up and left her coffee sitting and walked out the door. I had no choice but to follow her.

Despite Irvine's sentimental notions about my fellow worshippers, the congregation turned against me. The downside of being such a great hero that you are able to perform healings is that you just might be held responsible for your failures. Mrs. Greene had stopped appearing among us, and a rumour began to circulate that I had seduced her and was probably, in some mysterious way, responsible for Jimmy's death. The congregation listened. It was plain in the way they watched me and in the way they nodded nervously when I so much as smiled at any of them. It was also made clear when Pastor Tuttle announced, after the children had gone off to Sunday school classes, the subject of his sermon the next Sunday morning: "I want to talk to you about S-E-X."

Lilly Banks glanced towards me. Her mother, back in her wheelchair, was somewhere deep in the past and didn't seem to hear.

"Yes, that's right," Pastor Tuttle continued. "Every time you turn on the television they're talking about it, and every time you pick up a magazine or a newspaper they're talking about it; seems every time you turn around somebody's got something to say about it, and now you can't even get away from it on Sunday morning. Even Pastor Tuttle's talking about S-E-X. That's probably what you're thinking, and I don't blame you if you are. I don't blame you one bit. But what I want to say to you is a little different from what you're likely to have heard before: I'm not going to tell you how to have more or better S-E-X. I'm not going to tell you that it's good for you—'if it feels good, do it.' I'm not going to tell you that. Because that's not true. Lust is not good for you. It is that kind of attitude—that kind of worship of the ways of the flesh—that has led society down the path to destruction we are on."

I glanced at Irvine and he was staring off into space.

"It is that kind of attitude that leads to child abuse and teenage pregnancy and abortion and adultery and sinful, perverted acts that are performed sometimes even within the sanctity of marriage. That's right: even within the sacred bond of marriage, people are led astray. They tell themselves, 'It's only my wife I'm degrading in this way: God can't condemn me for what I do with my own wife.' As though marriage were a licence to sin. Is that what marriage is to you? Is marriage a licence to sin?"

Pastor Tuttle cast his gaze around the congregation.

"It is not. It is not. It is not!"

He actually hammered his fist on the pulpit.

Gloria, very pale, did not look my way when I glanced at her.

After church that day, Gloria snuck down to my room and we made love, but for the first time I could feel her feeling self-conscious, and it made me angry, even though she insisted she was worried her parents might hear us. I told her that Pastor Tuttle was a fool and that

I was glad I'd be gone from Broken Head by next Sunday and I'd never have to hear one of his sermons again.

"Yes, Dwight will be in Calgary. And I'm supposed to throw away my entire life and come and meet him there. And what exactly is it we're going to do in Calgary? Where and how are we going to live?"

"You don't like Calgary? We'll go to Vancouver. We'll figure it all out when we get there."

"So you keep saying. That's not much of a plan. You've never even been to Calgary. Or Vancouver."

"What difference does that make?"

"No difference. I just wonder if you've really thought about my position in all of this. What's my family going to think? Are you asking me to give up my family? Just because you don't have a family doesn't mean my family isn't important to me."

"I'm sure they're very important to you. Where's this coming from all of a sudden?"

"From me. From Gloria. The woman you're asking to give up her life to be with you. Gloria has had to start thinking about what's important to her."

She wouldn't look at me.

"I'm sure Nick's very important to you. Isn't he practically family?"

She got up and grabbed her panties and started putting them on. "Maybe he is. Maybe he's a lot smarter than you give him credit for. Nick wouldn't be taking off to Calgary with no plan whatsoever."

She put on her bra.

"I guess he'd have his daddy's credit card. Is that what you mean by a plan?"

"It's more of a plan than you've got. Do you think you can make fun of people just because they have money? It's not their fault they have money."

"Maybe I don't think money's quite as important as you do."

She stepped into her jeans. "No, money's not important and family's not important. We'll live off manna from the sky, won't we, Dwight?"

"Not if we don't have faith."

"Faith in what? Faith in the goodness of Calgary?" She buttoned up her blouse.

"You're ashamed of me. I can see that you're ashamed of me."

"Yes," she said. "I'm ashamed. What do you expect? What is there to be proud of? That you shot your father through the head?"

Gloria walked out, slamming the door behind her.

A few hours later I frantically rushed to the door to answer two faint knocks, imagining that it was her, but it was her father. He was pale, his eyes sunken into his skull. Every time I saw him he looked weaker, and I wondered why Gloria never mentioned this and why I never mentioned it to her. I assumed he was feeling the stress of planning the coming wedding and of having me in their lives. Broken Head was watching, and all those eyes were hurting.

"You all right?" I asked.

"I'm fine. A little tired, but I'm fine. Gloria told me you told her that your windows at the farm have all been smashed, I'm sorry. I reported it to the police, and I've called someone who's going out tomorrow to replace them. Your insurance will cover it."

"My insurance?" I said.

"Yes. I thought the place needed to be in a better state if you're thinking of selling it and going away. Can I come in?"

I wanted to ask him why he never asked me up out of the basement of the Irvine house for our little talks, but instead I stood back and let him in. He sank into the chair at the table, breathing deeply as if to catch his breath from the effort of the three steps across my tiny room. I sat down across the table from him.

"Shall we have tea?" he said.

I nodded and obeyed, running some water in the kettle and placing it on the stove. "I'll be gone in a week," I said.

"It's your decision."

I was at the sink, rinsing out the teapot with hot water, and I glanced at him, but he wasn't looking at me. I'd expected him to insist I shouldn't go, as he'd done so many times before. "You're certainly welcome to stay," he finally said.

"I'm not welcome. Mrs. Irvine doesn't want me here."

He didn't answer. I dropped the tea bags into the pot.

"I'm sure Gloria would like you to stay for her wedding," he said. "You're definitely invited."

I didn't respond. When I turned back to him, he was holding his head in his hands. Finally, he sighed and looked me in the eye. "What makes you think everyone hates you?"

"I see it in their eyes."

He shook his head. "All you see is your own reflection."

"What do you mean by that? You mean I hate myself? Maybe you're right. After all, I am a killer. And not just because I killed my father. I have other blood on my hands. But it's God who kills for me. The Old Motherfucker has killed so many for me. So many dead and rotting. I wish them dead and they die. I've been chosen. I'm my father's son."

He kept shaking his head, refusing to look at me. "I wish you wouldn't blame God," he said.

"Who else is there to blame? God warned my father I'd kill him."

"Even if that were true, He'd only have been telling your father what you would do. It was you who acted."

"Okay. You're right. I'm responsible. I'm not trying to duck responsibility. I have the blood of the man who killed my mother in my veins. I wonder how many he killed in Europe. You could see it in his eyes. That's the man who fathered me. And he was me. And I am him. How else could I have killed him so easily?"

He was still shaking his head. "I've told you, your father didn't kill your mother."

"I don't believe you. I don't believe your scientific conclusions. I believe in God, and God tells me my father is guilty."

"No," he said, springing to his feet so alarmingly fast that I stepped back. "God didn't tell you any such thing. God doesn't lie." His eyes were full of a strange kind of light. "Turn off the kettle. Let's go for a walk."

He stepped out the door and crossed the basement to my private entrance, not even bothering to glance back to see if I was following. I switched off the kettle and hurried to keep up with him.

The world was immersed in brilliant orange light. The trees were heavy with green leaves that would soon change colour and drop to the ground. You could already see the fall in that orange light. I strode down the street beside Gloria's father. Despite the weariness he'd claimed when he entered my room, he walked so fast that I could barely keep up with him. Neither of us spoke. A few cars passed, and I felt the drivers watching. When we reached the hospital, he led me around to the back, past the garbage bins, and we entered through the basement door to the morgue.

Inside, he switched on the bank of overhead fluorescents. There were his tools, all clean and gleaming and lying in their rows exactly as I'd imagined them.

"I want to show you something," he said. "Are you ready?" I nodded and he pulled out a sliding gurney that held a body. It was covered with a sheet, but I could make out the form of a man beneath it, and for a second I thought it would be my father, still waiting for me to collect him here over a year after I'd killed him. Irvine pulled back the sheet. It was an elderly man I'd never seen before.

"Dwight, do you know Mr. Gardner?"

There was no soul to face in Mr. Gardner, so I turned to Irvine and looked him in the eye. "No. How are you, Mr. Gardner?"

I couldn't help myself. It sounded like he was introducing me.

"Not well," Irvine said. "Not well at all. You see, Mr. Gardner had a weakness for the elixir of the gin berry, a passion that he brought with him from England and had been indulging ever since, with no great harm to anyone, until yesterday afternoon, when he tripped on the edge of his carpet, a carpet he'd walked over who knows how many million times. He must have stepped backwards and caught his heel. You see?"

He strained to roll the corpse on its side, and I helped him. He pointed out a contusion on the back of the corpse's head. "That's all it took."

I stared dully at the wound. "He's an old man," I said. "My mother wasn't old."

"He didn't die of old age. He died of a knock to the head. We're much more fragile creatures than we sometimes imagine. A hard knock in the wrong place and we're gone." He allowed the body to roll back and raised his hands slowly, palms towards me, to show me the old man's and my mother's souls exiting to the sky.

"How can you be so sure he wasn't pushed?"

His face fell and his hands descended until they were hanging at his sides. I could see tears in his eyes. "His wife came home from visiting a neighbour and found him."

"His wife could have been upset by his drinking. That sometimes happens in families. How do you know she didn't push him?"

He sighed with a fatigue so great that it sounded as if he might have lain down and slept right there. "The blow killed him," he said. "His wife didn't have the strength to hit him that hard."

"But wouldn't she have had the strength to push him and make him fall? He was drunk. He was old. His balance wasn't good. It wouldn't take much."

"The fall killed him," he said, pulling the sheet up over Mr. Gardner's face and pushing the gurney back into the wall. He turned and walked to the door. I still hadn't moved. He opened the door for me and stood with his hand over the light switch, suddenly impatient to go. Something about being there, among the dead, fascinated me: the sharp smell of disinfectant, the polished floor, the gleaming tools. I wanted him to show me more.

"It was an accident," I said.

His hand was still at the switch, threatening to plunge us into darkness, but he waited for me to lift my feet and walk past him into the night, and finally I did.

It was dark. There was a sort of sweet smell in the air that was probably beef barbecuing but made me think of gopher poison. Six years before, my father had given me careful instructions on how to mix the tiny tin cans of Fairview poison with wheat, and I had walked around the pasture with a pail, spilling the poisoned grain down the gopher holes with a plastic scoop so the gophers would eat and die underground.

I could hear Irvine's heavy footsteps beside me. "I'm sorry," I told him without looking at him, but he didn't respond.

When we reached the end of the block, he turned instead of heading for the house, and I followed him. At the end of that block we came to a small park and he led me into the trees, heading towards the grey outline of the playground equipment in the far corner. The playground was empty. Before we had reached the playground, he stopped.

"I'm dying," he said.

And I knew that it was true. I knew that it was this he'd brought me there to tell me. He was dying. He was practically dead.

"What do you mean?"

"Gloria doesn't know," he said. "No one knows except for me. I've done some tests. I've found a cancer. I'm not going to have it treated."

He had turned away from me, so that I was listening to his voice moving off into the trees, getting farther and farther away.

"Why not have it treated? Why would you do that?"

He shrugged and turned to look at me, but instead of answering he began to walk again until he reached the swings and, to my surprise, sank down onto the plastic seat. He smiled, his face pale and beaded with sweat. I stood there and watched him. He was dying. I could see him dying in front of me.

"It was me who pushed your mother," he said.

He threw his head back and lifted his feet off the ground, pumping his legs furiously until he was swinging and swinging higher and higher. I stood there watching him until he'd drained his strength and was clutching the chains of the swings in the crooks of his arms, riding his spent momentum.

"What?" I asked.

For a long time he didn't answer. I clung to an assumption that there was some trick to what he'd said, some lesson he wanted to teach me, and I stood waiting for him to portion it out to me. He didn't mean a real push, of course, but some parable of a push in his own life that led to the place where she had arrived and made her fall too heavily.

"Your mother," he finally said. The swing was still moving, but it had lost most of its energy. He lifted his head to look at me, and I could see that he was frowning. "I pushed your mother, and she fell and hit her head on a rock." There was no scorn in his face. It was a different sort of frown.

"Pardon?" I said.

I was floating in the air above us, looking down at the tops of our heads, watching our shapes breathing in the night.

He began to cry, bitterly, and he might have been Jimmy crying that he would not be allowed to watch the end of the movie until tomorrow because he needed his sleep.

"I just pushed her. She would not stop touching me. She was trying to make love to me. She had asked me out to your farm under false pretences. She was working on the cancer campaign I was organizing, and she told me she needed to talk to me about something important that had to do with the campaign. She left me a map she'd drawn and a note to meet her. I was curious and I went. The map guided me to what turned out to be your pasture, and when I got there she tried to make love to me. I told her *no*, it could not be the way she wanted it to be. I could not make love to

219

her. I did not make love to her. I *never* made love to her. I would not. She tried to seduce me and I would not be seduced. I've never been unfaithful to Emily. Mrs. Greene, too, wanted me to be unfaithful. I wouldn't do it to Emily and Gloria. But your mother would not give up, so to make her feel what I felt, I gave her a push. I am a married man and she would not respect that, so I pushed her away and she tripped. Just like Mr. Gardner. She fell straight backwards. There was this rock. I told you about the rock. It wasn't in the creek, but there was a rock. I did not lie about the rock. I could take you out there and show you that rock right now."

He stopped talking and stared at me, his eyes pleading for God to descend from the sky in a beautiful machine and rescue him. There were crickets. I don't believe I noticed them until that moment. They were just there, rubbing their legs together the way they always do, and I didn't really hear them until his tongue stopped moving. I was thinking about my father's look before he fell backwards. My father, innocent for the first time in my lifetime.

"Just a push," I said. "And how did she get in the creek? And how did the blood get on the rock in the creek?"

Still swaying very slightly on the swing, he looked at the ground.

"You want me to give you a push?" I asked.

He looked up but didn't answer.

"God killed her," I said. "She died for our sins."

"She wasn't innocent," he protested, shaking his head.

"But you are. It's God who killed her."

"All I did was push her," he said. "A little push. I can show you the rock."

"No," I said. "I don't want to see the rock."

"I'm sorry. I can imagine what you're feeling right now."

"Can you?"

"I wanted to tell you. I've wanted to tell you right from the start, that day in your hospital room. It was very hard not to tell you. But now I've told you, and I'm glad."

There were so many things I had wanted to say to my father when I thought he'd killed her that suddenly occurred to me.

"I'm so happy you feel satisfied. And what is it you want from me now? You want me to forgive you? You want me to forgive you for killing my mother? And blaming my father?"

He was looking right at me. "I never blamed your father. You did. What we both need to think about right now is Gloria."

He was looking directly into my eyes with those gentle grey eyes of his, which I suddenly realized were more terrible than any eyes I'd ever seen. I wanted to grab a stick and poke out those eyes. I turned and walked away from him for a few steps and then whirled around and walked back towards him.

"I'd like to kill you," I shouted.

"I understand," he said. "But as I've told you, I'm already dying. I haven't even sought out treatment. Emily has been trying to convince me to see my doctor, but I haven't, and it's already too late now. It's God's will. I started feeling it growing in me the day I pushed your mother. Being part of her death is killing me. Do you understand? Sometimes I'll forget, sometimes for a whole hour. But then I remember."

Blood pounded through my brain. Maybe God had already answered me. He was dying. If I was chosen, wasn't he doomed? I thought of the mark of the bullet appearing on my father's forehead and the look of surprise as it passed through his brain. Jacob Froese the innocent.

"So confess," I said.

"I just did."

"That's not good enough."

The swing had lost all energy by now and hung straight down, but his arms were still locked around the chains, clinging on for dear life. He opened his mouth, but didn't speak. After a few moments he managed to form the words. "You want me to do that to Gloria? You want Gloria to go through that hell? Think about it. Think about Gloria."

Gloria. He didn't really want Jacob Froese to be innocent in the eyes of Broken Head and the world. He was still bargaining. He was looking for loopholes. He wanted a pardon.

"You make me want to puke," I said.

He sighed and wearily stood.

"Good evening, Dwight," he said, and he walked away.

EIGHT

"I'm in here," she says, raising a sheet of paper with her right hand.

"Yes. You're in there."

"Why am I just called 'the nanny'? Why don't I have a name?"

"Your name is a secret," I say.

She lowers the paper and sets it back on the pile, her eyes still on me. "But you wrote this for Caroline. Her name is in here. Caroline knows my name."

"I haven't finished it," I say. "I can put in your name if you want."

I'd made her a cup of tea, and she'd moved from the couch to the table in the kitchen nook. I'm at my desk, the computer the only light in this half of the room.

"No," she says, looking down at the next sentence, already reading again. "My name is a secret."

There's an alleyway in Broken Head where at night you can approach the floodlit front of the courthouse, a great stone building with fluted columns (in the style of the Americans copying the Romans copying the Greeks) at the top of a long staircase. You walk uphill as you approach. The stairs and the building are framed by the darkened alley. Once you've reached the courthouse, you can walk past the grand building and around it to the back. There, across the street, another alley begins. If you walk up this alleyway, you are approaching the oldest school in Broken Head, but instead of the front door, you approach a gothic, arched red wooden side door. The school dates from a time when boys and girls had separate entrances, and in the daytime you can see the word "Boys" etched into the stone above the red door. A single dim bulb lights the door so that only the red arch of the entrance is visible as you approach from the darkened alleyway.

I approached that door and stood there staring, but it did not open.

I went home and Gloria was there waiting for me, wondering where I'd been. I told her I couldn't sleep and so I'd gone for a walk.

"You were at Mrs. Greene's," she said.

"No," I said. "I wasn't. I was just walking around."

"I don't believe you. You're lying. I can see that you're lying."

It's hard not to look like you're lying when you're lying. At least, it is for me. I'd already learned that you need to look a person in the eye when you're lying, but sometimes that's just too difficult.

"I was with your father. He told me something. A secret."

"What secret?"

"He asked me not to tell you."

"What did he tell you, Dwight?"

"He asked me not to tell you. He'll have to tell you himself. I told him to tell you."

She started to ask me again, but I told her it wasn't for me to say. Instead, I told her about my walk and my approach to the courthouse and the old school, but she wasn't interested. She nodded blankly and turned away from me. I didn't want to let her go, and so I tried to embrace her, but she shrugged me off.

"I don't know what to do, Dwight. When are you leaving?"

"The day after tomorrow. You know what to do."

And then she let me kiss her, and we went to the bed and made love for the last time. I think I even knew it would be the last time. Afterwards, I must have drifted off to sleep, because when I woke up she was dressing and had left before I could tell her that her father was a killer and so she should have no need for her family anymore.

I rolled over and tried my best to sleep.

Our entire union lasted less than three weeks from first kiss to last. Or was it three days? Or three minutes? My entire life is focused on those three parts of time. There were all the years of dreaming about her before the three weeks, and there have been all the years since of remembering those three weeks. Remembering and dismembering the memories: laying them out and cutting them up and holding them to the light for inspection. And asking to be forgiven. But there could be no forgiveness without a confession.

Sometimes I wonder if it ever happened at all. Maybe the second Gloria was as much a devil as the first. After all, the person who I began the three weeks with doesn't correspond with the person who dismissed me when the three weeks were over, and certainly has nothing in common with the woman I see through the kitchen window when I'm sitting and watching her house from under her neighbour's pergola. I'm not sure who *she* is. And she's looking after Caroline. Has the devil moved inside her and taken control of my daughter's life? I worry about that. Here I am, nothing but a janitor, when what my daughter really needs is a father.

The final week is the blurriest of them all. I must have gone for many walks, wandering past the library and down to the creek, walking the pathway they'd built there for walking. Mothers strolled by pushing strollers. There were joggers and in-line skaters in sweatsuits, burning off calories and making their hearts work harder. Maybe they stared at me because they recognized me as the hero from the news the year before. Maybe it was because I looked as though I'd been sleeping in my clothes and my dazed expression made them think I might murder them or their children. Heroes may become dangerous once they've stepped down off the pedestal.

Mostly I stayed in my room and waited for Gloria, but she came less and less and for shorter and shorter visits. Her mother needed her. Her father needed her. Nick needed her. No one needed me. I didn't ask how the wedding arrangements were going.

It bothers me particularly that I can't with any certainty remember anything about making love with her that last time. I might remember, but I could just as well be remembering some other time. I do remember that I woke up afterwards and it was the middle of the night, but she was up and slipping into her clothes.

"Gloria?"

She froze. "Sorry I woke you," she whispered. "I gotta go. I'm sorry."

"It's okay," I said. "It's your family. We have to do what our family needs us to do. Don't we?" I didn't whisper, and my voice in the dark sounded like some great being declaring some great truth.

She turned and was gone.

It was past noon when I woke again, halfway through another day. Another half-day of my life I'd missed, and I wished I could go back to sleep and not wake up. I tried my best to pretend that what had happened the night before hadn't happened. I didn't want to think about what I didn't want to think about. If she hadn't been my mother, what difference would it make? She'd be another dead woman buried under the earth. And I was alive, and I was in love, and she couldn't be brought back. It wasn't for her I'd be doing it. She wouldn't have wanted it. Why would she want someone to stand up and swear on a Bible and tell that filthy story. Her part was just embarrassing. To have thrown herself at him and have him push her away. What a pitiful woman. Always needing to be looked at, always needing to be touched. It wasn't the way to be remembered. Better to be murdered by your husband and die innocent of your own death.

I made coffee and sat at the table, breathing in the smell of ground roasted beans grown far away. The smell wound through my brain and made the memory of the night before all too clear. A knock came at the door, and I got up and opened it. Dr. Andrew Irvine looked ready to fall. All it would take was a little push. He seemed surprised that I'd answered the door so quickly, as if he'd expected I'd have to walk miles to let him into that tiny room.

"I need to talk to you," he said so softly it was almost a whisper.

"Sit down," I said, but he just stood in the doorway, looking at me.

"What do you want from me?" he asked.

"Nothing," I said.

"What did you say to Gloria?"

"I told her you told me a secret. I said you'd have to tell her."

He nodded slowly. "She came and asked me. I told her I'm ill. I told her I'm dying."

"Is that what you said?"

"What good would it do anybody to tell her more?"

I looked up and stared at the ceiling. There was a spiderweb there, wavering in a draft, but I'm sure he thought I was looking at God. Perhaps it was a kind of evidence of a god that had once been near, that spiderweb: a small god with eight legs and a taste for flies.

"Gloria might even be proud of you," I said. "For confessing." I looked down to see if he was looking up, but he was staring straight into my eyes.

"You don't really believe that," he said. "This is just revenge."

I looked back up at the spiderweb. It was amazing the draft it revealed in what seemed such a still place. Both the strand of web and the shadow of the strand were wavering in a breeze I couldn't feel.

"There's a draft," I said.

I looked back down at him, and I could tell he thought I meant something more than what I'd said, which fascinated me. I really didn't mean anything more than that there was a draft. I wanted to ask him what it was that he believed I meant, or what it was the spider meant, or what it was the shadow meant. I wanted to tell him that none of it meant anything and that there was no possibility of God in a world so full of accidents.

"She'll hate you, you know," he said, as if that were an answer. "She'll never forgive you."

And he turned and walked away, past his own dirty laundry. It was lying there, beside the washing machine, that literal dirty laundry. Later that day, the woman they hired to do that kind of thing came and dealt with it.

Gloria didn't come down for the rest of the day. When she finally did that evening, she explained that she'd had to spend time with her mother, who was distraught. She'd gone with her to the doctor to get her a sedative.

"She's losing it completely. She couldn't stop crying. I didn't really believe she even loved him, but when I made him tell her, she just dissolved. She must really love him."

"She's sleeping?" I asked, and she nodded. "Is that the only reason you came?"

"Pardon?"

"You couldn't come when she was awake. You didn't want her to notice or to upset her any more than she was already upset, and coming down to me would upset her. Telling her the wedding was off would upset her. Moving to Calgary with me would upset her."

She looked me in the eye, and I could see fear and shame and anger in her eyes. I wanted her to confess.

"I wanted to be with her," she said.

"And where was your father?"

"At his doctor's. He had an appointment."

"An appointment," I said.

"Mom and I wanted to go with him, but he wouldn't let us because Mom would have made too much of a spectacle."

I was going to tell her. Her eyes were begging me not to tell her, as if she already knew, and that made me very angry. The words were almost out of my mouth, but I managed to stop myself. I brushed past her, opened the door and stepped into the basement, wanting to get away before I said what I wanted to say.

"Where are you going?" she called, but I didn't answer.

I drove out to the farm. The windows had been replaced, paid for by my insurance. I was nineteen years old, and I was having windows paid for by insurance. It made me feel very mature. There was nothing but wisdom between me and old age.

I got a grain shovel and a broom and began to clean up the broken glass and the bird shit. I was a janitor, and it felt good sweeping the mess into a shovel. There was so much order to be had in the removal of fragments of jagged glass and shit and plain old dust from my mother's linoleum.

In the corner by the sofa and below the window beside the stove, I found a dead pigeon and a dead sparrow. The glass people hadn't even bothered to try to chase them out before they'd put in the windows. Too much of a hurry. I swept the birds into the shovel and dumped them into the old pesticide pail I was using to collect the garbage. Birds and glass and dirt and shit.

That night there was moonlight coming through my slot of window into my basement room. My last night of work started at nine. Tomorrow I would go to Calgary and wait for Gloria to come to me. I was lying on the bed with my eyes closed, and something passed across me. I opened my eyes to see what was there and saw the moon. Outside my window, in the sky, where the moon belongs, was the moon. A pink moon, obscured by the sheen of a layer of thin cloud.

Sometime in the next hour, Gloria came to me very happy and excited. "He's okay!" she said.

"Who? What do you mean?"

229

"Dad. The doctor talked to Mom. They've done all sorts of tests and the doctor can't find anything wrong with him."

I sat up in the bed, and she waited for me to say how pleased I was that her father was well, but I didn't and so she kept talking. "There's nothing wrong with him. It's like a miracle. It's all in his head. Something mental. All the stress, I guess. He needs a rest. All he needs is a rest."

"All the stress," I said. "It's going to be difficult to tell him that you're not going to marry Nick. How can you possibly tell him?"

Her smile faded and she looked grimly at me. "We need to talk, Dwight."

I could see what she was there to tell me, hoping I might take it reasonably well because it was all for the sake of her father, and so I thought I'd have my say first.

"My dad didn't kill my mother."

She stared at the wall above me. "I believe you," she said.

"Your dad did. Your dad killed her."

Her face went through a slow transformation that marked her changed forever. "That's not funny," she said.

"No. It's not funny. He pushed her. He was having an affair with her, and he got rid of her because he was scared she'd tell your mother. She threatened to tell your mom. So he killed her."

It was a very strange sort of calm that had come over me and now came over her. She began to move towards the door.

"He says he did it for your sake. That doesn't mean it's your fault. It isn't your fault."

I didn't like the way she was looking at me, so I looked up for the strand of spiderweb. It was still there, still moving in the breeze I couldn't feel.

"You liar," she said.

I lowered my eyes to her, expecting to see the devil, but she didn't have the same easy smile. It was her, though. She had returned, or she had been there all along.

"Your dad killed your mother," she said.

She turned and walked out the door, slamming it closed behind her.

The next morning, after my last night of washing away the pestilences of Broken Head, I was drinking a cup of coffee when the door burst open and Irvine walked in. He stood staring at me but didn't speak.

"Hello," I said. "I hear you're much better than you think."

He went to Gloria's chair and sat there across from me. His face was a funny shade of purple, and he was sweating like he'd just finished a race.

"Too hot for tea?"

He didn't answer. I got up, filled the kettle and put it on the stove. Irvine watched me all the while, but didn't speak. I rinsed out the teapot with hot water and put in two tea bags. When I was finished, I sat back down across from him. He kept staring at me, his eyes burning. I decided he must be waiting for me to explain myself.

"I think you're right about my being chosen," I said. "It's a painful thing to be in the hands of the living God."

He was staring at me, and I stared back at him. He didn't look away. I got up and took some cups from the cupboard and placed them on the counter. When I turned back, Irvine had a pistol pointed at me. His hand was shaking, but I could see that it was one of my father's pistols—a pistol I may have watched my father making on his lathe. I wondered where he might have come across my father's pistol. Maybe he got it from Chandler. Or from the police. I stared into his eyes, begging him to shoot.

A minute passed. He was still pointing the pistol, his hand still shaking, and I knew that he wouldn't pull the trigger. He didn't have the courage to turn his back completely on his god. The kettle whistled. I turned my back on him and went to the stove, picked up the kettle and poured the water into the teapot.

"Milk, but no sugar?"

He lowered the pistol and stood. "Come to church tomorrow," he said.

He walked out the door.

I poured myself a cup of tea and breathed in the steam.

Later that morning I heard a chair pull back, and when I looked up from staring into my cup, my father was sitting across from me.

"Hello," he said.

I set down my spoon. I'd been stirring, simply to hear the sound of the metal tinkling the porcelain.

"Hello," I said.

He looked around at the room, scratching his chin with his good hand in exactly the way he had always scratched his chin with his good hand. "I see you've found a home to match the size of your soul," he said.

He lifted his left hand from his lap and placed it on the table, and it was a real hand, of real flesh and blood. At least, it looked that way, and I wanted to reach out and touch it. But it was my father's hand, so I couldn't.

"You mother-fucking son of a bitch," I said.

"Fathers are supposed to fuck mothers," He said. "It's part of the job description."

"But not conceive Himself. That's just disgusting. Who could think that was anything but disgusting?"

"Is it really?" He said. "I always thought it was beautiful. But you wouldn't recognize beauty if it shot you between the eyes."

I waved the spoon in his face. "I'll give You beautiful. If this were a knife, I'd kill You right now. I'd kill You and I'd cut You up into pieces and flush You down the toilet one by one until there was nothing left of You but the blood and the bones. And then I'd wash away the blood. But I'd keep the bones. I'd put them in the sun and let them bleach nice and white, and I'd sell them to the first man who'd have them."

232

"Be wasting a lot of good eating. There's a knife over there in the drawer," He said, pointing the six feet to the other side of the room. He reached out with that left hand of His, and I let Him pinch my cheek.

"Are you God, or are you the devil?" I asked.

"Has anyone ever seen us in the same room at the same time?"

I got to my feet and walked across the room and opened a drawer. I found a pad of paper and opened another drawer.

"What are you looking for?" He asked.

"A pen," I said. "I want to write that down."

"Write it down," He said, and when I didn't respond, He smiled and said, "Then burn it."

He got up and walked out the door.

"You really believe you're Caroline's father?" the nanny asked.

She'd stopped reading long before the end, and I was filling her in with the details.

"I am Caroline's father."

"And you really believe that you've spoken to God."

"No. I don't really believe that. I remember it, but I don't really believe it could have happened. He was sitting as close as you, but I don't really believe He was there. At the same time, I wish I could believe in Him. I wish I could believe in something. Anything at all. That's what I want, more than anything else in the world. But I'm afraid of what He wants. I'm afraid He might want me to kill someone else."

"You really believe that? Why would God want that?"

"Read the newspapers. Read your history books. Isn't that mostly what God wants? Isn't that mostly what He's always wanted?"

"You should talk to someone," she said. She was already edging her way towards the door.

"I am. I'm talking to you."

She nodded, but it wasn't like she was nodding at me anymore. She was nodding at someone else who neither of us had met. "That's good. But I have to go now. You should talk to someone else."

"I should talk to someone else?" I said. "Who should I talk to?"

"I don't know," she said. "I've got to go now."

"You're going to tell her, aren't you?" I said. "You're going to tell Gloria."

She opened the door, about to walk away, but she stopped and met my eyes. "Yes," she said. "I think I'd better tell her."

She waited for me to respond, and when I didn't, she stepped outside.

"Goodbye," she said.

She closed the door.

Oh, to be chosen.

While snow-blowing the walks yesterday (the school has one of those ride-on snow blowers), I watched a group of boys playing soccer in the snow, first dividing up into their teams. Some of them danced around, swinging their arms in the air, trying to get the captains' attentions, shouting "Pick me, pick me!"

God is not a captain on the playground, Caroline.

But He is looking for me. By the time you read this, He'll likely have found me, and I'll have said goodbye to my little room with the red door and gone up to Him. Unless that was Him who passed away the other day.

You girls, too, like to be chosen. Don't you? There are those special groups you all want to belong to, and later on, at school dances, you'll wait in the dark for someone to choose you. It's an eternal recurrence. Maybe it's actually the girlfriends who tell the boys who to choose, but you still have to wait for the boy you've chosen to brave your rejection and choose you. No one even notices how perfectly clean the floor is, and when they're through they go away and leave their messes with the confident expectation that when they return on Monday morning for gym class it'll all be clean again. An eternal recurrence.

I chose your mother and she chose me, and together we made you whole. Or were we chosen? What difference does it make in the end? We aren't together, and you, my daughter, don't even know who I am. If we were chosen, we were chosen to be apart. Your grandfather chose to bring us together so that he could tell me his secret. He gave me the choice to stay silent, and I made the mistake of telling your mother. Irvine chose and I chose and your mother chose. I don't really believe it was God. I don't want to believe in a God so terrible that He would make those sorts of choices. He allowed us to choose and that is His great beauty. There is no beauty in a god who chooses for us.

And now I've chosen you. I'll give you this terrible confession and so absolve myself in the eyes of a God who recently froze, alone, on a subway grate. Did you not read about it in the newspaper? He, of course, was the man with no name, and I've written this for you and for Him. It's all so neat and tidy. Why bother to wait when to eternity it's all the blink of an eye? I'll stow these pages and words in your backpack tomorrow while you're out at recess and let you decide what to do with it all. If they don't fire me when I arrive at work tomorrow.

If that's the case, I'll have to take you away somewhere with me, on a boat (or maybe all we'd need right now is a skidoo to get across the ice) out to one of those islands in the bay where your cottage is, and we'll break into one of those log cabins with a fireplace that burns large logs and I'll read the whole thing to you. I'll bet you like to be read to. I need for you to know that I killed an innocent man who was your grandfather. He wasn't innocent of much, but he was innocent of my mother's death, which was what I chose to kill him for. It was really your other grandfather who was guilty. And I chose not to kill him.

So what does my life mean?

I arrived a few minutes before the service began and sat in a pew near the back, where I looked around at the people watching me. Every time I turned, there was someone looking, holding their gaze a breath too long before they looked away. All those yellowed old eyes. The congregation was mostly old and wrinkled and grey, even there, in that church that had striven to attract the radical youth. They were not

235

so successful. In Broken Head, the average age is old, and most youth are not radical enough to go to church.

Gloria and her father were there, as I'd expected, but I was shocked to see her mother there too. Gloria caught sight of me, and for a moment I fantasized that she might call me forward to sit with her and her family, but she turned away. A moment later, Irvine turned and saw me, and then he turned away too. I knew for certain in that moment that I had lost her. I considered getting up and leaving, until I remembered that she was not the reason I was there. I was there for my mother. No. I was there for my father.

Mrs. Greene was nowhere to be seen that Sunday. She had given up on God. I didn't know where to look, so I stared straight ahead at the cross adorning the wall behind the pulpit. If He'd died two hundred years ago instead of two thousand, there might have been a guillotine up there; fifty years and it might have been an electric chair. I wished they hadn't stuck so literally to the commandment against graven images so that He might have been represented hanging there, staring back at me through His calm, suffering eyes. I wondered if the cross itself was not a graven image. I needed to see Him seeing me. There's a great beauty in Christ, and I needed to believe in that beauty even when I couldn't look Him in the eye.

I thought of the woman at the well, and I thought of Him saying, "Let he who is without sin cast the first stone."

Pastor Tuttle appeared in the doorway he always appeared from and walked up to the pulpit. He was such a serious man, and that day he looked particularly serious as he surveyed his flock, his eyes halting when he saw me watching him from my pew near the back. He gave me a long, grim look to scold me before he announced the first hymn.

They stood and sang together about the glory of God. I remained seated, thinking about that woman by the well whom the crowd was about to stone for her sins. Jesus saved her. Did Jesus ever do anything more beautiful than that? I did not feel like singing. The old woman next to the old man at the other end of my mostly empty pew kept glancing over at me.

Next, Pastor Tuttle led them in a prayer pronouncing the glory of God. He spoke and they answered, and at the end they said Amen. I didn't answer.

Once they'd sat down, and after he'd called Mrs. Banks forward to make a few announcements about the flea market and other fundraising efforts, Pastor Tuttle began to speak. Like many of his sermons, his words were directed at the evils and temptations of the world that existed just beyond the doors of his church. On that day, though, he was particularly passionate, and during his entire sermon he kept his eyes on me.

"There are those who question the existence of God. He is all around them, and yet they persist in questioning His existence. He stands before them and asks them to feel the holes in His hands, but they turn away and say that they would prefer not to feel. They do not want to touch their Lord. They want to be alone. They are ashamed, and so they do not want to believe that God looks down on their shame and weeps for them.

"These same people often question whether Satan exists. Incredible, isn't it? With all the pain, the horror, the wallowing mire of sin that we see around us in the world today, how could anyone question whether the devil exists?"

He stared at me so steadily I was tempted to stand and answer him. But I didn't have the courage.

"How could anyone possibly question that this world is under the grip of an evil dictator? Think again. Think about it a little harder. To whose advantage is it if people begin to delude themselves into thinking that the devil does not exist? Why, to Satan's advantage, of course. If people are off their guard, he can operate unopposed. He can steal their souls without them even knowing their souls have been lost. For he's fooled them into believing that they have no souls. The soul is of no more consequence to them than the cork they pull from the bottle to get to the wine. 'You don't want that cork, do you?' he asks them, and they shake their heads and throw him the cork and he catches it and drops it into his pocket for his collection. And they drink down the wine until they are passing out with drunkenness. They prefer to believe that their souls are worth nothing. But that illusion will be as temporary as their life on earth, for when their body dies, that soul they refused to believe in will be thrown into hellfire! And believe you me, then they will believe."

It was at precisely that moment in Pastor Tuttle's sermon that Dr. Irvine rose and solemnly began his walk up the aisle. Pastor Tuttle paused when he saw him approaching, but continued speaking as he watched him come closer, perhaps hoping that he might head through the door that Pastor Tuttle always appeared from and find his way to some necessary relief in the washroom.

"And what will hell be like for those sinners? Imagine the bodies of all the sinners in history piled on top of each other—Cleopatra, Caligula, Attila the Hun, Marie Antoinette, Napoleon, Adolf Hitler, Eva Braun, Marilyn Monroe, John Fitzgerald Kennedy, Pierre Trudeau—all the sinners in history piled on top of each other and rotting, but forced to suffer their own putrefaction, their own burning at the flames of the foul, stinking brimstone, and you can imagine hell. A place of no light, for the hellfire burns without light . . ."

He stopped as Irvine began to climb the stairs to the pulpit.

"Andrew? What is it . . . ?"

A moment later Irvine stood beside him, looking calmly into his eyes, waiting for the microphone. Pastor Tuttle tried to return the look, but was forced to turn away.

"Friends, it would seem that our friend Andrew Irvine would like to speak to us today . . . about something."

Pastor Tuttle shuffled over and down one step, and Irvine took his place behind the pulpit. He searched for only a moment until he found my eyes, and then he hung his head.

"I have something I need to tell all of you." He cleared his throat. "A little over a year ago, I killed a young woman. Eva Froese. Dwight Froese's mother. And then, in my professional capacity, I called that murder an accident. And it was an accident. But that accident was also a murder, and I stand here today to confess it . . . before God. As proof of what I say, here is a note she wrote to me the day before she died, inviting me and giving me directions to visit her in the pasture on her farm where she died." He handed a scrap of paper to Pastor Tuttle, who took the paper but continued to gaze up at Irvine. "And I went and visited her there. She claimed an attraction for me and tried to embrace me. I did not want to embrace her, so I pushed her and she fell and her head hit a rock and she died. It was an accident. I killed her by accident. I am a murderer."

By the time he'd finished speaking, Mrs. Irvine had already begun to scream. A flair for the dramatic. Or perhaps what he'd said really had unhinged her and she couldn't help screaming. I shouldn't judge. Irvine sat down beside the pulpit, his head in his hands. Mrs. Irvine's screams continued. She sounded like she was being held down and branded with a hot iron. The rest of the congregation sat silently, listening to her screams as though it had all been planned and was a continuation of the sermon, wondering what should happen next. Pastor Tuttle did not know what to do. He reclaimed his place behind the pulpit, placed a hand on Irvine's shoulder, opened his mouth to speak and found he didn't know what to say. Should he announce the next hymn? I stared at the back of Gloria's head, waiting for her to turn and look at me or to try in some way to comfort her mother, but she just sat there beside the screaming woman, staring straight ahead.

A few of the parishioners turned and gaped in my direction, apparently expecting something from me. I got up and fled. They watched me go, wishing that they could follow and escape Mrs. Irvine's screams.

Using cardboard boxes I found in the basement, I packed my clothes, my mother's red blouse, the radio, my father's dress shoes, and the other few things I possessed, and carried the boxes one by one out to the Fargo. A woman across the street watched me from her window. Another sunny Sunday, so I suppose it was a good enough day to move. I couldn't remember the last time it had rained. Maybe months. Maybe even years. Everything was dying. Soon there'd be nothing left but dust. The lawns were still green, but only the sprinklers kept them alive. Or maybe it wasn't that unusually dry. It never rains that much in Broken Head. I really don't remember. I hadn't been keeping track.

I got in the truck and drove out of Broken Head. Instead of heading for Calgary, where I knew I'd wait for Gloria forever, I went to the farm. When I got there, I drove into my yard and saw Mom's clothesline, and it made me ashamed. The next thing I knew, I had driven the truck right into it, and it went down before me and under the truck, making that odd shrieking sound of metal screaming against metal, which at that moment reminded me of Mrs. Irvine screaming. I turned off the engine and got out to inspect the damage. There was fluid pouring down. An angle iron had sprung up once it had passed under the bumper and smashed the bottom of the radiator. I went into the house and lay down on my bed and went to sleep.

When I woke up, it was already dark, and I was hungry and realized I had no food. I sat at the table in the kitchen, wondering what to do about that. It was a relief to think about something as simple as my own hunger and how I would survive, but before I'd made any plan I saw two headlights turn off the grid and aim down my driveway. Irvine's white Mercedes. I walked out of the house. The car stopped before me, and I saw that it was Gloria driving.

She'd come to me.

The electric window descended in its perfectly engineered way.

"I thought maybe you'd come here. Dad's asking for you. He wants to talk to you. He wants you to come right now."

I nodded, hoping that she'd say more; that she'd come to me because she wanted to see me and talk to me. But she didn't say anything else. Her eyes avoided mine when I tried to look into them. Her upper lip quivered with the effort of having to be so close to me. She bit her finger and looked at the marks her teeth left. She hated me. I could see that she hated me.

"There's something wrong with my truck," I said, pointing at where it was still parked atop the mangled clothesline.

She saw and nodded. "Get in," she said.

I got into the car and she put it in gear and drove out of the yard.

Neither of us spoke for some time. The waning moon followed us as we drove, travelling the same speed that we travelled along the grid road. The dashboard gleamed like the cockpit of a spaceship, and I hoped we might take off and go to some other planet in some galaxy where they hadn't invented shame.

"Is he in jail?"

"No," she snapped. "He's not in jail."

She was silent for some time. I didn't ask why he wasn't in jail, but she understood that was what the silence meant, so she finally answered, "He insisted we go to the police station, and we sat there all afternoon while they talked to him, but in the end they sent him home."

She drove too slowly, with both hands clutching the wheel, afraid that the gravel would throw her into the ditch. She had a fear of gravel roads.

"Why did they send him home?"

"Because it was an accident. It wasn't his fault. They don't believe it was his fault. No one believes it was his fault. They know you made him say it."

I didn't answer for a moment, and she sniffed hard.

"How could I make him say it?"

"I don't know. You seem to have some power over him."

"You don't really believe that, do you?"

She didn't answer.

"So, if he's not in jail, how come he didn't come out here to see me himself?"

She glanced at me with a malevolence that made me glad I couldn't see her eyes more clearly.

"He's in bed. The doctor gave him a sedative, but he's been fighting it for hours. He keeps babbling away about how he has to see you. He still insists he's dying. He thinks he might be dead by morning."

"I love you," I said.

She flexed her hands on the wheel, and I thought she was going to shout, but when she spoke it was with the same tone of eerie calmness she'd been speaking with all along.

"Well, I don't love you. We were never meant to be together."

I measured her words and then measured my own. "No. I guess it's all chance, our being together. Chaos."

She nodded, staring at the grid road, and answered, "Well, I'd just as soon not embrace chaos, thank you very much. I'm engaged to Nick Campion. I'm going to marry Nick Campion. I'd always planned to marry Nick Campion."

The digital readout of the speedometer told me we were going sixty-three kilometres an hour.

"Congratulations," I said.

"How could you do this to my father?" she asked. "After everything he did for you?"

"What about my father?"

"What about him? You killed your father. And now you're trying to kill my father."

I didn't answer for a moment, and she reached over and turned on the radio to show me that she wasn't interested in anything else I had to say. A pop song played. It doesn't matter which one. It was a love song, of course. They're almost all love songs. You'd think the only thing people want to listen to is people declaring their new love or damning their old love or lamenting their lost love.

We didn't speak again, even after she'd pulled into the driveway, got out of the car and led me up the stairs and down the hallway to his bedroom. All of my time in that house, and all that had happened, and I'd never been as high as the second floor before that moment. We passed an open door that was obviously Gloria's room, and I wanted to stop and look, but she glanced back at me with a scowl and I followed.

Irvine resembled one of his corpses. He lay in a king-size bed with a heavy oak frame, the sort of bed that, even without four posts and a canopy, suggested a dead king lying in state. I had never seen that room before. The oak dressers. The window looking out over the swimming pool glowing so invitingly in the warm evening. I pictured myself opening the window and diving.

Gloria walked up beside her father and touched his pale hand. "Dad? Dwight's come."

He didn't open his eyes, but his lips curled into a smile. I sat down beside the bed. Gloria turned and left.

It was a full minute before he opened his eyes and focused them on me. "Why didn't you come sooner?"

"A little busy."

"I'm dying."

"Yeah. Sure. Me too."

He gave me a sad look and closed his eyes again. "I wanted to thank you," he murmured. "I've never been happier in my life. You've saved me. Thank you."

"You're welcome," I said, and I stood and headed for the door.

"They've forgiven me. I tried, but they've forgiven me."

That stopped me before I could escape.

"Apparently," I said. My back was still to him, but I'd made the mistake of stopping. I was looking at a couple of pairs of his socks on the top of his dresser because I didn't want to turn back and have to look at him. They were black socks.

"It's God's mercy. It's God's mercy on my wife and daughter. I can feel the hand of God on me."

"That's wonderful," I said.

"Yes. It is," he said. "Wonderful."

243

"It doesn't change the fact that you killed her," I said. "I've lost everything. And you're happier than you've ever been. That's the power of confession and forgiveness, I suppose. That's our great moral code. Congratulations."

I couldn't help but wonder if he'd opened his eyes, but I didn't want to look at him.

"You still have the farm," he said.

I laughed and turned to face him. He had opened his eyes.

"I was sitting at home just now wondering how I'd avoid starving to death."

Immediately, he began to struggle to sit up, and I watched the corpse raise himself until his head almost reached the top of the oak headboard. "My chequebook is in my jacket," he said, motioning to where the jacket was hung over the back of a chair. "Bring it to me."

I did as he told me. He opened the drawer in his bedside table, took out a pen, opened the chequebook and scrawled something on it. When he ripped it from the book and held it out to me, I reached out and took it. Ten thousand dollars.

"Will that do?" he said.

Without answering, I put it in my pocket and walked away. I heard him say, "Thank you, Dwight," as I stepped out the bedroom door.

The door to Gloria's room was closed, so I knocked. It opened a crack and she peeked through at me.

"I'm ready to go," I said.

"Could you . . . could you take a cab, please?"

She reached out, opening the door a little wider, and offered me a twenty-dollar bill. I looked at that bill, clutched between two of her fingers. I almost took it, but a rush of adrenaline flared through my veins, and I put my hand on the door and pushed it open. She stepped back and let me enter.

"He killed my mother," I said. "What was I supposed to do? What would you have done?"

"Please leave," she said.

"I could have killed him. But I did that once already, and it was all just a bigger mess. I couldn't do that again. I couldn't do that to you."

"Please leave," she said again.

I sat down on her bed.

"All right, then," she said. "I will."

She walked to the door, opened it and turned back to challenge me with another dark look, her eyes trying to tell me something I didn't understand. Apparently she had decided against surrendering her room. I sat watching her. There was something in her eyes I hadn't seen before: something beyond anger and fear, and even beyond hatred. She put one finger of her left hand against the door frame, opened the door a little wider with her right hand and, with all her strength, smashed the door shut on her finger. Groaning, she staggered back towards me. I'd already jumped to my feet, as if there was something I meant to do to help her; to save her, the way I'd saved her father. She sat down on her bed, examining the blood oozing from under her purple nail.

"Jesus, Jesus, Jesus, Jesus, Jesus . . ." she said.

There was no point saying anything else to her. I was alone. She was alone. We had both chosen. I was not even there. It was only her and her finger and the terrible pain. Finally, I stood and left her room as she'd ordered me to do, closing the door behind me.

As I walked down the stairs, I caught sight of Mrs. Irvine, almost as pale as her husband, watching me from the kitchen doorway, drinking a glass of her mineral water. I stopped and looked in her direction, and she shrank back for a moment into the darkness of the kitchen, as if to hide, before she relented and loomed into the light.

"Goodbye, Mrs. Irvine," I said.

"Goodbye, Dwight," she answered.

I deposited the cheque at an automatic teller machine, withdrew the forty dollars it would allow me to withdraw, ordered two pizzas, ate one of them at the restaurant and took the other home with me for breakfast and lunch the next day. The cabbie made me give him twenty dollars before he'd leave Broken Head.

The next morning, the alarm woke me at six. I got up and started demolishing the passage between the house and the shop, using a hammer mall my father had used to drive posts to smash the Cindercrete blocks that shut out the light to my bedroom. At noon I left that project, ate what was left of my pizza and started work on the truck. I managed to halfway plug the radiator with goo and limped into town by carrying enough water that I could top it up every few miles. It got me to the grocery store. The other shoppers, mostly women, snuck looks at me that matched the tone of the Muzak. I had shopped there many times while living in the Irvines' basement, but I suddenly remembered shopping in that same store with my mother, arguing over a box of sugar-coated cereal, and when I remembered, I bought myself a sack of the oatmeal she used to make me eat some-times, telling me it would stick to my ribs. I hated that oatmeal.

Now I eat it every morning.

The cashier had gone to school with me. I said hello and she said hello because that's what cashiers are expected to do, and otherwise we pretended not to know each other. I loaded the groceries into the truck, filled the radiator and drove home (stopping to fill the radiator twice), put the groceries away, made my dinner, gathered the dishes into the sink, read until ten and went to bed. The next morning, I got up at six and continued demolishing and hauling away those Cindercrete blocks.

I could have made that the shape of my life, changing the projects with the seasons. I could have worked the farm and made a small living by keeping my overheads low. I could have bought a few cows and a bull and sold the steers in the fall and kept the heifers as replacements and bought another bull so I wouldn't have to breed them to their father. I could have made a religion of making ends meet.

But instead I sold the farm and moved to Calgary and got a job cleaning office towers. I did consider the burning that God in the form of my father had ordered me to do. Went so far as to dump a pail of gasoline in the living room, but before I could strike the match, I changed my mind. Perhaps it was Satan, visiting me in my father's form. And even if it was Him, I didn't want to believe in such a wasteful God. And even if He existed, I wanted to show Him that I refused to believe in Him. Like my father had. And so I went to Calgary.

For all I know, Dr. Irvine and his wife still live in the same house in Broken Head. Maybe Caroline has even been there to visit them. They were there the last time I visited my parents' graves, eight years ago. I was parked on the street in front of the house when Irvine walked past, on his way home from the hospital. He saw me and stopped to say hello.

"Dwight? How are you doing?"

"Just fine. Just fine. And you? You're looking well."

It was true. He looked fit and healthy.

"What are you doing here?"

"Just driving around. Visited my parents' graves."

"That's good."

"I suppose. Just a stone. And you paid to have it put there. How's Gloria?"

"She and Nick are doing well. They're both down east, going to school."

I nodded. He didn't tell me about Caroline. He kept her a secret.

"Have you moved back to Broken Head?"

"No. Don't worry. I'm in Vancouver now. I'll never come back."

He nodded. "I like the beard."

I shrugged. "It just grows there."

He nodded again. "Nice seeing you."

He walked across the street and into his house without once looking back over his shoulder. I admired that. I sat for a couple minutes more, wondering how long it would take a police car to show up if I stayed. But I decided I didn't want to know, and I started the truck and drove away.

A couple of years ago, I was walking past a row of televisions in a department store and a row of Nick Campions were talking out of the screens. His name was there, below his face, and the name of the bank he worked for below that. He was talking about something to do with the stock market, and at the end of the clip it said that he worked in Toronto.

It wasn't like I got in the car the next morning or anything, but when it was time to take my holidays, I went to Toronto. His name was in the phone book with his address, so it wasn't hard to find the house. When I saw Caroline and saw how old she was and saw my mother standing there as a little girl, I decided I should move to Toronto.

She's my daughter. I wanted to see her.

I went in to do the morning routine early so that I was out of the way in my room with the red door by the time the kids started showing up. Not long after the bell, Choppy opened the door and shook his head at me. "Somebody here lookin' for ya."

The nanny was standing behind him, and I told her to come in, but when she did Choppy stood there staring at us.

"Can you give us a minute, Choppy?"

"I don't know." He gave her a long once-over. "I guess you're knocked up, are ya?"

"I guess I'm not," she said. "Are you?"

"Not that I know of," said Choppy.

"Well, the rumours must be wrong, then."

"Can't trust rumours." Choppy smiled. You could see he liked her despite himself. "Okay, I'm gonna leave you two alone. But if I hear anything funny, I'll call the principal, you hear?"

He closed the door on his own wicked grin.

"Isn't he full of piss and vinegar this morning," the nanny said.

She looked things over in our little room, and I felt more than a bit exposed.

"I couldn't do it," she said. "I can't tell her. But I don't know what the fuck to do, because she's bound to find out sooner or later, so when she does, you've got to promise me that you'll pretend I didn't know anything."

"I promise," I said.

"And I've thought about it a lot, and I think it's better that Caroline doesn't know. She shouldn't know. It's not the same as me. She has a dad who she thinks is her dad, and I can't see it doing her any good to know about you, even if I can understand you wanting to know her."

I didn't say anything.

"You're gonna have to promise me that you won't tell her anything and that you won't ever show anybody what you wrote. Can you promise me that?"

It was obvious from the way she looked at me that she needed me to give her this one thing. What else did I have to give?

"I promise," I said.

She took a deep breath.

"All right, then. Here's what we're gonna do. Gloria's not getting home until late tonight, and I told her I'm gonna take Caroline after school for a movie and pizza. You can meet us at the theatre. Just pretend it's by accident and you can sit with us, and even if she mentions it, her mother probably won't think anything of it. You probably shouldn't come for pizza, though. If Gloria hears you came for pizza, she's bound to get interested."

"By accident."

"Yeah. Is that okay? That's the best I can do."

"I appreciate it," I said.

She told me the theatre and the time of the movie and stood there looking at me for a few seconds before she kissed me on the cheek. She was gone before I could think of anything else to say.

The burning has been surprisingly easy. I expected to have a hard time making myself do it, but the only problem has been disconnecting the smoke alarm, which was wired right into the grid. There's nothing worth saving in here at any rate. I see that now. It's a nasty little story that makes even the beautiful into something ugly. Caroline, for instance. She's so beautiful, and so she's barely in here. And there's so much good about her mother and my mother and even my father that I never came close to getting across. I've made them all into monsters.

I'm burning the pages in my kitchen sink, ten sheets at a time. The windows are open to let out the smoke.

I've made a religion of making ends meet and of writing this confession I'm now burning. By the time I'm finished writing this page, it will be time to burn another ten pages. It will not be many minutes before it's time to print and burn this very page. One puny voice silenced. No more significant than an insect consumed by a nit-picking ape. I tell myself that I am connected in my insignificance to everything in the universe and burning my false image makes me more connected: my molecules might at any moment disperse and merge with everything around me. I might explode. I might scream first before it happens. I might just sit and stare at the walls before I pass right through them. I tell myself I've finally discovered the meaning of my life in destroying my own pitiful creation. I don't really believe.

She looks like my mother. A little like my mother and a little like her mother. You can really see it when she leans on her elbow and talks to you. I did go for pizza with them, and she let me eat her crusts. She asked me if I liked pepperoni, and she smiled when I said that I did.

There's nothing more than that. I really wish there were. I wish I had some glimpse of God that might help everyone. I wish I knew. I wish I'd asked Him something important when I saw Him. I wish I could give something more to be burned, because the burning is so important that there needs to be more fuel. I wish I could say that I'd come to know Him or He'd come to know me, or that I myself could serve as some cautionary tale for future generations. But I have nothing else.

That's all I have to say. That's all I have to burn. There aren't so many other shameful things that have happened to me that I could also confess, and in the end, at any rate, it would all be ash.

At the theatre, after we'd gone through the motions of our accidental meeting, the nanny went to the counter to get popcorn and left me with Caroline. She stood there on one leg, looking at me out of the corner of her eye.

"This movie's for kids," she finally said.

"I heard it's good. I like kids' movies."

She didn't respond for a while, twirled around on one foot, practising her dancing. "Are you Louise's boyfriend?" she asked.

"No," I said. "We're just friends. She doesn't have a boyfriend."

She rolled her eyes at me.

"Whatever," she said.

Editor's note:
This manuscript was recovered by Toronto Police from a deleted
file on the hard drive of a computer discovered in the apartment of
caretaker Jonathan Froze. The computer had been confiscated by
police as Mr. Froze was under investigation for assaulting a child
who attended the school where he worked. Mr. Froze committed
suicide before the investigation could be completed. The child and
her nanny made corroborating statements that he'd done nothing
more than attend a movie and gone for a restaurant meal with them.

ACKNOWLEDGMENTS

The author wishes to thank Boris Rodriguez, Su Rynard, Michelle MacAleese, Claire Tallarico, Janice Dexter, Berniece Gowan, and Marc Amfreville for helpful comments.

Thanks to my editor, Michael Schellenberg, and my agent, Hilary MacMahon.

Special thanks to Elizabeth Mulley for all her feedback on the manuscript.

And thanks to Alison.

LEE GOWAN is the author of *Going to Cuba*, a collection of stories, and the novels *The Last Cowboy* and *Make Believe Love*, which was a finalist for the Trillium Award. An award-winning screenwriter, he is the coordinator of the Creative Writing program at the University of Toronto School of Continuing Studies. He lives in Toronto.